The Curious Affair of the Third Dog

"Patricia Moyes is almost impossible to resist and her new thriller . . . has much more than a glorious title. This is another lovely English, well-bred, well-balanced middle-class police procedural, comfortable and cozy." —*Library Journal*

"All the ingredients are present—a small town, London, an urbane Chief Superintendant, chatty dialogue, convincing villains."
—*The New York Times*

"Another highly entertaining and amusing English mystery."
—*Publishers Weekly*

THE HENRY TIBBETT MYSTERIES
by Patricia Moyes

Night Ferry to Death
A Six-Letter Word for Death
Angel Death
Who Is Simon Warwick?
The Coconut Killings
Black Widower
The Curious Affair of the Third Dog
Season for Snows and Sins
Many Deadly Returns
Death and the Dutch Uncle
Murder Fantastical
Johnny Underground
Murder by 3's (*including* Down Among the Dead Men, Dead Men Don't Ski, *and* Falling Star)
Falling Star
Murder à la Mode
Death on the Agenda
Down Among the Dead Men
Dead Men Don't Ski

A RINEHART SUSPENSE NOVEL

The Curious Affair of the Third Dog

Patricia Moyes

An Owl Book
HOLT, RINEHART AND WINSTON • NEW YORK

Published by Holt, Rinehart and Winston,
383 Madison Avenue, New York, New York 10017.

Library of Congress Cataloging in Publication Data
Moyes, Patricia.
The curious affair of the third dog.
I. Title.
[PR6063.O9C8 1986] 823'.914 85-17610
ISBN: 0-03-009534-4 (An Owl bk.) (pbk.)
First published in hardcover by Holt, Rinehart
and Winston in 1973.

First Owl Book Edition—1986

Printed in the United States of America
1 3 5 7 9 10 8 6 4 2

ISBN 0-03-009534-4

To my sister,
Barbara Nicholson,
who is the RSPCA representative
in a village which is nothing
like Gorsemere

1

It was a beautiful day in May, and the fresh sunshine of early summer danced over London, working that familiar magic that paves the dourest of the city's streets with gold—or at least pinchbeck—and transforms parks and squares into enchanted gardens. Outside Buckingham Palace, severe, dumpy Queen Victoria became a fairy princess, as the sunshine dazzled off the white marble of her sugar-icing memorial, and in Trafalgar Square young lovers held hands beside the splashing fountains, lost in their private Arcadias.

The sunbeams were even making an impudent attempt to penetrate the dirt-encrusted glass vaulting of that most austere of railway stations, Waterloo. They had no real hope of success, but their influence was there in the light, bright clothes and laughing voices of the travelers. Not even the sonorous tones of the train announcer, alternating with a hideously blaring version of the Skaters' Waltz booming over the loudspeakers, could disperse that lightness of heart and step which comes to London on the first real day of summer.

Emmy Tibbett felt it, as she stood at the open window of her compartment on the 1:45 P.M. to Guildford, Farnham, and all stations to Westmouth-on-Sea. She was aware of a ridiculous, heady excitement, out of all proportion to the occasion. After all, she was not off on any great adventure—just going to spend a fortnight in the country with her elder sister and brother-in-law. Women in their forties, she told herself, had no right to feel like ebullient schoolgirls at the end of the term; and even as this thought occurred to her, another part of her mind riposted—"And why not?"

Henry, her husband, had sacrificed his Wednesday lunch hour to come and see her off, and was now standing on the platform, afflicted by the distressing dumbness which always sets in at such moments. Everything necessary, and quite a lot that was not, had already been said; and still the train did not move.

"Give my love to Jane and Bill," Henry said, for the third time.

"Of course I will."

Silence descended again. Henry looked at his watch. "You should be off any minute now."

"Don't bother to wait, darling."

"No, no. I'll stay and see you off."

"After all, I'm not going forever. We'll see you at Gorsemere on Friday evening."

"Barring emergencies," said Henry.

"Don't forget to ring and let us know which train you'll be on so that Jane can meet you."

"I won't." Another endless pause. Then doors slammed, a whistle blew, and the train began to move slowly out of the station.

Immediately, a host of vital instructions, as yet unspoken, crowded into Emmy's mind. "Leave a note for Mrs. Harrison about the laundry!" she shouted.

"What laundry?"

"And tell Madge I can't lunch on Thursday!" But it was too late. The train had gathered speed, and was racketing out of the cavernous station and through the sunlit suburbs, heading southwest.

Henry smiled, waved—and then turned away with a small, affectionate sigh. He made his way to the Underground and embarked on the short but inconvenient journey which would spew him out above ground within walking distance of his office in Scotland Yard's new building in Victoria Street.

As he sorted through the papers on his desk, Chief Superintendent Henry Tibbett reflected on the basic dreariness of his job. The glamorous cases, the ones which had brought him a certain celebrity and which people always wanted to hear about, were few and far between; many of them had arisen not in the course of his ordinary work, but because of the flair, which his colleagues called his "nose," which so often prompted Henry to smell out something fishy in an apparently innocent situation.

Between these oases of interest and excitement stretched the deserts of routine: the domestic quarrels erupting into violence; the drunken brawls outside sordid public houses, which ended in the flash of a knife, the pounding of fleeing footsteps, and a body bleeding to death in the gutter; and, most boring and least savory of all, vicious squabbles within the criminal fraternity—a bunch of uniformly unpleasant characters who, by definition, resorted to violence more readily than other people.

In most of these cases, there was no element of mystery, no doubt at all about the identity of the killer. The distraught husband or wife seldom denied the crime. The scared, suddenly sobered-up youths were easily traced. And as for the avowed crooks, there was nearly always an informer ready to sell out an associate to the police, if the price was right.

Henry sighed, and thought wistfully of the classic murders of fiction: the aristocratic house party, neatly cut off by snow or floods to limit the number of suspects; the multiplicity of unlikely motives and opportunities; the tortuous investigations of the amateur sleuth; and the final dénouement, in which the murderer turns out to be the elderly, gentle maiden aunt—beloved by all, but unmasked as a subhuman fiend in the final chapter.

Gorsemere, now—the little Hampshire village to which Jane and Bill Spence had retired—that would make a good setting for just such a story. The aristocratic houseparty would have to go, of course—although there was that chap, Sir Somebody Something, who lived in a biggish house; but the village was certainly close-knit, everybody knowing everybody else. The only trouble was that people didn't get murdered in places like that. Or if they did, it was a case of Joe Soap coming home drunk and hitting his wife harder than he meant to. No chance of a mystery. The whole of Gorsemere would know every detail long before the police were even called in.

At any rate, thought Henry, let's hope none of them start murdering each other next weekend. He was tired, and looking forward to a couple days of relaxation in the country—well away from London, well away from crime.

On the train, Emmy relaxed and gave herself up to pleasurable anticipation. She was fond of her elder sister, Jane, and her brother-in-law Bill. She considered them with affection as the wheels thudded rhythmically down the iron way.

Jane Blandish had met and married Bill Spence during the Second World War, an unbelievable thirty-plus years ago. Bill was in his early thirties then, and had left his father's farm in Dorset to join a famous infantry regiment. He had been commissioned just before the wedding and sent overseas just after it. Emmy still had the wedding photographs somewhere—Jane in a square-shouldered, short-skirted suit and a ridiculously perched hat with a veil, clutching a posy of carnations and gazing up adoringly at Bill, who looked ill at ease in his new khaki uniform. Emmy herself stood behind Jane, beaming complacently in trim Air Force blue, with the two stripes of a corporal on her arm—it was before she had become an officer in the WAAF. The two sets of parents were sharply contrasted —the London-based Blandishes as chic as wartime shortages would allow (Emmy remembered how her father had wanted to unearth his morning suit and top hat and been thwarted by an outraged Jane); and the Spences, bluff and four-square, exuding an aura of wide acres and newly ploughed earth. The whole group had the air of slightly frenetic gaiety which characterized such occasions in wartime. The shadow of the swastika hung over all of them.

Ironically, the uniformed members of the Services—Emmy and Bill—had survived. So had the elder Blandishes, who had resolutely refused to leave London, even during the worst of the bombing. But in 1943, a low-flying German sneak raider, bent on destroying a southcoast radar station, had made a mistake and dropped its bombs on the Spences' quiet Dorsetshire farmhouse. They had both been killed as they sat eating their lunch in the big, red-tiled kitchen.

After the war, Bill had come home to what was left of the farm. He and Jane had worked hard to rebuild the farmhouse and get the land working again. Jane—blonde and pretty and vivacious and apparently a city sophisticate—had taken to country life like a duck to water. Soon she was even more the complete farmer's wife than her late mother-in-law had been. She had always loved animals, and before long she had her own small poultry farm and would tramp out to the cowsheds at night to help to deliver calves, while her kitchen frequently harbored ailing newborn lambs, not to mention the numerous cats and dogs endemic to a farm.

Well, all that was long ago. Now, the greatly enlarged farm was being run with computerized superefficiency by Giles and Hamish, the Spences' two sons. Their young daughter Veronica, born after the war, had long since moved to London, where she continued her successful career as a fashion model, in spite of the fact that she was married and had a baby son of her own. Emmy smiled as she remembered how determinedly Jane had refused to be shocked by an enormous photograph of Veronica on the *Daily Scoop* fashion page, eight months pregnant and showing off the latest thing in maternity wear.

"I must confess, though," Jane had said to Emmy on the telephone, "that I'm relieved we've moved to Gorsemere. People here are very much with it—we're on the edge of commuter-country, after all. I can't think what they made of it back in Dorset."

For Jane and Bill, feeling that it was rather late for them to learn the new tricks of modern farming, had handed the farm over to the younger generation and retired to a comfortable, red-roofed, white-painted cottage in the village of Gorsemere, in Hampshire.

Retirement is supposed to present all kinds of problems—too much leisure, lack of interests, and so forth. As far as Emmy could judge, it had brought nothing but happiness and fulfillment to the Spences. Bill, a keen golfer, was working hard to reduce his handicap. He was also a lay magistrate, a member of the Parish Council, chairman of the Gorsemere Wildlife Conservation Society, and secretary of the local gardening club. Too much leisure was not his problem.

As for Jane, she still had her house to run, which is a full-time occupation, especially with a man around the place all day. In addition, as well as her voluntary charitable works in the village, she had what she proudly called her job. This was the position of full-time, salaried representative of the Royal Society for the Prevention of Cruelty to Animals. Her telephone was the busiest in the village.

It was shortly after three o'clock when the train pulled into Gorsemere Halt. Emmy was the only passenger getting off at the station. Soon—between five and seven o'clock—the London trains would be disgorging their dark-suited hordes of commuting businessmen, and the little station yard would be full of comfortably opulent cars driven by comfortably opulent wives meeting their husbands; now, however, Jane's slightly battered green station wagon had the place to itself. Jane herself was just climbing out of the car as Emmy, lugging her suitcase, emerged from the station.

"Darling—so sorry I'm a bit late . . . Mrs. Denning's cat has had kittens *again* and she kept me for hours on the phone about finding homes for them . . . why she can't have the animal spayed, I don't know . . . here, give me that case . . ." Jane kissed her sister briefly on both cheeks, and then opened the back of the station wagon and swung in the heavy case with the practiced ease of a countrywoman used to hefting weighty loads.

"You're looking marvelous, Jane," said Emmy sincerely. "Retirement suits you."

It was true. Jane, in her fifties, had hardly a gray hair in her honey-blonde head, and—as Emmy acknowledged ruefully—she had kept her tall, slim figure apparently effortlessly, in contrast to Emmy's continual running battle against overplumpness. Jane's pale blue linen trouser suit was certainly appropriate for the country, but it was in no way reminiscent of a dowdy farmer's wife. Her total acceptance of rural life had not obliterated her flair for wearing clothes to their best advantage, and Emmy knew that Jane, in old blue jeans and a T shirt, could look better dressed than many women who bought expensive clothes and contrived to make a mess of them.

Jane grinned. "It certainly does," she said. "I've never been so busy in my life, nor has Bill. We both adore it. By the way, Bill's sorry he couldn't be here to meet you—it's his turn today to sit on the bench and dispense justice to local drunks and erring motorists in Middingfield. How's Henry? Have you seen Ronnie and the baby recently?"

The drive back to Cherry Tree Cottage, the Spences' house, was pleasantly filled with exchanges of family news. Emmy gazed with deep pleasure on the gentle summer landscape of dappled fields, leafy woods, and flowering gardens. The village of Gorsemere itself was typically attractive without being in any way a showplace. The village green, with its Victorian stone horse trough and ugly but touching war memorial, could be duplicated in a dozen neighboring hamlets. The gray stone church dated from the nineteenth century, and was no architectural gem. The small houses around the green were mostly of pleasantly mellow red brick, with the exception of a row of hideous council houses built in the thirties of cheap, jaundiced brickwork. Even these, however, had been softened by the passing years, and their unregimented gardens, bright with rhododendrons and dahlias, helped to create an effect of pleasing smugness. The one building which had some claim to distinction was the White Bull—a black-and-white timbered structure, leaning at several interesting angles, which had been a coaching inn on the main London road in the old days when the latter passed through Gorsemere. London–Westmouth traffic now took the so-called New London Road, which was a mere two hundred years old.

Around the nucleus of church, inn, parish hall, and small shops, residential Gorsemere was in the process of spreading itself further into the countryside each year, as house-hungry Londoners found themselves forced to accept a longer and longer journey to work in order to be able to come home to space, fresh air, and a decent-sized garden of their own. Only Gorsemere House, the rambling and inconvenient home of Sir Arthur Bratt-Cunningham, Bart., had existed before the beginning of the twentieth century. A few other sizable houses, each in two or three acres of garden, had been built by well-to-do retired people before the First World War. The twenties and thirties had seen more building, with the houses and gardens shrinking in direct relation to the date of their construction; but it was not until the fifties and sixties that the real building wave had hit Gorsemere. It was difficult now to find an open field or cultivated farmland within several miles of the village. Cherry Tree Cottage was a product of this epoch in Gorsemere's expansion.

"And just about the last of the decent houses to be built," Jane had told Emmy when she and Bill had bought the place a couple of years earlier. "At least we have half an acre and the house isn't jerry-built. You should see what's happening now—great development estates of beastly little mass-produced boxes, about ten to an acre. We feel pretty safe, though, because the woods behind us are Crown Property and can't be built over. Or so we hope. We're keeping our fingers crossed."

The station wagon nosed its way along the narrow road which had previously been known as Gurton's Lane (because it led nowhere except to Gurton's Farm) but which a hopeful Rural Council had rechristened Cherry Tree Drive. Outside the cottage, Jane pulled the car onto the grass verge.

"I won't put her in the garage," she said, "because I've got to collect Bill from the station at five. Come on in."

The garden of Cherry Tree Cottage was surrounded by a workmanlike wire fence, which Jane was—as yet unsuccessfully—trying to disguise with various creeping plants. The reason for this barrier was soon obvious, for as Jane and Emmy approached the gate, they were greeted by a cacophony of barking.

"What's the state of the menagerie?" Emmy asked.

"Not too bad at the moment," said Jane cheerfully. "Three assorted dogs, two cats, an injured rabbit, and a canary—apart from our own lot, of course."

"I think you're a miracle," Emmy said. "I don't know how you cope."

Jane laughed. "This is nothing," she said. "Up till yesterday I also had a Great Dane and a nanny goat. I'm thrilled about the Great Dane—his people couldn't afford to feed him any longer and brought him to me, and I've found him a marvelous home. Amanda Bratt-Cunningham—Sir Arthur's daughter—dropped in for coffee and fell in love with him. She collected him yesterday."

"And the goat?" Emmy asked.

"Some children found it straying along the New London Road, of all places. I eventually traced the owner—a farmer from Upper Gedding, about five miles away. His wife kept it as a pet, and for milk, and some clot had left the farmyard gate open. She was nearly in tears of joy when she came to fetch it home. I must say she was welcome to it. I'd been keeping it in the toolshed next to the garage, and the place still stinks to high heaven. Bill's furious. Hello, what do you lot want?"

Emmy turned to see that Jane, in the act of opening the gate, had been surrounded by a group of four small children who had apparently materialized out of thin air. The largest, a tow-haired girl of about nine with several front teeth missing, seemed to be the spokeswoman of the party. She gazed up earnestly and almost accusingly at Jane, and said, "Are you the cruel-to-animals lady?"

"That's right," said Jane gravely.

"Well, we've brought you this." The girl unclenched a grubby fist, to reveal five shiny ten-penny pieces. "There's one from each of us and one from Sandra but she's still doing hers."

"Still doing her what?"

"Her good deed for ten pennies. Hers is looking after her baby brother while her mum's out and she's not back yet so Sandra couldn't come. Go on, take them," she added encouragingly. "They're for the animals."

"That's very kind of you," said Jane, taking the money.

"And now can we see the goat?" It came out in a rush, and at once the chorus was taken up by the other three. "Please can we see the goat? Betty Humfrey and John Adams saw the goat and they only brought ten pennies between them."

"Oh dear," said Jane. "I'm so sorry. The goat's not here any more."

"It was here yesterday," said the tow-haired girl mutinously.

"I know it was," said Jane, "but we found out where it lived and its mistress came to collect it last night. It's safely back home again now, so that's good, isn't it?"

Four small, pouting faces indicated that it was far from good. Emmy wondered if they were going to ask for their money back.

Jane said, "I'll tell you what, though. If you go round to the police station and ask Mrs. Denning nicely, I expect she'll let you see her new kittens."

"What color?" asked the smallest child—a dark-haired boy—suspiciously.

"All sorts of colors. There are five of them—black and white and tabby and—"

"Kittens aren't the same as a goat," remarked the gap-toothed girl, with remorseless logic.

"And if you come back here after you've seen the kittens," Jane went on smoothly, "you can collect your badges."

"Badges?"

"Yes. To show you're helping the animals. You can wear them to school."

This argument tipped the balance. "All right," said the girl.

And then, to the others, "Come on! Race you to the p'lice station!" The whole party took to its heels and vanished down the lane as suddenly as it had come.

Jane pushed open the gate and led the way into the garden, to be once more surrounded—this time by a leaping, barking, welcoming canine chorus. "They're sweet, aren't they?" she said. "The kids, I mean. You'd be surprised how much money they collect—and it's all their own idea. Yes, all right, boys—dinnertime soon. No, leave Emmy alone. Just shove them away, darling—they're too affectionate by half. Here we are."

And so at last the two sisters were inside the house, and Jane showed Emmy into the small, cheerful spare bedroom and invited her to unpack before tea. Then they took a turn in the garden, accompanied by a bodyguard of assorted dogs and a dignified and unobtrusive escort of cat outriders, and Emmy picked flowers for her bedroom while Jane filled a trug basket with freshly cut salad and beans and parsley for supper.

They were still having tea when the children turned up again —this time accompanied by Sandra, a serious and bespectacled eight-year-old. The kittens had proved a great hit, and there were high hopes that, if the mothers approved, homes might have been found for at least two of them. Badges and cookies were distributed, and the children were allowed a quick, respectful peek at the injured rabbit, which was convalescing in a comfortable box in the kitchen. Then it was time for Jane to go off to the station again to collect her husband.

Emmy, left alone, stretched out luxuriously on the drawing room sofa and gave herself up to pleasant relaxation. She knew that she was not, and never would be, a countrywoman like Jane; but, for a bit, it was a marvelous change from the racket of the city. Small things and small creatures became suddenly and beautifully important down here, and time seemed to expand to accommodate the minutiae of existence. Emmy was happily indulging in such leisurely meditation when the telephone rang. She heaved herself up off the sofa and went into the hall to answer it.

"Gorsemere 387."

"Mrs. Spence? This is Police-Constable Denning speaking. Sorry to bother you, but—"

"It's me that's sorry," said Emmy. "I'm afraid Mrs. Spence is out at the moment. This is her sister speaking."

"Oh." P.C. Denning sounded taken aback, and a note of distress crept into his pleasantly burred voice. "Will Mrs. Spence be long, then? It's rather important, you see."

"She should be back soon," said Emmy. "She's only gone to the station. Can I give her a message?"

The voice hesitated. "Yes. Yes, if you would, madam. Ask her to ring the police station, would you? Tell her it's about Harry Heathfield's dogs. Tell her . . ." the country voice was obviously distressed. "Tell her it's urgent, will you?"

2

Jane and Bill were back at Cherry Tree Cottage within half an hour, and while Bill went off to have a shower and "get out of these damned town clothes," Emmy delivered the police constable's message to Jane.

"I suppose he's the husband of Mrs. Denning who has kittens," Emmy remarked.

"That's right. The village policeman—a darling man. We work together a lot. Harry Heathfield, you said? Oh dear. Well it was only to be expected."

"What was?" Emmy asked.

But Jane was already at the telephone, dialing a number. "Hello? P.C. Denning? Mrs. Spence here. I believe you wanted me . . . yes . . . yes . . . well, there wasn't really any hope, was there? . . . Of course he must be, poor man . . . yes, I'll go round there right away . . . tell him not to worry—that is, can you get a message to him? . . . Oh, good. Yes, I'll see to everything . . . thanks a lot . . . goodbye for now. . . ."

Jane hung up and turned to Emmy with a smile and a resigned sigh. "No peace for the wicked," she said. "I'm terribly sorry. I have to go out. And there'll be three new arrivals to cope with."

"New arrivals?"

"Dogs. Poor things. Lucky I've got a good supply of dog food."

Emmy, intrigued, said, "Do tell me, Jane. Who's Harry Heathfield, and why wasn't there any hope, and what's it got to do with the village policeman?"

Jane was pulling on a stout pair of rubber boots and thick leather gloves. "Oh, well—they rang him from the prison, you see."

"Who rang who?"

"Look, Emmy—I must go. You can come along and help if you like, and I'll explain it all in the car."

"O.K. I'll come."

Jane glanced critically at her sister. "I'm not sure that you're suitably dressed," she said. "You look a bit posh to me. I expect the poor things will tear us to pieces."

Emmy grinned. "Don't worry. I never wear anything that I care about when I come to see you."

They both laughed, and went out to the car.

"Now," said Emmy, as she settled herself in the passenger seat, "for the third time, who's Harry Heathfield and what about his dogs?"

Jane frowned at the road ahead of her. "Poor Harry," she said. "He's such a nice man. Lives a couple of miles out of the village, on the Middingfield road. Everybody told him he hadn't a hope, but he thought being drunk would be a defense."

"A defense against what?"

"Sorry. I'm not being very lucid, am I? The fact of the matter is that Harry is in prison, and of course he's in a state about his dogs."

"You mean—?"

"His case came up today at the County Assizes. He's been free on bail since the committal proceedings at Middingfield. He was convinced he'd get off. He can't remember anything about it, you see."

"I don't see at all," Emmy said. "What did he do?"

"Oh, he's not a *criminal*," said Jane, swinging the station wagon around a tight bend in the road. "It was only a motoring offense—but unfortunately he killed somebody."

"Driving while drunk?"

"Apparently. I told you, he can't remember a thing about it, but Bill says it was an open-and-shut case. He was on the bench of magistrates that sent Harry for trial. And he does so love dogs."

"Bill?"

"No, idiot. Harry. If I haven't room for a stray, I can always get Harry to take it in for a day or so. That is, I could. I haven't seen much of him recently. Anyway, Denning tells me that he was given a year in jail—and of course he's desperately worried about his dogs. He left them chained up in the yard this morning, you see."

"Are they strays or—?" Emmy began.

"Oh, Harry has his own mongrel bitch, Tessa. Had her for years. I'll look after her myself till he comes out. Otherwise, he tended to accommodate a floating population, rather like me—Denning says there are three altogether. Here we are. Oh, lord. Listen."

Jane had pulled the car onto the side of the road, and Emmy saw that they were on the outskirts of the village. Houses were few and far between, but the car was parked outside a pair of ugly red brick semidetacheds, which would have looked more at home in a London suburb than isolated in the middle of the countryside. From the back of one of the houses, canine voices were raised in complaint—an ear-splitting mixture of wailing and barking.

Jane jumped out of the car. "Tessa!" she called. "It's all right, old girl. Here we come!"

The door of the second house opened, and a middle-aged woman with a kindly, work-lined face came out.

"Are you from the cruelty people?" she demanded.

"Yes," said Jane.

"Oh, thank goodness you've come. Those poor creatures—I've rung the police. I mean, it isn't right, is it? It was bad enough having to give evidence, and now poor Mr. Heathfield's been sent to prison."

"So I hear," said Jane briskly. She was obviously not keen on being drawn into a lengthy conversation.

"Well, I don't care what anybody says, I call it a shame,"

remarked the woman belligerently. "A nicer gentleman you couldn't hope to meet, and I told the judge so, evidence or no evidence. The best next-door neighbor a widow woman could have. And now those poor dogs with nothing to eat—"

"Well, you needn't worry about the dogs anymore," said Jane. "We've come to take them away."

"You're not going to—? I mean . . . have them put down, like?"

"No, no. I'm taking them to my house. Then I'll find homes for them until Mr. Heathfield can have them back again."

"It's very good of you, I'm sure," said the woman. "Ever since I got back from the court, they've been barking and carrying on something dreadful, poor dumb creatures. I told the policeman—"

"Yes, yes, you did quite right." Gently but firmly, Jane extricated herself from the conversation and led Emmy around the corner of the house and down the narrow, fenced-in alley that led to the backyard.

The yard was small, but meticulously neat and cleanly swept. There was a lean-to shed whose open door revealed a workbench and gardening implements. There were also two dog kennels, warmly lined with straw, outside each of which stood a bowl of water and an empty feeding dish. A long chain was firmly fixed to the interior of each kennel, and each chain terminated in a frenziedly barking dog. The larger—a shaggy black mongrel with a beautiful head—recognized Jane at once, and the barking changed to yelps of welcome.

"Good girl. Good old Tess." Jane fondled the mongrel's ears. "Just a minute, now . . . let's get you off your chain and onto this lead . . . Emmy, love, will you take her? She's gentle as a lamb, just a bit boisterous. Thanks. Now, what about you, old chap?" She addressed herself to the second dog—a biggish, nondescript terrier who cowered in snarling fear as Jane approached him. She knelt beside the kennel and let the dog sniff her hand; soon, reluctant but at least partially reassured, he allowed her to detach his chain and clip a lead to his collar.

Jane stood up. "Well, we'd better get them into the car."

Emmy said, "I thought there were three dogs."

"So did I—P.C. Denning said three, but he must have made a mistake. There are obviously just the two." Jane put her head briefly into the shed. "Nothing there, and the house is all shut up. No—this is the lot, and I must say I'm not sorry. I've got enough on my plate as it is."

They led the dogs down the alley and to the front of the house. Mr. Heathfield's next-door neighbor was still in her front garden, spinning out to impossible lengths the chore of sweeping her doorstep. She smiled briefly. "There you go then," she remarked approvingly. "Poor Mr. Heathfield. Wouldn't hurt a fly. I was only saying to my married daughter—" She broke off. "Where's the other one?"

"What other one?" Jane already had the back door of the station wagon open, and was propelling Tessa's posterior through it.

"Why, the third dog." The woman, still carrying her broom, came down to her garden gate. "Three dogs, Mr. Heathfield had."

"I can assure you," said Jane, a little tartly, "that there are only two dogs."

"But—"

"Mr. Heathfield used to take in stray dogs and keep them for a few days until he found homes for them," Jane added firmly. "Tessa was his only regular pet, you know."

"But there was the new one . . ."

"So we'll be getting along. Good girl, Tessa. Sit. Now, Emmy, help me with this chap. In you go, boy. Right. Now we'll be off."

Emmy climbed into the car and shut the door. Jane switched on the ignition, and the engine roared into life. As they drove away, the woman was still leaning on her garden gate. She was saying, "But there was a *third* dog . . ."

In the car, Emmy echoed, "But there was a *third* man . . ."

"What's that?" Jane's eyes were on the road.

Emmy laughed. "Sorry. I was just quoting from the film. You remember . . . Harry Lime. He was the third man."

Jane was not listening. She said, "These two will have to sleep in the shed where the goat was. Lucky they're used to living in kennels. Sorry you've been let in for all this, Emmy."

"I don't mind," said Emmy staunchly. The ragged terrier, who seemed to have taken a fancy to her, settled himself more comfortably, half on her lap, distributing a liberal allowance of coarse ginger hairs over her trousers. Emmy bore him no malice, but was glad, all the same, that she was not dressed in her best.

After supper, Amanda Bratt-Cunningham telephoned. For some minutes, she and Jane chatted about the Heathfield trial, for Amanda had happened to see Harry on the fatal evening, and so had been called briefly to give evidence. But really, Amanda was calling to reassure Jane that the Great Dane, whom she had christened Wotan, had settled down splendidly. Wouldn't Jane and Bill come to Gorsemere House on Friday for lunch—and bring Jane's sister, of course? Then they could see for themselves how happy Wotan was in his new home. Jane said they would be delighted.

Mrs. Denning then rang to thank Jane for having found homes for two of the kittens—apparently both mothers had been agreeable, and Jane spoke long and earnestly to Mrs. Denning about the minimum age at which the kittens should leave their mother.

Hardly had Jane resumed her half-cold cup of coffee than the front doorbell rang. The visitor turned out to be a fussy clerical gentleman, whom Jane introduced as Mr. Thacker, the vicar of Gorsemere.

"I am so very sorry to disturb you at this hour, Mrs. Spence . . . oh, well, if you insist . . . yes, a cup of coffee would indeed be welcome . . . it's about your RSPCA stall at the fête next week. . . . I've just been to see Mr. Yateley and he . . . yes, with milk and sugar, please . . . he's agreed to put on a greyhound-training demonstration . . . should be a great attraction . . . and it seemed to me that if you and he were to get together . . ."

The result was that Jane and Mr. Thacker got together for a good half hour of technical discussion. At last, when the general outline of the canine contribution to the fête had been thrashed out, Mr. Thacker turned with a wide smile to Emmy.

"Welcome to our little village community, Mrs. Er . . ." he beamed.

"Tibbett," said Emmy.

"Mrs. Spence's sister, I believe? . . . Such a *very* valuable new member of the parish . . . Mrs. Spence here, I mean . . . and Mr. Spence too, of course. . . ."

Bill Spence grunted, and retreated even further behind his copy of *The Times*. It was clear that Mr. Thacker came high on the list of people whom Bill could do without.

The vicar turned to Jane once more. "You've heard about poor Harry Heathfield, I suppose?"

Jane grinned. "I've not only heard about him," she said, "I've got his two dogs in my shed."

"His dogs! Of course! I had quite forgotten them. Dear me, what will become of them, Mrs. Spence?"

"Well," said Jane. She glanced a little doubtfully toward Bill. "I . . . I thought I'd keep Tessa myself. Harry's black mongrel." *The Times* gave an indignant rustle. The addition of an extra member to the household was obviously news to Bill. Jane went on quickly, "The other is one of Harry's strays. I'll have to try to find a home for him. If you hear of anybody, Mr. Thacker . . ."

"Of course, of course. I'll do what I can. What sort of a dog is it, Mrs. Spence?"

"Oh, a very nondescript sort of brown mongrel terrier—not very attractive, I'm afraid," Jane said.

To her own surprise, Emmy heard herself saying defensively, "But he has a sweet nature, Mr. Thacker. A most affectionate creature." She remembered the ginger head resting trustfully on her knee in the car, the big brown eyes, the wagging banner of a tail. He had cowered away from Jane, but he had accepted her, Emmy, as his friend. It seemed the least she could do to stick up for him.

Jane gave Emmy a quizzical look, and Mr. Thacker beamed. "I see you share your sister's love of our dumb friends," he said unctuously. "Even in the short time that she has lived among us, we have all come to rely on her. Anybody who finds himself in difficulties—like Harry Heathfield, for example—knows that he can turn to her for help. How happy the wretched man must be to know that his pets are being cared for! When such an unexpected calamity overtakes a man—"

The newspaper rustled again, and from behind it came a distinct snort, and the word "Fiddlesticks!"

Mr. Thacker stopped in mid-sentence, his mouth open. "I beg your pardon?"

Slowly, Bill lowered his paper. "I said 'Fiddlesticks!' Mr. Thacker."

"So I understood, Mr. Spence. But—"

Emmy guessed that by now Bill was regretting ever having intervened in the conversation, but it was too late to retire again behind his protective camouflage of newsprint. Gruffly, he said, "The man must have known he'd be sent to prison. He had proper legal advice, and any competent lawyer must have told him he hadn't a hope. It was pure irresponsibility on his part to go off to court leaving his animals unprovided for."

Mr. Thacker looked surprised at this outburst. "Indeed? I fear I have no direct knowledge of the case, Mr. Spence, but there has been a lot of talk. The general climate of opinion, if I may call it that, was definitely in his favor—"

"Then the general climate of opinion," remarked Bill scathingly, "is talking through its hat. Look, Mr. Thacker, I was on the bench for the committal proceedings. I know."

"How very interesting, Mr. Spence." Mr. Thacker was as keen on the scent of gossip as any spinster of his parish. "Strictly speaking, Heathfield was not one of my parishioners—did you know that the parish boundary runs along Riverside Lane? Rather interesting . . . not many people realize . . . In any case, in the circumstances it was not up to me to offer . . . em . . . consolation to the poor man. But I should be fascinated to hear . . . unless there's a question of professional secrecy, of course . . ."

"My dear man, I'm a magistrate, not a doctor or a priest. Nothing secret about it. It was a very bad case. Heathfield had been drinking at the White Bull all the evening, and—not to put too fine a point on it—he was dead drunk. When he left the pub, he simply drove off—"

"Drove off?" echoed Thacker. "I didn't know he owned a car."

"He didn't," said Bill, grimly.

"But he knew how to drive?"

"Yes, unfortunately—otherwise he wouldn't have got as far as he did. Apparently, he used to drive a van in connection with his market-gardening business, but when he retired he gave it up—let his license lapse. No—he simply stole this car, which belonged to another of the pub's customers, and drove off in it. He managed to get almost as far as his own house, and then he lost all control of the car and smashed it into his own front wall. Unfortunately, there was a wretched passerby between the car and the wall, and he was killed. When the police arrived, they found Heathfield at the wheel—passed out cold—and the other man lying dead under the car." Bill snorted, with a certain grim satisfaction. "The police threw the book at him, of course. Causing death by dangerous driving, driving with more than the prescribed blood-alcohol level, driving without license or insurance, taking away and driving a car without the owner's consent . . . you name it, they charged it."

"Dear me. I had no idea . . . yes, a very bad case." Thacker was trying to sound virtuously distressed, but could not keep the underlying glee out of his voice. "So he pleaded guilty, I suppose?"

"No, he did not. Against all advice, he insisted on pleading not guilty—on the grounds that he remembered nothing at all that happened after he left the pub, that it was not the sort of thing he would ever have done, and that he'd only drunk so much because he'd been egged on by what he called 'London men.' "

"That's perfectly true!" Jane's intervention was emphatic and surprising. Bill looked at her severely.

"What do you mean by that?"

"I mean that it wasn't the sort of thing he'd do. I know Harry. I've seen him with his dogs—"

"Oh, really, Jane. Nobody ever suggested the man had a bad record. All his neighbors spoke up for him. Nevertheless, nobody can commit a serious crime and then avoid the consequences by claiming that he was drunk at the time. In fact, in a driving offense, it makes it infinitely worse, not better. He must have known he'd be sent to prison, but he stubbornly persisted in being optimistic, and as a result we're landed with yet another bloody dog." Bill picked up his paper, shook it ostentatiously open at the leader page, and retired behind it.

Jane said hotly, "Well, Amanda was at the trial, and she says the judge said that man was wrong—"

"Which man?" Bill growled from behind his newspaper.

"You know. The man whose car it was. The man who'd been drinking in the pub with Harry. The judge said that he and his friend had obviously been encouraging Harry to drink too much, and that they should have known better."

Bill lowered his paper slowly and with dignity. "I do not intend," he said, "to get involved in this conversation. I merely point out that these men in the pub—who had never met Harry Heathfield before—had no reason to think he would be driving later in the evening. In any case, nobody can blame his own drunkenness on anybody else. Heathfield could have refused to drink with them, couldn't he?"

"Well, the judge said that being a publican himself—"

"A publican?" interrupted the vicar, greatly intrigued. "You mean, the judge who tried the case is also a publican?"

"No, no," said Jane. "The witness. He came from London and ran a pub of his own there. I can't remember his name."

"My dear Jane." Bill Spence did not often sound pompous to Emmy, but he had put himself into a position where it was difficult to avoid it. "Even the judge appears to have been infected by this general climate of opinion that Mr. Thacker mentioned—but not, I am glad to say, unduly. A man who gets drunk in a pub has nobody but himself to blame for it—or for his subsequent actions. Is that clear?"

"Yes, dear," said Jane meekly.

On Friday morning, in his office at Scotland Yard, Henry Tibbett studied a report which had been put on his desk. Then he rang for Sergeant Reynolds.

"Yes, sir?" The sergeant, correct and eager as usual, waited like a well-trained gundog.

Henry indicated the file in front of him. "This shooting affray at the Runworth Stadium last night."

"Yes, sir?"

"Any ideas on it?"

Reynolds gave a little shrug of distaste. "The usual thing, sir. Couple of rival dogtrack gangs shooting it out. Lucky nobody was killed."

"The man who was seriously wounded—Marsh, isn't it? Richard Marsh?"

"That's right, sir. Red Dicky, they call him."

"On account of his politics?" Henry asked, dryly.

The sergeant smiled. "I should say not, sir. Red Dicky's about the strongest supporter of private enterprise you could meet —especially if it's dishonest. No, he got his nickname on account of his hair. Regular carrot-top. Nasty piece of work."

"What do you know about him?"

"Just the usual. Small-time villain, gambler, always hanging around greyhound tracks."

"You spoke to him at the hospital, Sergeant?"

"If you can call it that," replied Reynolds, with infinite contempt.

"You mean—he wasn't saying a thing."

"You've put it in a nutshell, sir. No earthly idea who shot him. Didn't even see anyone he recognized at Runworth all evening."

"Any ideas of your own?"

"Well . . ." Sergeant Reynolds hesitated. "I wouldn't want to do any guessing, sir, but . . ."

"But what?"

"Well, it did just occur to me that Larry Lawson was killed a few weeks ago."

"Lawson," repeated Henry thoughtfully. "He was another of them, wasn't he? The dogtrack boys."

"That's right, sir. Red Dicky and Larry—well, let's say they didn't see eye to eye. In fact, they were leaders of rival mobs—only Larry Lawson was doing well for himself before he died. Moving up into a higher class altogether, as you might say. So now, when Red Dicky gets shot up—well, one's mind does sort of turn to one of Larry's pals, doesn't it? Shorty Bates, for instance."

"But you've no proof?"

"Not a shred, sir. The only other witness who might have been some help is a washout. He's in the hospital, too."

"Another of the mob?"

"No, no, sir. Very respectable. Bank cashier. Name of Hudson. Immediately after the shooting, Red Dicky's pal pulled a gun and shot wildly back at the attacker—only succeeded in hitting poor Mr. Hudson in the leg."

"And Hudson didn't see who fired the original shot?"

"With all those people milling around, sir . . . the best I could get from him was that there was a tall, blonde young woman standing close to Marsh, which gets us precisely nowhere. If it wasn't one of the Lawson gang, sir, I'll eat my hat."

Henry said, "But there was no question of Lawson being murdered, surely? He died in a motor smash, if I remember rightly."

"Not exactly, sir. He was run over by a drunken driver."

Henry looked interested. "A drunken driver belonging to a rival gang, you mean? A hit-and-run job?"

Reynold's gloom deepened. "No, sir. Naturally, I was suspicious, and I had Detective Constable Wright read up the com-

mittal proceedings. The driver was a retired marke
a real countryman, never been in any trouble of any
and certainly nothing to do with the stadium lot.
got plastered in the local pub one night, borrowed a car to drive home in, and passed out at the wheel. He was sent up for twelve months only the day before yesterday, at the Middingfield Assizes. All perfectly straightforward. No doubt about anything."

"Then why are you so sure—?" Henry began.

Sergeant Reynolds grinned faintly. "Because I've got a nasty, suspicious nature, sir. You ask my wife. Oh, I'm not suggesting that this retired gardener character was anymore sinister than any other idiot who goes in for drunken driving and has an accident. No—but it did cross my mind that someone like Shorty Bates might not be so well-informed as we are. If he thought Red Dicky had a hand in Lawson's death—well, he's not the kid-glove type. Or, of course, it could just have been a clash of business interests. Whatever it was, we'll never get anything helpful out of Marsh. Might as well close the file, if you ask me."

"Until it happens again," said Henry, "and some innocent bystander gets in the way of a bullet—and isn't as lucky as your Mr. Hudson."

"Well, there's always that risk, isn't there, sir? I'll keep at it, don't worry—there's always a chance that somebody'll lay information, but I doubt it. If Marsh dies—and the doctors say he's in a bad way—then we might get some information—a murder often scares the small-timers. But if he recovers—" Reynolds shrugged. "I daresay Red Dicky will have his own methods of retaliation, once he gets out of the hospital."

"That's just what I meant," said Henry. "More violence. Well, so long as Marsh is out of action, that gives us a breathing space. Nothing else urgent on our plate for the moment?"

"No, sir."

"That's good," said Henry, "because I'm off to Hampshire for a country weekend, and I don't want to be disturbed."

3

Emmy, Jane, and Bill arrived at Gorsemere House just after twelve noon on Friday. The rhododendrons were in bloom, throwing out a blaze of red, purple, and white which mercifully masked the blatant ugliness of the big Victorian house. As they climbed out of the station wagon, an enormous dog came bounding out of the front door to greet Jane with embarrassing enthusiasm. He was closely followed by a slim, fair-haired girl in corduroy trousers and an open-necked shirt.

"Hey, there!" she called. "Wotan! Here, boy! Heel!"

To Emmy's surprise the huge dog hesitated, his big eyes alight with intelligence. He looked from Jane to the girl, then back again.

"That's right, Wotan," said Jane softly. "Go to your mistress."

With a joyful bound, Wotan sprang back toward the girl, very nearly knocking her over with his great front paws, and then lay down at her feet, thumping the ground with his tail.

"You see?" said the girl.

"It's marvelous, Amanda," said Jane. "He's accepted you completely."

"He was just waiting for me to come and find him, weren't you, boy?" said Amanda Bratt-Cunningham.

Jane beamed. "I call that a real storybook happy ending," she said. "I only wish I could find such good homes for all my strays."

"How many have you got at the moment?" Amanda asked, as she led the way into the house.

"Oh, not too bad," Jane said. "I don't suppose you know anybody who wants a canary? I've got one that some children found with a broken wing. It's almost well again, and I've enquired all over the village but nobody claims it. Anyhow, the goat's gone."

"Praise be," said Bill piously. "Another day, and I'd have wrung the brute's neck and stewed it for supper."

"You've got no soul, Bill Spence," said Amanda.

"I don't know about a soul," retorted Bill, "but I've certainly got a nose. Jane shut the miserable beast in my toolshed. I've still not succeeded in fumigating it."

They had moved into a dark-paneled, chintzy drawing room, which showed signs of the shabbiness which Emmy had observed in other large houses owned by impoverished aristocrats. Sir Arthur might be the local squire as a matter of tradition, she reflected, but it was likely that many of the commuters in their shiny new bungalows could buy him out several times over, and this huge house was clearly a financial burden. It had compensations, however. The drawing room windows gave onto a stone terrace, from which steps led to a downward-sloping lawn bordered by enormous rhododendron bushes. The big flowers—white, red, purple, and mauve—glowed against the dark, shining leaves, making two avenues of blazing color, one on each side of the clipped green sward. Emmy exclaimed in delight.

"Yes, they are spectacular, aren't they?" said Amanda. "What will you have to drink, Mrs. Tibbett? Sherry? Fine. Jane . . . Bill . . . ? Three sherries." She busied herself at a trayful of decanters. "Of course, this part of the world is famous for rhododendrons. We locals get a bit blasé about them, but they are quite a sight at this time of year." Amanda distributed glasses of amber sherry. "You must get Jane to drive you around—the country's looking lovely just now."

"Yes, I'm looking forward to that," Emmy said. "When my husband arrives this evening—"

She broke off at the sound of a door opening. Turning, she saw to her surprise that a section of what she had taken to be paneled walling in fact concealed a door, which opened into a smaller, book-lined room. This door was now open, and two men were coming through it—a tall, thin, tweedy man with sparse gray hair and pince-nez, who was ushering out his visitor. The second man was shorter, sturdier, and younger. He had fair, crinkly hair and a merry, circular face, and he wore the uniform of a police constable. His dark blue dome-shaped helmet dangled from his hand by its leather chin strap.

"Ah, there you are, Father," said Amanda. "Come and meet everybody. Hello, Mr. Denning. Have a drink."

"That's very kind of you, Miss Amanda." The policeman's voice had a pleasantly soft country burr to it. "Since I'm not actually on duty . . ."

"Sherry, whiskey, or beer?" Amanda asked.

"Sherry, if you please," said Denning.

"Father?"

"I'll have a beer, thank you, my dear." The tall man looked around the room, peering shortsightedly at his guests, and fixed on Emmy. "Ah, you must be Jane's sister. Mrs. . . . Er . . . ?"

"Mrs. Tibbett, Sir Arthur," said Jane. "Emmy, may I introduce Sir Arthur Bratt-Cunningham?"

Sir Arthur shook hands with old-fashioned ceremony, and muttered a few words of greeting. Then, thankfully grasping his beer tankard, he bore Bill Spence off into a corner to discuss matters relating to the local parish council.

P.C. Denning said, "I was just having a word with Sir Arthur on a few routine matters." He was evidently doing his best to rid his speech of officialese, and Emmy could not help smiling sympathetically. She knew how easy it was to drop into prescribed jargon. Denning went on, "I'm glad to have the chance of a word with you, Mrs. Spence. I was going to ring you."

"Were you, Mr. Denning? What about? Not more kittens, I hope. I was talking to your wife last night—"

"No, no, Mrs. Spence. Well, that's to say, not kittens, but not so far off. I got your message through to Harry Heathfield that his two dogs were being looked after."

Jane looked pleased. "Oh, I am glad. I hope that's set his mind at rest."

"Well . . ." Denning hesitated. "In a manner of speaking, no. I mean, he's very grateful, but . . ."

"But what?"

"The fact of the matter is, Mrs. Spence, that Heathfield insists there were three dogs."

"That's what the woman next door said!" Emmy exclaimed.

With a trace of impatience, Jane said, "I can assure you, Mr. Denning, that there were only two. Weren't there, Emmy?" She appealed to her sister.

"We certainly couldn't find a third one," Emmy said. "There were just the two kennels, with a dog apiece—and the shed, which was empty. The other dog couldn't be locked in the house, could it?"

"No, no, madam. Harry says there was one dog in each kennel and one in the shed. It's really preying on his mind."

"Well," said Jane firmly, "I'm very sorry, Mr. Denning, but the plain fact is that the third dog must have slipped its collar and escaped. After all, Tessa was Harry's only real pet; the others were strays. If one of them managed to get free, it's only natural it should have run away. Will you explain that to Harry? Of course he's upset at the moment, with everything that's happened—but tell him not to worry. The dog certainly isn't shut up in the shed, and it'll probably have found itself another home by now. And tell him that I shall keep Tessa myself until he can have her back. She's settling down very well."

P.C. Denning drained his glass. "I'll get a message to him, Mrs. Spence," he said—"And I'm sure you're right. Someone will have taken the dog in—or if they haven't, then you'll soon hear about it. And now I must be off—the wife's expecting me for lunch."

After P.C. Denning's departure, conversation became general. The forthcoming village fête was discussed at length, with

Sir Arthur and Bill agreeing on Mr. Thacker's general incompetence. The vicar had, it seemed, further incensed Sir Arthur by proposing to hold a raffle.

"Raffle!" snorted the baronet. "Just another word for a lottery, which is just another word for plain gambling." Amanda whispered something to Jane, and Sir Arthur—whose hearing was very sharp—wheeled around and said, "I heard that, young lady. All right, perhaps I do have a bee in my bonnet—but I've seen the misery that gambling can bring, and you haven't. I'm glad to say nobody in this house has ever placed a bet—and I don't intend to let the habit in through the back door with Thacker and his Church Restoration Fund."

Amanda said, "Oh, really, Father. Sixpence on a raffle ticket—"

"That's how it starts," retorted Sir Arthur. "Next thing you know, it's a hundred pounds on a horse." He glared at his daughter.

The slight awkwardness in the atmosphere was relieved by Jane, who asked Amanda about her new venture—a small market-garden which she was cultivating in the old walled vegetable garden of Gorsemere House. Amanda replied enthusiastically that it was doing splendidly—selling fresh fruit, flowers, and vegetables not only to passing motorists from a stall at the gate, but also supplying the local general stores and a newly opened greengrocery at Middingfield.

Amanda's home-grown produce was in evidence at the excellent lunch which followed—and then it was time for Emmy and the Spences to say good-bye, if they were not to be late in meeting Henry's train.

Emmy and Jane were waiting on the platform at Gorsemere Halt when the London train pulled in. Bill had been dropped off at Cherry Tree Cottage, where he was now mowing the lawn, and his place in the car had been taken by the brindle mongrel, who had been christened Ginger.

"He did so want to come," Emmy explained, with faint apology, to Henry. "He loves riding in the car, don't you,

Ginger?" The dog jumped up enthusiastically and licked Emmy's hand.

Henry laughed. "You'd better keep an eye on my wife," he said to Jane. "She seems to have designs on your dog."

"He's not my dog," said Jane. She sounded amused. "Just a temporary lodger."

"Oh." Henry had stopped laughing. "He'll soon be going back to his own home, then?"

"I'm afraid not," said Jane cheerfully. "He hasn't one to go to. But he'll have to go somewhere. I can't keep him."

Emmy said nothing, but caressed Ginger's head. Henry gave her a suspicious look, and was unusually silent in the car on the way back.

Later, relaxing in a deck chair on the lawn, with a cool glass in his hand and the comforting whirr of the lawn mower as background music, Henry said, "Sorry if I'm not being very conversational, Jane. It's just so marvelous to sit here and do nothing."

Jane grinned. "You should retire," she said. "Not that we do nothing, but the tempo is different. Is Scotland Yard being particularly bloody?"

Henry closed his eyes. "I wouldn't say that. Just dreary and busy at the same time, which is a bad combination."

"I thought you were a fanatic about your work." Jane was mocking, gently. "Dedicated and all that."

"Hardly. I admit, interesting cases do fascinate me—but nothing seems to be coming my way at the moment except the most predictable and sordid affairs."

"Poor Henry." Jane sounded amused. "Well, we've got a perfectly riveting mystery for you, right here in the village."

"No," said Henry firmly.

"The Case of the Third Dog!" said Jane dramatically.

"The what?"

"Mystery Hound Vanishes Without Trace. Is International Gang Involved?"

"Well, is it?" His eyes shut, Henry leaned further back in his chair and turned his face to catch the last rays of the sun.

"That's for the Wizard of the Yard to find out," said Jane.

"Seriously, though," Emmy remarked, "I wonder what did happen to the creature? I mean, it certainly wasn't there when we picked up Ginger and Tess."

"You mean, there should have been yet another stray to add to your collection?" Henry was drowsy and gently amused. It was all a delightfully long way from Red Dicky Marsh and the Lawson gang.

"Tess isn't a stray," said Jane. "Harry's had her for years."

"Then why are you—?"

"Because poor Harry is in prison," Jane explained.

Bill, who had finished his mowing, came across the newly cropped grass, mopping his brow with a large red handkerchief. "What's this? Poor Harry? Don't tell me you're trying to enlist Henry in this ridiculous argument."

"But Bill—"

"Now, you listen to me, Henry." Bill poured himself a glass of beer and took a swig at it. "Jane maintains this man isn't a criminal. I don't know what women use for logic. If causing death by dangerous driving when drunk, uninsured, and without a license and in a stolen car isn't . . ." He paused for another draught of beer. "Well, if that's not criminal, just tell me what is."

"Of course, people tend to take motoring offenses less seriously than other crimes . . ." Henry's eyes were still shut, his voice lazy.

"My dear Henry, this wasn't a question of speeding or parking in the wrong place. It wasn't even a straightforward drunken driving charge. The man stole the car, for a start. If anybody ever richly deserved to be inside, it's Harry Heathfield."

"But he couldn't remember anything about it!" Jane protested.

Bill snorted into his beer mug. "There! You see! Typically female reasoning—just because the man was kind to stray dogs, every sort of farfetched excuse has to be made for him. Of course he couldn't remember anything—he was dead drunk!

He'd been in the Bull since opening time—he didn't attempt to deny it."

"Those men from London—"

"I know, I know. Villains from the big city who plied him with drink. Well, he didn't have to accept, did he? Good God, the man's not a child or an imbecile. He's responsible under the law for his own behavior—"

The conversation rolled to and fro across Henry's semisomnolent form. Something about what the judge had said . . . a man who was a publican himself should have known better . . . Harry just wouldn't have done a thing like that . . . if you could have seen him with his dogs. . . . The voices blurred, retreated. Henry's head lolled back against the deck chair. He slept.

After dinner that evening, the Spences' telephone began its usual shrill series of summons. Sir Arthur Bratt-Cunningham wanted to consult with Bill over a matter relating to the horse trough on the village green, which was currently causing passions to run high on the parish council. A distraught lady—the wife of a newly arrived commuter from London—implored Jane's assistance in coping with her cat, which was having a fit. Jane put her in touch with the local vet. A neighbor rang to invite the Spences to a coffee morning in aid of Oxfam, and the vicar to make sure they intended to support the Bingo Evening organized by the Red Cross.

For Bill, this was the last straw. "For God's sake, can't that man Thacker leave us in peace for two minutes?" He looked at his watch. "It's only nine. Let's go down to the Bull for a beer. At least we'll be safe there from the Man of God."

Jane protested that she had too much to do, what with the washing up and bedding down her menagerie for the night; and Emmy said that she would stay to help her sister and have a good old heart-to-heart. So it was only Bill and Henry who walked down the dark, May-scented length of Cherry Tree Drive and into the bar of the White Bull.

The saloon bar was delightful—as Bill pointed out, it had been used as the setting for a big color advertisement put out by the brewers, and one could see why. It was paneled in dark wood, with inglenook seats and a huge fireplace. Chintz and polished brass abounded, and the beer handles glowed with polish and years of constant use.

Bill and Henry moved slowly from the doorway to the bar, their progress hampered by the fact that Bill knew everybody and everybody knew Bill. By the time they arrived at the mahogany counter, Henry had been introduced to the village doctor, two of the local commuters and their wives, Tom Hayward the butcher, and P.C. Denning—the latter out of uniform and comfortably relaxed. Behind the bar, a very tall man with an impressive wingspan of gray mustache was busy pulling pints of ale. He looked up with a smile as Bill and Henry settled themselves on stools at the bar.

"Evening, Bill. Lovely weather, isn't it? What can I get you?"

"Pint of bitter for me, Paul," said Bill. "How about you, Henry? The same? Good. Make that two pints and one for yourself. And meet my brother-in-law, Henry Tibbett. Squadron-Leader Paul Claverton, our genial host."

"Delighted to know you, sir. And less of the Squadron-Leader, if you don't mind, Bill. Very much ex-RAF these days, thank God. Two pints it is."

The landlord swept Bill's money expertly from the bar and deposited it in the till. Henry's memory stirred. Paul Claverton —"Crazy" Claverton, they had called him then: one of the great fighter pilots of the Battle of Britain, one of the few who had survived, to come at last to this peaceful haven of a country pub.

Bill said, "If you want people to forget the RAF bit, Paul, you'll have to shake off the face fungus."

Paul Claverton rubbed his chin thoughtfully. "You're quite right, of course. It's often occurred to me—but somehow, I've had the thing for so long, I'd feel naked without it. Cheers." He grinned. "Anyway, it does the business no harm. Mustn't be hypocritical."

Henry remarked that his wife had been a WAAF during the war, and for a few minutes conversation turned to those long-ago days. Then Claverton said, "Well, I always swore then that if I came through in one piece, I'd buy myself a country pub. Not a very noble or original ambition, but at least I've achieved it, which is more than a lot of chaps can say. I'm very lucky. Especially as the Bull is a real country pub, not a tourist trap."

"I noticed when we came in," Henry said, "that everybody seemed to be local, and to know everybody else. It's rather surprising, considering what an attractive place it is, and not too far from London."

"Ah, but we're off the main road," Claverton pointed out. "The Fox and Pheasant on the Middingfield road gets all the passing car trade, and frankly they're welcome to it."

"You surely must get some outsiders as well as local people," Henry said.

"Very few, sir. Very few. And most of them we could do without. You've heard about Harry Heathfield?" Claverton added to Bill, with an abrupt swerve of topic.

Bill groaned. "I seem to hear of nothing else," he said. "Don't tell me you're joining the whitewash brigade."

"The what?"

"My wife and Amanda Bratt-Cunningham," said Bill, "are convinced that because Harry was kind to dogs he should have been acquitted and awarded costs against the police. Women!" He buried his nose in his tankard.

"I certainly wouldn't go so far as to say that," Claverton replied, "but I can't help feeling a bit sorry for the fellow, all the same. Of course, I'd never have let him leave the pub in that state if I'd had the remotest idea he was planning to drive a car. In fact, I wouldn't have let him get that way at all, but I never realized what was happening. That's what I mean about outsiders. A couple of the most objectionable types I've ever had in my bar. Never seen them before and never want to see them again, I assure you. I didn't realize that Harry was in the inglenook over there, and that they were plying him with Scotch. Mild and bitter was his usual tipple, and not much of that—couldn't afford it. He came in every evening, regular as clockwork, had one pint or maybe two—made them last an hour or so. Then off home." He took a drink of beer, and pulled thoughtfully at his mustache. "Funny. Can't think why they did it. Just amusing themselves, I suppose—slumming among the yokels. One of them was a parody of a Colonel Blimp type, bogus as hell, and the other was a lah-di-dah smoothie with pointed shoes. Well-spoken and all that, but if you ask me—Yes, of course, Doctor. Two pints, coming up."

As Claverton moved off down the bar to serve the doctor, Henry heard a rich, fruity voice behind his left shoulder saying, "My good friend Mr. Spence, if I'm not mistaken." He turned to see a squarely solid man in a worn tweed jacket settling himself onto a stool on the other side of Bill.

"Evening, Simon."

"Jane not with you?" the newcomer went on, and without waiting for an answer, added, "Pity. Wanted to talk things over with her about this bloody fête. You've heard Thacker's latest idea?"

"No," said Bill, "but nothing would surprise me. What are you having?"

"Large pink gin, if you please, Paul." The man pulled out a pound note and laid it on the bar.

"No, no," said Bill. "Have this one on me. And you'll have another pint, will you, Henry? Two more pints and a large pink gin, Paul. Henry, this is Simon Yateley. Simon—my brother-in-law, Henry Tibbett."

"Ah, yes—Jane's sister's husband. She told me you were expected. Welcome to Gorsemere."

"Now," said Bill, "tell me what the unspeakable Thacker has been up to?"

"Well, it's just such a lunatic idea," said Yateley. "He badgered and badgered me about this blasted fête until I gave in and agreed to put on some sort of training demonstration with a couple of dogs. You know how he won't take 'no' for an answer."

"Do I not," said Bill gloomily. To Henry he added, in explanation, "Simon breeds and trains greyhounds, you see. Has a big place up on the hill, beyond the Bratt-Cunninghams."

"Well, that was bad enough," Yateley went on, "but now he's insisting that I get together with your good lady, and that we somehow put on a joint sideshow of greyhound training and RSPCA work. I told him, it's just bloody impossible. The two things don't go together at all. Unless Jane has some sort of brainwave—"

"Brainstorm, more like," said Bill, peering morosely into his beer. "Why don't you simply tell Thacker you won't do it?"

Yateley laughed briefly and bitterly. "What, and have him on my doorstep morning, noon, and night for weeks? No, thank you." He downed his drink in one gulp. "Tell Jane I'll be in touch, will you? I suppose we can work something out. Is she as busy as ever?"

"Not unduly, as a matter of fact," said Bill. "We have our usual assortment of waifs and strays, of course. Harry Heathfield's dogs are the latest additions."

Yateley looked interested. "Oh, you've got them, have you? Good. Bella will be glad to hear that. Here, drink up and have another. And you, Tibbett. Paul! Same again, if you please."

The evening passed quickly and pleasantly. Henry, enjoying a delightful sense of relaxation and noninvolvement, was content to sit quietly drinking his beer and letting the tide of village talk swirl around him. The forthcoming fête was obviously arousing great interest, and Yateley snorted sardonically when Bill related Sir Arthur's outburst over the proposed raffle. However, Bratt-Cunningham's detestation of gambling was clearly a well-known foible, and Henry had the impression that the villagers were secretly not unpleased that their squire should display at least one harmless eccentricity. Other burning topics were the rearrangement of the railway timetable, which was greatly exercising the commuting contingent; the birth of twins to somebody called Maisie, who Henry only realized later was a thoroughbred mare; Amanda Bratt-Cunningham's market-garden; and the threatened removal of the horse trough from the village green.

It seemed to Henry no time at all before Paul Claverton was

calling "Last orders!" and he and Bill walked out into the warm, lantern-splashed darkness of the pub's courtyard, bidding cheery good-nights to their erstwhile drinking companions.

Walking back up Cherry Tree Drive, Henry found himself engaged in an all-too-familiar mental struggle, a silent but acrimonious argument between his sybaritic self and that inconvenient instinct which his colleagues called his "nose."

"Go on," urged this relentless persecutor. "Ask him."

"I'm on holiday."

"You won't be on holiday on Monday. You'll have to face up to it sooner or later."

"I'm damned if I'm going to ruin my weekend. Anyhow, it's a ridiculous idea."

"Are my ideas usually ridiculous?"

"No—but this would be stretching coincidence too far."

"In that case, there's no harm in asking, is there?"

"He may not know."

"There's only one way to find out, isn't there?"

"If I do ask him, I don't promise to follow it up."

"All right. One thing at a time. Just ask him. Go on."

"Oh, very well . . ."

Bill said, "You're very silent, Henry. I hope you weren't too bored. Our village society isn't very lively."

"No, no. Sorry. I was just thinking." Henry took a deep breath. "Can I ask you something, Bill?"

"Of course." Bill sounded surprised.

"You were on the bench which committed this man Heathfield for trial, weren't you?"

"Yes. I told you so earlier on."

"Well, then, you may remember. What was the name of the passerby who got killed? The man Heathfield ran over?"

Bill hesitated. "Wait a minute. It's on the tip of my tongue. An ordinary sort of name. Thompson . . . Dawson . . . no, I've got it. Lawson. Lawrence Lawson."

"A local man, was he?" Henry was clutching at straws.

"No, no. He came from London. Was spending a few days down here on holiday, poor devil. Why are you so interested?"

"No reason," said Henry. "No reason at all."

"I told you so," remarked his nose, complacently. "Now what are you going to do?"

"I don't know," said Henry, and realized that he had spoken aloud.

"You surely know why you're interested?" said Bill.

"Oh, that . . . no . . . probably nothing to do with it . . ."

"Well, here we are." Bill unlatched the gate of Cherry Tree Cottage and stood back to let Henry enter first. Funny, he thought. Old Henry must have had one too many. Not like him Usually holds his drink well. Probably been working too hard. Do him good to have a nice quiet weekend with nothing to worry about.

4

The next day, Henry made a determined and largely successful effort to ignore the tugging of his professional instincts. With Emmy and the Spences, he went for a long and leisurely pre-lunch walk through bluebell woods and across sandy heaths, finishing up at a somewhat bleak establishment on an open hill-top which Jane described as "Simon Yateley's place," but which a wooden signboard designated as Hilltop Kennels. The barrack-like appearance of the buildings was enhanced by the presence of a high wire fence, topped by rolls of barbed wire and dangerous-looking spikes. Inside were several long, low structures, whitewashed and looking much like stables, each compartment giving onto a wired-in enclosure. As Bill pressed the bell beside the formidable iron gate, a cacophony of barking greeted the visitors; and Henry saw that the whitewashed buildings were in fact rows of kennels, and that many of the runs were occupied by slim, nervous-looking greyhounds.

Glancing up at the fortified fence, Henry said, "Your friend Yateley certainly makes sure that his dogs don't escape."

Jane laughed. "It's the other way round," she said.

"How do you mean?"

"The fence isn't to keep the dogs in. It's to keep out any possible—oh, hello, Simon. I heard you wanted to talk to me, so we thought we'd take our constitutional in this direction."

The bluff, four-square man whom Henry had met in the White

Bull had come from the kennels, and was now engaged in the complicated process of unlocking the gate. He had exchanged his tweed jacket for blue overalls, and a whistle hung around his neck on a lanyard. He grinned in welcome.

"Good show. Always delighted to see you, Jane my dear. And Bill. Yes, I met Henry last night over a beer. How d'ye do, Mrs. Tibbett? Come on in, all of you, and have a drink. I was just about to pack in the training session and have a snort myself."

He pulled open the heavy gate to admit his visitors, and then relocked it carefully after them, before leading the way past the line of kennels toward an ugly, upright, red brick house which was presumably the residential part of the establishment.

"Come on in," said Simon Yateley. He opened the front door and ushered the party into the hallway, which was hung with sporting prints. Raising his voice, he called, "Bella!"

A distant female voice answered. "What is it now?"

"Company. Bill and Jane and a couple of friends. We'll be in the lounge."

The voice shouted an unintelligible reply which did not sound enthusiastic, and Yateley grinned. "My lady wife," he explained, "will be very cross with you."

"Oh, I'm so sorry—" Emmy began, distressed.

Yateley went on, with a grin. "Don't you worry yourself, Mrs. Tibbett. Jane knows what I mean, don't you, dear? The fact is," he went on in a confidential tone, to Emmy, "Bella has been dying to meet you and she'll be miffed as all hell not to have had time to tart herself up. Now, come and name your poison."

Mrs. Yateley appeared as her husband was handing out the drinks. For no very good reason, Emmy had expected a slick, enameled beauty; to her surprise, Bella Yateley turned out to be a capable country girl in corduroy breeches and a khaki shirt. Her chestnut hair was short-cropped, and her strong, attractive face was patently unused to the application of cosmetics—although, in honor of the occasion, Bella had put on a smudge of lipstick and a sprinkling of powder which failed to hide her freckles.

She greeted Bill and the Tibbetts with a wide, friendly smile, and then went over to Jane. She came straight to the point. "Simon tells me you've got Heathfield's dogs."

"That's right," said Jane. "Pro tem, anyhow. I'll keep Tess myself until Harry comes out, but I'll have to find a home for the other one."

"You want to be a bit careful who you give her to," Bella said. "She's a sensitive bitch."

Jane looked surprised. "She? What do you mean? It's a male —a sort of brindly mongrel Airedale. Rather a nice animal."

"Oh." Bella dismissed Ginger with a shrug. "That must be another one he picked up. I meant the third dog."

"Now, don't you start, for heaven's sake." Jane was laughing. "This is becoming the mystery of the century. What became of the third dog?"

"Well, what did become of her?"

"I don't understand."

"I'm talking about Lady Griselda."

"About *who?*"

"Lady Griselda of Gorsemere. By Lord Jim out of Patient Griselda. One of our biggest disappointments," Bella added.

"You mean, Harry Heathfield had a *greyhound?*" asked Jane. She became aware that Henry was standing beside her, listening with interest.

"That's exactly what I mean," said Bella.

"But . . ." Jane was bewildered. "What on earth was Harry doing with a racing greyhound?"

"I'll tell you." Simon Yateley's voice boomed genially, as he joined the group. "Bella gave the bitch to Harry."

"You must have been mad," Jane remarked, to Bella.

"Not at all," said Simon. "As Bella said, Griselda was one of our biggest disappointments. We bred her ourselves, you see. Most of our dogs," he added, to Henry, in explanation, "belong to other owners, and they send them here for training. Rather like an exclusive finishing school for young ladies. But we do breed some of our own, and we thought we had a winner in Griselda, didn't we, Bella?" His wife nodded.

Henry said, "So what went wrong?"

Yateley shrugged. "Nothing exactly went wrong," he said. "It was just a question of temperament. Some dogs are racers, some aren't. Griselda had the looks, the breeding, the class, and the speed, too—but temperamentally she must be a throwback to some undesirable ancestor. She's a delightful creature—affectionate, gentle, perfect as a pet—but a dead bloody loss on the track. She'd go like the wind on training runs—do anything for Bella. But show her a racing track and a mechanical hare and—phut. Like Ferdinand the Bull. He didn't want to fight, Griselda didn't want to race. No competitive spirit at all. Well, it does happen, and there's no sense wasting valuable kennel space on an animal like that. So we let Harry have her. Glad to find her a good home. How is she?"

Jane was looking distressed. "I don't know," she said.

"What d'you mean? I thought you'd taken in Harry's dogs—"

"So I have," said Jane. "The other two. But there was no sign of a greyhound—was there, Emmy?"

Emmy shook her head. "There certainly wasn't. She must have escaped sometime during the day, before we got there."

"Oh, poor Griselda!" Bella Yateley was patently upset. "We must find her. What can we do?"

"Give me a complete description of her, for a start," said Jane. "Then I'll circulate it to the police and other RSPCA representatives. Now—color?"

"Pale fawn, white forefeet, white star on her forehead," said Simon promptly. "Most distinctive. Can't miss her."

"In that case," said Jane, "I'm sure we'll find her quickly. Somebody's sure to have picked her up. And if she's an obviously valuable-looking dog, you needn't worry about her being sold for vivisection or anything like that."

"No," said Henry, "but whoever found her may be planning to sell her for a good lot of money."

Yateley said, "She certainly looks like a top-notcher, but it'd take a full-blown classic mug to buy a greyhound off a stranger, with no pedigree and no idea of her form. No, I reckon she'll turn up. Now, Jane Spence, what are we going to do about the Reverend Wretched Thacker and his fête worse than death?"

Back at Cherry Tree Cottage at lunchtime, Jane started on her round of telephone calls in search of the missing Lady Griselda of Gorsemere; but she drew blanks. No such dog had been reported as found, or turned in, either to the police or to any of the animal societies. Lady Griselda had, it seemed, just disappeared.

"The plot thickens," remarked Bill Spence with heavy humor, as he sharpened a dangerous-looking knife prior to tackling the joint.

"It certainly does," said Henry. But he was not smiling.

5

Monday morning. A pale, watery sun did its best to struggle through the high layer of clouds lying over London, while a sharp wind from the north sent scraps of paper flying down the gutters of Victoria Street, and made the scurrying crowds of work-bound typists wish they had worn their winter maxi-coats. In an office on the fifth floor of Scotland Yard's clinically pale new building, Detective Sergeant Reynolds faced Chief Superintendent Henry Tibbett across the latter's desk. He looked puzzled.

"The Heathfield case? You mean, the drunken driver who ran down Larry Lawson? But I told you, sir—I checked it out."

"You got Detective Constable Wright to do it, didn't you? He's a new boy."

"Well—yes, sir, he is. But very conscientious. Shaping up well."

"All right, all right, Sergeant. I'm not getting at him." Henry smiled. He knew about Reynolds' fierce championship of his men, and he approved of it. "What I mean is that in the nature of things he's not acquainted with the name and face of practically every villain in London, as you are."

"Of course he's not, sir. Couldn't be. But like I said, he's conscientious. He told me he'd checked with CRO on every witness in that case, and not one has a criminal record. So—"

"All the same," Henry said, "just check once more yourself,

will you? Get hold of the trial transcripts and read them through. Just see if there are any familiar names."

"But, sir—"

"Look, Sergeant," said Henry, "you know me well enough by now. Call it my nose, or anything else you like. Call me a bloody fool—but do as I ask, will you? I'm off to the Old Bailey to give evidence, but I'll be back."

Reynolds grinned. "Anything you say, sir."

Henry spent the greater part of the day in court—most of it waiting in bleak corridors, but culminating after lunch in a satisfactory half hour in the witness box, which was instrumental in convicting an habitual robber-with-violence. He got back to his office at three in the afternoon, to find a message that Sergeant Reynolds would like to see him as soon as possible. He picked up the telephone.

"Ask Sergeant Reynolds to come in right away, will you?"

As soon as the sergeant came into the office, Henry knew that his instinct had been right. Reynolds' expression of mingled admiration and exasperation was one which Henry had seen before. He carried a sheaf of papers in his hand.

Henry said, "Well? Any luck?"

"Once I don't mind. Twice is a bit much," said Reynolds enigmatically. He threw the papers down on Henry's desk. "You knew all along, didn't you, sir?"

"No," said Henry. "I guessed. You mean—it was Weatherby?"

"That's exactly what I mean, sir. Major George Weatherby, licensee of the Pink Parrot public house in Maize Street, Notting Hill. Talk about an old friend. No criminal record, of course. By golly, he gets around, does the major. I thought we'd heard the last of him, after the Byers case."

Henry sighed, but with a certain satisfaction. "I thought of him at once, when I heard that one of the witnesses had been a London publican," he said, "but I hardly dared hope . . . What's he been up to lately, Sergeant?"

Reynolds shrugged. "Nothing—as usual. He still runs the Pink Parrot, and the upstairs Private Bar is still the meeting place for prosperous villains specializing in gambling, racetracks, and the dogs. The major has been especially careful about keeping his own nose clean, since we got so close behind him on the Byers case. I thought he'd maybe given up the profitable profession of being a convenient witness, but the temptation must have been too much this time."

"Tell me about it, Sergeant," said Henry. "Who were the other witnesses? What was Weatherby's evidence?"

"Well, sir." Reynolds took a deep breath. "The fact is, it was Weatherby's car that was stolen—and wrecked, into the bargain. It'd be funny, wouldn't it, if it was all just a coincidence? I mean, suppose it's true what he said—that he'd been having a quiet drink in this country pub, and this drunk nabbed his car and crashed it—"

"With Larry Lawson under the wheels?"

"Well, sir—"

"I know. Try to prove it. Well, go on. What happened?"

"According to Weatherby, he was on holiday. The Pink Parrot was closed for redecoration, he said. It was a fine evening, and he and a friend decided to drive down to the country for a meal and a drink. All innocent enough, on the face of it."

"Who was this friend?" Henry asked.

"Not a CRO man, you can be sure, sir. Never heard of him before. A Mr. Albert Pennington of Chelsea. Occupation, Company Director. The two of them drove down to Middingfield, in Hampshire, in Weatherby's car—the major driving—and finished up at a pub called . . ." Reynolds consulted his papers . . . "called the White Bull, in a village by the name of Gorsemere, a few miles from Middingfield."

"I wonder why," Henry said.

"Well, now, sir—not that I hold any brief for Weatherby—but it was a lovely spring evening, and from all accounts it sounds a very pleasant pub. Inglenooks and oak beams and so on. There's plenty of London people like to drive to the country of an evening—"

"The White Bull isn't on the main road," said Henry. "It's on the old London–Westmouth road and used to be a coaching inn—but now the road passes to the north. It's most unlikely that a stranger would go out of his way to find the White Bull —and the landlord says he'd never seen either Weatherby or his friend before."

"He does? But how—? I mean, you've actually spoken to the landlord, sir?"

"I have. I'll explain in a minute. Go on, Sergeant."

"Well, like I said, sir, Weatherby and Pennington went into this pub, leaving the car parked in the yard outside. Weatherby said he didn't bother to lock the car, not in the yard of a quiet country pub—but he did admit that he hadn't intended to leave the key in the ignition. Pure forgetfulness, he said. Well, I suppose we've all done it one time or another, haven't we? Anyhow, Weatherby and his friend went into the White Bull and sat down in one of these inglenook things, where they got into conversation with the man Heathfield. Never met him before, of course, but Weatherby said he was a great character, with plenty of local anecdotes to tell. They were amused by his talk, and brought him drinks to keep the flow going. Whiskey, it was."

"His usual drink was mild and bitter," said Henry. "Go on."

"Heathfield got a bit merry, it seems, but both Weatherby and Pennington insisted that he seemed OK. Then, suddenly, the drink seemed to hit him. About ten o'clock, that was. He got to his feet—Heathfield did—swayed about a bit, and said he'd be off home. Very unsteady, and speech badly slurred. Weatherby says he asked him if he was all right, and Heathfield said yes, it was only a few minutes' walk to his house, and the fresh air would do him good. And off he went. Weatherby and Pennington had another drink and thought it was all a bit of a joke. Then, at half-past ten, the pub closed. The two men went out into the car park—and lo and behold, no car. They went in and told the landlord, who phoned the local police. By that time, news of the accident had reached the Gorsemere Police Station, so of course they were able to identify the car right away. It was a write-off, of course. Weatherby and Pennington hired a local taxi into Middingfield, and caught the last train back to London. All perfectly straightforward."

"Perfectly," said Henry dryly. "Now, what about the rest of the evidence?"

"Just routine, really, sir. P.C. Denning, from Gorsemere, received a phone call at twelve minutes past ten, from a Mrs. . . ." Reynolds consulted the paper again ". . . a Mrs. Donovan. The accused's next-door neighbor. A widow lady living on her own. She testified she was in bed and asleep when she was woken by the crash outside. She got up, put on a dressing gown, and looked out of the window. The road's not lit there, but she could see the car, with its nose smashed into Heathfield's front wall. She says she could see Heathfield, slumped over the wheel, unconscious. She knew him well, of course, living next door. She rang the police right away. It was only when they got there that they found Lawson. He'd been caught between the car and the wall—killed outright, the doctor said. Heathfield was still out cold. At first, they thought he was concussed—but when they got him to the hospital they found he wasn't injured at all. Just dead drunk. And that's all there is to it."

"And Heathfield says he remembers nothing about it," Henry said.

"That's right, sir. He remembers going to the White Bull, like he did every night, and sitting in the inglenook, and the two London gentlemen talking to him and buying him drinks. Then, he said . . ." The sergeant sorted out the appropriate sheet of paper, and began reading aloud. "He said, 'I came over queer suddenly. I remember saying I must go home—and after that I don't remember nothing till I woke up in the hospital.' And he seemed to think that was a defense!" Reynolds laughed sardonically.

"Any other witnesses?" Henry asked.

"Just enough to sew the case up tight," said Reynolds. "Nobody actually saw Heathfield getting into the car—the pub yard was deserted. But a young lady did happen to see the car being driven in the direction of Middingfield. A Miss Amanda Something . . . double-barreled name . . ."

"Bratt-Cunningham," said Henry.

"That's right. She was driving home and happened to notice

the car. It's rather distinctive—or was—being bright yellow. She noticed that it was weaving about a bit, which made her take a second look, and she's certain she recognized Heathfield at the wheel. Reading her evidence, I'd say she liked Heathfield, and didn't enjoy ratting on him—I gather her old man's by way of being the local squire, Chairman of the Magistrates and so on. Reckon it was him insisted she tell the police what she'd seen. Anyway, it was an open-and-shut case without her evidence. The only other witnesses were the experts—doctors and police. Oh, and Lawson's widow identified him."

"What did she say? What was he doing in Gorsemere?"

Reynolds shrugged. "Your guess is as good as mine, sir. *She* said he was having a short holiday in the country."

"On his own? She wasn't with him?"

"Seems not, sir."

Henry and Reynolds looked at each other. Henry raised his eyebrows slightly, and Reynolds said, "I agree, sir. It stinks to high heaven."

"The question is," said Henry, "what are we going to do about it?"

"We could start with Weatherby, sir. I could haul him down here and give him an uncomfortable half hour or so—metaphorically speaking, of course. It'd be a pleasure."

"I'm sure it would," said Henry, "but I think not. Let's not put them on their guard. No, I think the person to see is Mrs. Lawson. You have her address?"

"The one she gave the court, yes, sir. You want me to get her in for questioning?"

"No, Sergeant. Just the address. I'll visit her myself."

The address which Sergeant Reynolds produced was in an opulent part of the North London suburb of Finchley, and the house turned out to be an ugly but luxurious structure of thirties stockbroker-Tudor vintage. It stood in a biggish garden, which, although neglected, was bright with blossoming fruit trees; and there was a large "For Sale" notice beside the front gate. Henry got out of his car, pushed open the gate, which was sagging slightly on its hinges, and walked up a gravel path which was already sprouting a crop of weeds.

There was no point in ringing the front doorbell. The place was obviously empty. Through uncurtained windows on each side of the door, Henry could see large rooms devoid of furniture, with dark rectangular marks on the wallpaper indicating where pictures had hung, and electric wires sprouting forlornly from the middle of the ceilings in place of light fittings. The house had not been hastily abandoned; efficient removal men must have stripped it systematically, crating furniture and household goods for storage or transfer to another house. The conclusion was obvious. Soon after her husband's death, Mrs. Lawson had sensibly decided to move to smaller quarters, and to sell the house for the huge sum it would undoubtedly fetch.

Henry walked around to the garden at the back. From the general state of neglect, he guessed that the property had been deserted for a couple of months at least. Lawson had been killed nine weeks ago. Either his widow had moved out as soon as she heard the news, or else the couple had already left the house before Lawson's accident. Henry wondered for a moment why Mrs. Lawson had given the court the address of this house, where she clearly no longer lived; then the obvious explanation occurred to him. She must undoubtedly have given evidence at the inquest immediately after Lawson's death, and probably thought it less complicated to use the same address. Since the house was still hers, he presumed she was justified.

At the back of the house, big French windows opened onto a paved terrace. Clumps of grass and dandelions were pushing up determinedly between the flat gray stones, and an ancient canvas swing chair sagged sadly from its rusting frame. The windows had been left shuttered, but one of the slatted wooden panels was broken, and through it Henry could peer into the empty drawing room—a large, handsome apartment with a polished parquet floor marked with the shapes of departed rugs, and the outlines of wall-bracket lamp fittings on the Regency-stripe wallpaper on either side of the open fireplace. Lawson had certainly come up in the world, as Reynolds had said.

Henry wondered why his widow had been in such a hurry to leave this pleasant home.

From the terrace, shallow steps led down to a lawn, around which the garden had been cunningly landscaped to appear larger than it actually was. This illusion was enhanced by the fact that the property was adjoined on all three sides by neighboring gardens abounding in trees and flowering shrubs, so that only a carefully hidden fence indicated the boundary of the Lawson domain. Trees had been placed so that no other house was visible at a casual glance. Henry could imagine admiring visitors exclaiming—"Why, you might be in the heart of the country!"

Equally ingenious was the placing of a bank of golden-flowering berberus bushes to screen the prosaic structures at the bottom of the garden—a small greenhouse, an open brick bonfire pit, and a garden shed. Henry was making his way toward the greenhouse when a voice behind him said abruptly, "What are you doing here?"

Startled, Henry swung around to find himself facing a short, sturdy man, with pointed features and a fussy manner.

"Just looking around," said Henry, "the house is for sale, you know."

"Thinking of buying it, were you?"

"I'm interested in it, yes."

The man seemed to relax. "Oh, I'm sorry to have to disappoint you, sir. You haven't visited our offices, I daresay."

"Your offices?"

"Rackham and Stout, Estate Agents. The property is in our hands. Surely you saw the board?"

"I'm afraid I didn't make a note of the agent's name," said Henry, apologetically. "I was just passing in the car, and saw that the house was for sale—"

"Yes, sir. Well, it *was* for sale, but I'm afraid you're just too late. A very desirable property, this. We sold it only this morning. Places like this get snapped up, you know." The small man smirked, giving his sharp face a foxy look.

"It's only recently come onto the market, then?" Henry asked.

"That's right. Very recently. And now, if you don't mind, sir . . ." The fussy manner became more marked. "I am here on behalf of the purchaser, and I have certain things . . . I regret we have not already removed the 'For Sale' board . . . it will be attended to . . ."

Henry beamed. "Of course. Do forgive me. I have no right to be here. What a pity the house is sold. Just my bad luck."

"That's right, sir. Just your bad luck." It was with evident relief that the small man shepherded Henry back to the front of the house, down the garden path, and into his car. Parked immediately behind Henry's car was a small, dark-blue van of the kind used by small businesses for delivery work; but there was no indication on it of the owner's name. Henry, making a quick mental note of the number, presumed that it had been driven here by the small man from the agency, who was now standing just inside the gate with a distinctly proprietorial air, waving Henry good-bye. Short of revealing his identity as a police officer, Henry could not linger and hope to maintain any credibility. He climbed into his car and drove off.

He did, however, make a circuit of the neighboring roads, which brought him back to the gate of No. 18 Sandown Avenue about five minutes later. There was no sign of the blue van, nor of the small man. The "For Sale" notice was still there. Thoughtfully, Henry drove to the offices of Rackham and Stout, Estate Agents, in Finchley Road.

Here, Henry was greeted by an attractive blonde receptionist, who appeared suitably impressed by the sight of his official identity card, and in a few minutes he was ensconced in a leather armchair in the private office of Mr. Rackham himself. The latter was a dark, rotund gentleman, with all the self-assurance and friendly bounciness of North London's well-to-do Jewish community.

"Chief Superintendent Tibbett? Well, well, well, this is an honor. Sit yourself down and have a cigar. No, go on. They're the best. Not worried about cancer, are you? These wouldn't do you any harm, you can rest assured—wouldn't dare, not at the price I pay for them. You're quite sure? Well, I hope you don't mind if I do. One of my little self-indulgences, I'm afraid." Mr. Rackham lit the fat cigar with care, and puffed at it with loving attention until he was satisfied with its performance. Then he removed it from his mouth, and went on, "And what can we do for you, then, Chief Superintendent? Interested in house property in this area?"

"Yes," said Henry. "As a matter of fact, I am."

"Well, now, fancy that. Any particular house, did you have in mind?"

"No. 18 Sandown Avenue," said Henry.

Rackham beamed. "A very highly desirable property," he said, rolling the words round his tongue. "A gentleman's select detached residence standing in its own extensive grounds of nearly a fifth of an acre. Central heating, parquet floors, modern kitchen, fixtures as found. Landscaped garden abounding in shrubs, trees, and floral . . . er . . . flowers." His pudgy forefinger flicked a switch on a small black box on his desk, which at once emitted an indistinguishable female noise. "Oh, Miss Farthing. Bring me details of 18 Sandown, will you? Thank you, dear. Yes," Mr. Rackman went on, once more addressing Henry, "that property is what I can only describe as a snip."

"So it's not sold?" Henry asked, getting a word in with difficulty.

"No, no. Not yet—you're still in time, I'm glad to say, Chief Superintendent. We've had nibbles, that I don't deny—but let us face it, the price is steep. Fair, mind you—but steep. It is what you might call a unique type of residence, and money is tight these days. Undeniably tight. But you're in luck, Chief Superintendent. I happen to know that the owner is anxious to make a quick sale—doesn't want the property hanging about on the market—and she's open to offer." Rackham leaned back and puffed on his cigar.

Before Henry could say more, the door opened and the blonde slipped in and placed a gray cardboard file on Mr. Rackham's desk.

"Thank you, my dear. That'll be all for now." Rackham pulled a pair of gold-rimmed spectacles out of his breast pocket, settled them on his broad nose, and began to scan the papers in the dossier. "You'll find all the details here, Chief Superintendent. Magnificent double living room, thirty feet by twenty, giving onto—"

"Yes, I know," Henry said. "I've already been to look at the house."

"You have?" Rackham was immediately suspicious. "I'm very surprised to hear you say that, sir, because we are the *sole* agents. If a key has been obtained by some other firm—"

Henry hastened to reassure him. "No, no. I didn't go inside. I just had a look at the place from outside, and explored the garden." He hesitated for a moment, and then added, "As a matter of fact, I met your representative there."

"My representative?" Rackham seemed genuinely bewildered.

"I don't know his name," Henry said, "but he was a small, dark man—about forty, I should think. Driving a plain dark-blue Austin van. He told me that the house was sold, and that he was there on behalf of the purchaser."

Rackham's face had assumed an expression of almost comical astonishment and disbelief. He burst out, "That's a load of old rubbish, sir, if you'll forgive the expression. Whoever the man was, he was an impostor, or worse. Certainly nothing to do with this firm, of that I can assure you. The house is *not* sold, none of our representatives drives a blue van, and nobody has any right to be on that property without authorization from this office!" He puffed furiously at his cigar, as if to prevent himself from exploding.

Henry smiled. "I rather thought as much," he said. "That's why I came to see you right away, Mr. Rackham. I must explain that I've no idea of buying the place. My interest is professional."

Enlightenment dawned on Rackham. "I know exactly what you mean, Chief Superintendent," he said, enigmatically. "Exactly. Young hooligans!"

"I don't—" Henry began.

"Breaking into unoccupied properties," Rackman went on, "Taking drugs and playing guitars and every sort of lark. No respect for law and order. Disgusting. I'd cut off their long hair and give them all a good thrashing if I had my way. We've had a lot of trouble with them. They started in Piccadilly, but they're creeping out into the suburbs. You mark my words. They're finding their way into the most select residential—"

Henry said, "I didn't mean hippies, Mr. Rackham. The man I saw could hardly have looked more respectable, and there was no sign that the house had been broken into."

"Then what—?"

"The property belongs to a Mrs. Lawson, I believe?"

"That is correct. The poor young lady was widowed not long ago, in tragic circumstances. Her husband was killed in a motor smash, so she told me. He was a well-to-do gentleman—something in the City, I believe—but of course, with the breadwinner struck down in his prime, as you might say, the lady has been left in reduced circumstances, if you get my meaning. She came to us shortly after his death, to put the house on the market."

"And where is she living now?" Henry asked.

"Well, now—I'm not sure if it's proper to divulge—"

"I am a police officer," Henry said. "I am investigating certain suspicious facts about the death of Mr. Lawson, and I must speak to his widow."

Rackham seemed relieved not to have to wrestle with his conscience any longer. He said at once, "Ah, well, that makes a difference, doesn't it, Chief Superintendent? Let's have a look." He thumbed through the file. "Here we are. Mrs. Marlene Lawson, 208 Nelson Buildings, Battersea." He raised his head and met Henry's steady gaze. "I can see what you're thinking, Chief Superintendent. Something of a comedown after Sandown Avenue. I understand Mrs. Lawson is staying with her mother, and that things . . . aren't easy. As I told you, she is very anxious to dispose of the property. In fact, she telephoned me only last week to ask if we'd been able to find a purchaser. I explained to her that the figure she had in mind was—well, a little unrealistic, shall we say? I suggested that if she wanted a quick sale, she should come down at least a couple of thousand. She said she would consider the matter and let me know."

"And has she?"

"Not as yet. But this is only Monday—"

"Very interesting," said Henry. "Now, Mr. Rackham, could we go and take a look at the house?"

"Well—naturally, if you think it's important, sir . . . but—"

"The man with the blue van," said Henry, "who had no connection with your firm, seemed to think it important to keep me away from the place. I'd like to know why."

As it turned out, 18 Sandown Avenue had apparently no clues to offer. Henry and Rackham explored it room by room, but it showed no signs of being anything other than a luxurious home beginning to display sad evidence of emptiness and neglect. Henry examined the kitchen with special care, but there was no trace of recent use or occupation. By the end of the unrewarding exercise, Rackham was glancing ostentatiously at his watch and showing signs of impatience. He did not react favorably when Henry, having at last closed the front door behind him, said, "And now the garden."

"Really, Chief Superintendent—I don't want to be obstructive in any way, but I really cannot see what useful purpose—"

"There's no need for you to wait if you're in a hurry, Mr. Rackham," said Henry pleasantly. "I can look at the garden by myself. Have you got keys to the greenhouse and the shed?"

"I really don't know," said Rackham irritably. He looked at the small bunch of keys in his hand. "Let me see. Front door, back door, French window—what's this? Ah, yes, garden shed. And greenhouse. Oh, very well—if you must see them, I'll come with you." He sighed deeply and led the way to the back of the house.

The greenhouse was warmly damp and stuffy. A few potted plants left behind by the Lawsons were expiring limply on the slatted wooden shelves. The water in the tank was green and uninviting. A couple of panes of glass had been broken, and the explanation seemed to lie in a bright yellow ball made of hard rubber. It must have been shied over the fence by neighboring children, and now looked incongruously new and bright as it lay among the peeling paint and dying ferns.

Mr. Rackham eyed the broken glass with a sort of furious resignation. "Vandals," he remarked. He stooped and picked up the yellow ball. "Young savages. The trouble we have with children, Chief Superintendent . . . there were no windows broken when Mrs. Lawson left here, of that I am sure. Of course, we've made it clear that any damage incurred while the property is vacant is the responsibility of the vendor, but it does not make the place easier to sell. No, it does not. I have a good mind to complain to the police."

"Since I am the police, Mr. Rackham," said Henry affably, "perhaps I can help you. If you give me the ball as evidence, I'll make some enquiries locally and—"

Mr. Rackham handed over the ball eagerly. "Most kind, Chief Superintendent. I really do appreciate that. If you knew the trouble—"

"Yes, I'm sure," said Henry hastily. "Now, if we can just see the shed, I needn't keep you any longer."

The garden shed was dark, dusty, and unremarkable. It contained a few rusty garden tools, a roll of ancient netting, an old gray blanket, an enamel bowl, and a few cracked flowerpots.

"Nothing to detain you in here, is there, Chief Superintendent?" asked Rackham, expecting the answer "no."

Henry looked around the small shed. "No," he said obediently. "No, nothing." As they went outside again, he added, "Do you mind if I lock up?"

Rackham looked surprised. "Of course, if you wish . . ." He handed over the key. As Henry turned it in the lock, he added another small piece of information to the one already stored in his mind—making two in all. First, that the enamel bowl had a little water in it; and second, that the lock had recently been oiled.

Mr. Rackham was only too keen to get away from Sandown Avenue. It was nearly half-past five, time to be shutting up the office and getting home to a change of clothes, a stiff drink, and maybe a couple of holes of golf before dinner. Assuring Henry rather perfunctorily of his willingness to cooperate with the police at all times, he climbed into his car and made off at high speed. Henry, with the yellow rubber ball in his hand, rang the front doorbell of No. 17—the next-door house whose garden bordered that of No. 18 near the greenhouse.

It was opened with unnerving promptness by an angular, gray-haired lady, who wore a dark-blue gabardine raincoat—despite the clement weather—and a sensible gray felt hat. She gave an exclamation of surprise at seeing Henry.

"Oh! You gave me quite a turn! What do you want?"

"I was hoping to speak to . . . the lady of the house," Henry said, apologetically.

"Well, I'm afraid you can't. Mummy is out. Mrs. Rosenberg, I should say. We were just going for a walk before supper. I had my hand on the door to open it when you rang," she added accusingly.

Henry now saw, in the hallway behind the woman, a large shiny perambulator with wisps of pink and white frothy lace peeping over its dark flanks.

"Mrs. Rosenberg won't be back till later, so if you don't mind—" The woman grabbed the handle of the pram and wheeled it expertly in a sort of skid turn, giving Henry a glimpse of a tiny bonneted head on a lace-edged pillow. Directing the pram purposefully toward Henry's stomach, the woman turned and called into the house, "Come along now, you boys! Nanny is waiting!"

From somewhere at the back of the house, footsteps came thudding into the hall, and two small boys with dark hair and mischievous faces joined the party. Henry judged them to be about four and six years old, respectively, and both were dressed with the neatness that only an English nanny of the old school can impose upon wayward youth when she intends to take it to the park.

"Ah, there you are. Come along now, one each side of the pram. That's right. No, Arnold, you may *not* look at Baby. She's asleep and a good thing, too. Least said, soonest mended," she added inconsequentially, and wheeled the perambulator carefully out over the doorstep. It was then that she saw what Henry was holding. "That's Master Simon's ball," she said.

"Yes," said Henry. "That's what I came about."

"Well, its no use blaming *me,*" said Nanny, instantly on the attack. "I've only got one pair of hands and I'm engaged to look after Baby Rebecca. Those two boys are as much trouble as a barrel-load of monkeys, and I haven't got eyes in the back of my head. If they've broken your window, you'll have to speak to Daddy about it."

She shot a devastating look at the two boys, and the smaller of them began to whimper. Nanny instantly changed gear, becoming the champion of the family.

"Now, now, Simon, there's no need to be upset. Nanny will send the nasty man away, and Daddy will deal with him when he comes home." She turned on Henry again. "And if you're from next door, I can only say that some people deserve to have their windows broken, disturbing others the way they do."

"Disturbing? I don't understand—"

"That dog. If it is a dog. More like a poor soul in torment, as I said to Mrs. Birch, who obliges in the mornings. All night, it goes on. Cruel and thoughtless, that's what I call it, and if you've a mind to complain about Master Simon's ball, there's two can play at that game, I can assure you."

Henry said, "I didn't really come to complain about the broken window, Mrs. . . . er . . . Nanny. I'm a police officer. From Scotland Yard."

Nanny was predictably unimpressed. "Police, are you? Then you might get something done about getting us a Panda crossing, that's all *I* can say."

"This howling dog," Henry persisted. "When did you hear it?"

"When? The last three nights, that's when. And you can tell your sergeant that if it happens again tonight, there's going to be a complaint."

"And it came from next door?"

"How should I know where it came from? It's nothing to do with me, I'm sure. Now come along, Simon—and you, Arnold

—or we'll never get to the park and back by six. You can just give Master Simon's ball to me—to *me,* I said, Simon—and keep that dog quiet in future."

Nanny took the ball, placed it in the pram, and shepherded her flock out onto the path. She closed the front door behind her with a decisive slam.

"Now, you remember. If the howling starts up again to-night—"

"I don't think," said Henry, "that the dog will trouble you anymore."

6

The journey from Finchley to Battersea was a long and frustrating one, involving as it did crossing London from north to south in competition with the evening rush-hour traffic. It was seven o'clock before Henry arrived outside the ugly, dark red structure, as forbidding as a Victorian barracks, which had the words "Nelson's Buildings" picked out in a curious sort of green and yellow tiled mosaic plaque over the main door. Further up the shabby street, identical blocks commemorated Frobisher, Drake, and Raleigh. The buildings were not exactly tenements, not exactly slums; in fact, Henry thought, they had probably represented a big step forward in enlightened Council housing when they were built, early in the century, but that was a long time ago.

There was no elevator, of course, and the halls and stairways—though clean enough—had the depressing yellow-tiled aspect and disinfectant smell of a public lavatory. Prams stood in serried ranks in the ground-floor hallway, and from many flats came the discontented wails of the very young, together with a permeating odor of boiling cabbage. As he trudged up the stairs to the second floor, Henry reflected that Mr. Rackham had been quite right about the contrast between No. 18 Sandown Avenue and Mrs. Lawson's present accommodation.

The door of No. 208 was opened by a middle-aged woman, heavily made up and still handsome—even though her brassy-golden hair was far too bright to be true and her waistline had thickened. No smell of cabbage emanated from the apartment; on the contrary, as the door opened Henry was greeted by an appetizing whiff which reminded him of Provencal cooking—garlic and tomato and herbs. The woman eyed Henry in silence.

He said, "Is Mrs. Lawson at home?"

"Marlene? No, she's not back yet. What is it this time?"

"I just wanted a word with her. Perhaps I could wait?"

"Who are you?" The woman was suspicious. "Another of Larry's lot?"

A brief temptation to claim to be one of the Lawson mob flickered through Henry's mind, but he dismissed it regretfully. For one thing, he did not approve of policemen who played at *agent provocateur*, even in a good cause—and more cogently, he was fairly sure that even if he succeeded in fooling Mrs. Lawson's mother, Marlene herself would quickly expose him as an impostor when she returned. He said, "No. As a matter of fact, I'm from Scotland Yard." He showed her his identity card.

"Oh, my God." The woman glanced quickly around the landing, as if to make sure that none of the neighbors had overheard. "You'd better come in. What's happened? Marlene's not—?"

"No, no. Nothing to worry about." Henry stepped into the flat, and the woman hastily closed the door behind him. "I'm just making a few more enquiries into Mr. Lawson's death, Mrs. . . . Er . . . ?"

"Bertini," said the woman. "I'm Mrs. Bertini. Marlene's mother. Both of us widowed now, and a cruel shame, with her so young and not married more than a couple of years." She paused, and looked shrewdly at Henry. "But what's this about more enquiries? It's all over and done with. Coroner's verdict of accidental death on poor Larry, and the man that did it got a year inside. Deserved more, I say—leaving poor Marlene as good as penniless, and her accustomed to the good things of life and why not? I always say—"

Henry cut short the flow. "Perhaps you can help me, Mrs. Bertini. I'm trying to find out more about Mr. Lawson's visit to Gorsemere. I believe he was there on business?"

Mrs. Bertini looked thoroughly scared. "I can't tell you anything. Of that I *am* sure. You'll have to wait for Marlene. She won't be long now."

She ushered Henry into an overcrowded sitting room. The mantlepiece was dominated by a large tinted photograph of a handsome, Italian-looking man—presumably the late Mr. Bertini. Clusters of empty Chianti bottles hung up like Breton onions, a plastic model of the Coliseum, and several Venetian glass bambis confirmed the original nationality of the household—or, at least, of its late master.

Mrs. Bertini said, "You'll excuse me if I pop into the kitchen a minute. Marlene's ever so particular about her risotto—just like her Dad, rest his soul." She hurried out in the direction of the delicious cooking smell—a middle-aged English Mum, curiously veneered with a bright splash of Mediterranean culture. Henry waited.

It was only a few minutes later that there was the sound of a key in the front door, and a young feminine voice called out, "Mum! I'm back!"

At once, the kitchen door opened. "Marlene . . . come in here . . ." There was no mistaking the urgency and alarm in Mrs. Bertini's voice. "There's a man in the lounge—" The kitchen door slammed on the lowered voices.

Oh well, Henry thought. Give them the benefit of the doubt. Nobody relishes the thought of a detective chief superintendent in their home, making enquiries. Especially Larry Lawson's widow and her mother.

Whatever was said in the kitchen, it was said quickly. It was no more than a couple of minutes later that Marlene Lawson came into the sitting room, perfectly self-possessed and very much in control of the situation.

Henry stood up. "Mrs. Lawson?" he asked.

"That's me. Mum says you're a copper, making enquiries about Larry. Well, fire away and get it over."

Marlene, relict of the late Lawrence Lawson, was a striking girl. She was small and slender, and she had inherited her mother's Anglo-Saxon features together with her father's blue-black hair, dark eyes, and olive skin. The combination was extraordinarily attractive, and gave the impression of power and personality, despite her lack of inches. Marlene Lawson was certainly no nonentity.

Henry said, "I'm sorry I have to trouble you further, Mrs. Lawson, but I'm making some enquiries—"

"Into Larry's accident." Marlene cut him short. "Well, you can't. It's finished and done with."

Ignoring this, Henry said, "You told the coroner at the inquest that your husband was on holiday in Gorsemere when he was killed. That wasn't true, was it?"

"Of course it was."

"Why weren't you with him, then?"

"None of your business."

"Where was he staying?"

For the first time, the girl hesitated. "I . . . don't know. He was touring around the country."

"Alone?"

"I've told you, haven't I? Don't you understand English?"

"Touring by car on his own?"

"For heaven's sake, how many more times? Yes, yes, yes!"

"Then what," Henry asked, "happened to his car?"

This time, Marlene was definitely shaken. "I . . . I don't know."

"What sort of a car was it?"

"I don't know that either." She was recovering her poise. "It was a hired car."

"No, Mrs. Lawson," said Henry. "If it had been, it would have been found and reported, and we would have heard about it."

Marlene evidently decided that attack was the best form of defense. She rounded furiously on Henry. "You've no right to come here questioning me, and upsetting Mum—as though we'd done something wrong. I've lost my husband, haven't I—not to mention my home and my money? Isn't that enough for you?"

"I'm only asking these questions, Mrs. Lawson, because I think your husband's death may not have been accidental, after all. If that's so, you surely want to help track down the—"

"Why should I?" She flung the words at him. "It won't bring Larry back, will it, to hound down some other poor bugger? It won't make any money for me—"

"It might," said Henry.

"I don't get you." But she was interested.

"I don't think your husband was on holiday in Gorsemere, Mrs. Lawson. I think he was there on business of some sort, and I think it's likely that he was robbed of something valuable. If we could recover . . . whatever it was . . . it would naturally become your property."

Marlene was looking thoughtful. "You just might be right," she agreed. "I never thought much of that accident story. Well, ask away. What do you want to know?"

"First of all," Henry said, "let's go back a bit. It wasn't a holiday trip, was it?"

She looked at him, sizing him up, assessing her answer. At last she said, "He told me it was a pleasure trip. I didn't believe him, but he wouldn't tell me any more. He never discussed business with me."

"What do you think he went down there for?"

"I thought he was after something—to buy, I mean. He was a general dealer, you know."

"Any idea what he wanted to buy?"

Marlene shrugged. "Nope. Could have been anything. He never discussed—"

"All right, all right." Henry smiled. "Now—Larry ran a car, didn't he?"

"Of course."

Taking a chance, Henry said, "A small, dark-blue Austin van, registration number X2ZE3?"

She answered at once. "Oh, no. That's—" She stopped.

"You know the van, then?"

"I never said so."

Henry let this pass. He said, "So what car did he run?"

"The Jag E-type."

"Have you still got it?"

She laughed, bitterly. "What do you think? Of course not. Sold it as soon as the will was proved. Couldn't afford to run it, apart from needing the cash."

Henry said, "But Larry didn't take the Jaguar to Gorsemere?"

"For crying out loud, how many times do I have to tell you? He went on his own, and he didn't take the car. So naturally I assumed he'd hired one." Marlene lit a cigarette, and blew out a cloud of smoke with a certain smug satisfaction. Her story, she seemed to say, tallied beautifully. Crack it if you can.

Henry said, "Can you think of any reason why he should have been walking along a country road by himself at ten o'clock at night?"

Marlene looked at him pityingly. "What d'you think I am—psychic or something? I suppose he'd come out of a pub and was going home."

"Where was he staying?"

"I've told you—I don't know."

"He was touring the country, but without a car. He was walking home at night down a country road, at least six miles from any hotel. He told you he was on holiday, but you thought he was trying to buy something. Is that correct?" Henry's voice was dead, official.

Marlene tossed her head, and said, "Yeah. That's right." But she sounded a little uneasy.

Henry made a note in his book, taking his time over it. Then he looked up and grinned widely at Marlene. "It won't do, will it?" he said amicably. "Let's think again. First, he wasn't touring and he wasn't staying anywhere. He went down to the country that evening to fetch one specific thing. He was on his way to get it—or perhaps he had it already—when he was run down by Heathfield's car."

"They didn't find—" Marlene began, and then stopped.

"No, they didn't, did they? So presumably he hadn't yet got it. Or else it was stolen from him after his death."

"Stolen?" Marlene opened her eyes very wide. "By who? He was on his own. And so was the chap in the car. And he was dead drunk. The judge said so."

"Yes, there's no doubt about that." Henry paused. Then he went on, "I was in Finchley earlier today. Took a look at your house in Sandown Avenue."

"So what's funny about that?"

"Nothing. It's a beautiful house. But you said just now that you'd lost your home. I suppose that means that Larry was buying the house on a mortgage, and now you can't afford the payments."

There was a little pause, and then Marlene said, "No. It wasn't on mortgage."

"But you're selling it just the same." Henry paused. "Oh, well, I suppose it would be an expensive place to keep up. A lovely house, though. I'm surprised it hasn't sold by now."

"Money's short," said Marlene laconically. And added, "And I want a whole lot of it. That's why I'm prepared to hang on till I get the right price."

"And yet," Henry pointed out, "you rang the agents last week, and they suggested lowering the price if you wanted to make a sale."

"I just told you, didn't I? I don't want to make a sale, not in a hurry. I'm waiting."

"Then why did you ring the agent?"

"Nosy, aren't you? Why shouldn't I ring him? It's a free country, isn't it?"

Henry said, "You kept the spare key to the garden shed, I suppose."

Marlene raised her eyebrows. "You barmy, or something?"

"I don't think so," said Henry seriously. "You had a spare key to the garden shed, and last week one of Larry's friends got in touch with you and borrowed it. The owner of the little blue van we were speaking about."

"I never—"

"Larry's friend," Henry went on, "got you to ring Mr. Rackham to make sure that the house was still deserted, and that no buyer had turned up. Once you were able to reassure him, he borrowed the key from you."

"I haven't got a key!"

"No, I'm sure you haven't. Larry's friend hasn't returned it yet. He was using the shed up until today."

Marlene stood up and glared at Henry. He could not decide whether she was simply angry, or whether there was fear, too, in her taut features. "You better get out," she said. "Get out and stay out, if you want to keep healthy. Larry's dead, and I've nothing more to do with . . . with his friends. But I warn you—don't start meddling with that mob. Just don't. That's all." Suddenly she raised her voice, and cried gaily, "Mum! How's that risotto coming on? I'm half famished!"

Mrs. Bertini came bustling in, beaming. "Just ready, dear. Won't be a moment. Had your little chat with Marlene, then, Mr. . . . that is, Inspector?"

"Yes, he has." Marlene's voice was light, but incisive as a whip. "He's going now. I don't think we'll be seeing him again."

"It's . . . all right . . . is it, dear?" Mrs. Bertini sounded anxious. "I mean . . . no trouble, is there?"

Marlene smiled. "No trouble at all, Mum. Good-bye, Mister Detective. You'll find the door over there as you go out."

Henry grinned. "Thank you very much, Mrs. Lawson," he said. "You've helped me a lot."

"You're welcome," said Marlene fiercely.

Henry drove thoughtfully back across the river to Scotland Yard's gray and white skyscraper, and made for the photographic section of the Criminal Records Office. The police portrait of Harold ("Shorty") Bates was hardly flattering, having been taken without much ceremony or attention to lighting effects on the occasion of his conviction for causing Grievous Bodily Harm to a member of a rival gang in a Soho back street some years previously; nevertheless, Henry had no difficulty in recognizing him as the pseudo-representative of Rackham and Stout, the driver of the small blue van. Henry called Sergeant Reynolds and issued some instructions. Then he looked at his watch, and sighed. It was a quarter to nine. Just time for a quick bite to eat in the Yard's canteen, and he could still get to the public house called the Pink Parrot, in Notting Hill, before closing time.

The Pink Parrot is an undistinguished pub which stands on the corner of Maize Street and Parkin Place. Its ground-floor bars, the Public and the Saloon, are unattractive to the point of repulsion, and consequently poorly patronized; the Private Bar, however, on the first floor, is an altogether more luxurious affair, with a faithful clientele drawn from the shadier elements of London's gambling scene.

The licensee of this dubious establishment was still Major George Weatherby—the military rank was, of course, no more than a courtesy title—who had shown amazing agility over the years in managing to keep his name and features out of the files of the Criminal Record Office. In a previous case he had sailed extremely close to the wind by turning up as a convenient witness to a contrived street accident. Afterward, Scotland Yard had debated whether or not to oppose the renewal of his liquor license. The generally held opinion was that he had had a severe fright and learned his lesson, and that it was more convenient for the long arm of the law to know the gathering place of this particular set of undesirables than to have to track down some new rendezvous. So the major had been left in peace, and had apparently turned over a new leaf.

Now, however, it appeared that he was up to his old tricks again. There were two possible explanations. Either he had been blackmailed or extravagantly bribed—or both—into returning to the perjury business; or—and Henry's mind shied away from the horrible possibility—the whole thing really had been coincidence, and Weatherby's car had in fact been driven away from the yard of the White Bull by the inebriated Harry Heathfield, without Weatherby's knowledge or consent. Henry sighed, locked his car carefully, and made his way through the dank, deserted Saloon Bar of the Pink Parrot and up the stairs to the Private Bar.

It was just as he remembered it. The tasteless, expensive, mock-"horsey" decor and furniture; the row of sound-proofed telephone booths from which the drinkers could place their bets; the smell of cigar smoke; the flashy clothes and sharp features of the customers; the brass ship's bell suspended above the bar; and, behind the bar, the broad, florid face and bristling gray mustache of Major George Weatherby himself.

The circumstances, however, were very different from those of Henry's previous visit. Then, a murder had been committed on the premises and the atmosphere was charged with suspicion and unease, as the clients of the Pink Parrot bent over backward to play the part of innocent bystanders. This time, it was an ordinary Monday evening, getting on for closing time, and the mood was genuinely relaxed. There were about half a dozen men drinking in the bar, and none of them paid the slightest attention to Henry when he came in. The major, who was sitting behind the bar reading *The Sporting Life,* looked up briefly and returned to his paper; then, as if doing an elaborate double take, he looked at Henry again, and a smile of apparently genuine welcome spread across his face, revealing his strong yellow teeth. He folded up his paper and laid it down with great deliberation as Henry approached the bar.

"Well, well, well. If it isn't my old friend Chief Superintendent Tibbett. Delighted to welcome you, sir. Long time no see. What may I get you?"

Henry swung himself onto a bar stool. "Half of bitter, if you please, Major."

"A pleasure, sir. A real pleasure." Indeed, the major did look pleased, as he manipulated the beer handle. He had never really expected to have his license renewed. "Yes, I'm delighted to see you. No hard feelings about our last little contretemps, eh?"

"None whatsoever," said Henry. He took a pull at his beer. "But you do keep at it, don't you?"

Weatherby looked surprised and a little alarmed. "Keep at it? I don't follow you, sir."

"This business of continually cropping up in courts of law, giving evidence," Henry explained. "First it was Pereira. Now it's Heathfield."

"Oh, come now, sir." The major was jolly and reproachful.

"You can hardly blame me if some drunk nicks my car. I was called as a witness by the police, I'd like to remind you. Hardly had a choice, had I?"

"No," said Henry. "No, you didn't. Tell me about it."

"You're interested in the case, are you, sir?"

"I'm interested," said Henry, "in finding out who shot Red Dicky Marsh."

Major Weatherby shook his head, smiling. "There you have the advantage of me, sir. I'm afraid I don't know the gentleman."

"I think you do," said Henry. "He's a regular patron of this bar, for a start."

"Ah, well . . . in that case, I might know him by sight, sir. But I can't be expected to know the name of every—"

"Oh, come off it, Weatherby." Henry allowed himself to sound impatient. "You not only know him, you also know very well that he's in the hospital, in serious condition, suffering from gunshot wounds. It's also very likely that you . . . well, never mind. Just tell me what happened the evening your car was stolen."

"Well, now . . ." Weatherby appeared to consider. "I really don't know what I can add to what I said in court."

"Then just say it again," said Henry patiently.

"It's very simple, sir. My friend and I were having a drink in this pub—"

"Not so fast, Weatherby," said Henry. "Start at the beginning. What were you doing gadding around the Hampshire countryside on a Wednesday evening, when you'd normally be behind the bar?"

Weatherby looked slightly ill at ease. "I suppose I'm allowed an evening off now and then, like everybody else," he said defensively.

"Certainly you are," said Henry, "but I understand you told the court that this pub was closed for redecoration."

"That's right." No doubt about the uneasiness now.

Henry looked around the room. "I don't see much sign of it," he said. "And the bar downstairs certainly hasn't been repainted."

"No, no. It was the . . . em . . . the outside of the house which was being redone. The roof," Weatherby added quickly, as though suddenly inspired.

"And that entailed closing the pub?"

"It did indeed. We had water coming in . . . plaster falling . . ."

Henry cast a skeptical eye at the ceiling of the Private Bar, which presented an undisturbed appearance. He sighed. "We'll let it pass for the moment," he said. "Go on."

"Well, as I was saying, my friend and I—"

"That would be Mr. Albert Pennington, Company Director, of Chelsea."

"Quite right, sir. And we—"

"Just what company is he a director of?" Henry asked.

"I really don't know, Chief Superintendent. A private company of some sort. I really think you should ask him."

"I will," Henry assured him. "Right. Go on."

"Well, as I was saying, Pennington and I decided to drive down to the country. It was a lovely evening. Birds, flowers, sunsets . . . all that sort of thing." Weatherby apparently realized the incongruity of presenting himself as a sentimental lover of nature. He hurried on. "So in due course we found ourselves at this hostelry—the White Bull, I think it was called."

"You hadn't been there before?"

"No, no. We found it quite by chance."

"I was wondering about that," Henry said. "It's a long way off the main road. I thought perhaps you might have been told about it by somebody."

"No, no. Nothing of that sort. We just . . . em . . . let the old car follow her nose, as it were. And there was this attractive-looking old place—"

"What time did you arrive there?" Henry asked.

"Around half-past eight, I suppose. Say a quarter to nine."

"So you'd already eaten?"

Weatherby hesitated. "We didn't have a meal—not a sit-down dinner, I mean," he said. "We stopped at a few other places first, and had snacks at the bar. Nothing more."

"And there were just the two of you?"

"Certainly." The major's pale-blue, bloodshot eyes regarded Henry steadily, if blearily. "As I told you. Pennington and myself."

"What other pubs did you stop at, before you arrived in Gorsemere?"

"I have absolutely no idea," said Weatherby blandly. "I didn't notice the names."

"That's rather strange, isn't it?" said Henry.

"It'd be a damn sight stranger if I *did* remember, after all this time." Weatherby was on the attack.

"All right," said Henry. "Let's get on. You arrived at the White Bull and parked your car in the yard, leaving the ignition key in the lock and the doors open."

"The ignition key was a mistake, that I admit," the major conceded handsomely. "But which of us hasn't done the same thing at one time or another, Chief Superintendent? To err is human—"

"All right, spare me the platitudes. Were there many other cars in the yard?"

"One or two. Not many. I got the impression that the pub was a real local, and that the patrons came on foot."

"Very wise of them," said Henry dryly. "Pity they didn't all go home the same way. So—you went into the pub, and there you met Harry Heathfield."

"Not right away. It's an old-fashioned house—oak beams and all that. We fixed ourselves up with drinks and installed ourselves in one of those inglenook things. Then we heard this character carrying on in the next booth."

"Carrying on?"

"Telling stories, singing songs, that sort of thing. Broad country accent. Real rustic type. We reckoned he might be amusing, so we moved in and joined him at his table."

"And bought him drinks?"

"Of course. Least we could do. He was a droll chap—kept us laughing with his tales. I suppose we should have realized that he'd had a spot too much—but the more he drank, the merrier he got. Then—around ten, it must have been—he suddenly stood up and said he'd be off home. He seemed all right—not quite steady on his feet, but OK. In fact, Pennington asked him if he was all right, and he said yes, he'd be fine, his house wasn't much of a walk away. And out he went. We thought no more about it, until we came out into the yard at closing time—and the car wasn't there. Could have knocked me down with a feather."

"So what did you do then?"

"What could we do? Went back into the pub—just caught the landlord before he locked up. He phoned the local police. The . . . em . . . accident had already taken place, so the constable knew all about the car. We made statements, formally identified what was left of the car—goodness me, Chief Superintendent, I don't have to tell *you* about police procedure in such cases. It was after midnight when we finally got away. Luckily there's a milk train back to London from this Middingfield place, and we caught it. Christ, what a journey! Stopped at every clump of grass on the way, and crawled in between. We finally got to Waterloo at four A.M. I can assure you, sir, that no man in his right mind would have gone through that night's experiences for fun."

"I believe you," said Henry. "On the other hand, if the money was right—"

"I beg your pardon, sir?"

"—or the pressure sufficiently strong—"

Major Weatherby dropped his expression of outraged innocence, perhaps remembering that he had tried it on Henry before, with singularly little effect. He substituted a grisly joviality tempered with resignation.

"Well, well, well, sir. I realize that I'm not going to convince you. Where you gentlemen at Scotland Yard get these nasty suspicions about people, it's not for me to say. Perhaps the nature of your work warps your characters and sours your natural benevolence—if you'll forgive me saying so. Still, that's neither here nor there, is it? You never proved anything in the Pereira case, did you, sir? And I think you'll find this one even more difficult. The facts are perfectly clear, and I'm sure you'll agree that I was more sinned against than sinning."

"The judge made a few uncomplimentary remarks about you, I gather," said Henry, with a grin.

"Very uncalled for, I thought," said Weatherby. "It was in the summing-up—he pointed out to the jury that being a publican myself, I should not have plied the man with strong drink to which he was not accustomed. Now, I ask you, sir, how was I to know that his usual tipple was mild and bitter? I asked the man what he'd like to drink, and he said 'Scotch.' Naturally, I'd no notion he was planning to drive a car later on. Yes, it really hurt me to hear the . . . er . . . the learned judge saying such things. But there it is. Heathfield was a local man, and well liked. The judge was doing his best to make what excuses he could for the fellow. One has to be charitable. After all, nothing the judge said could hurt me. I wasn't in the dock." Weatherby composed his face into an expression designed to indicate Christian charity and long-suffering, which ill became him.

Henry finished his drink, and said, "All right, Weatherby. There's nothing we can do for the moment. But I'm warning you—watch your step. One of these days, you'll trip up."

Major Weatherby favored Henry with a wolfish grin. "I appreciate your kind advice, Chief Superintendent. Really I do. But you mustn't worry yourself about me. I can take care of myself. Another drink? No? Then that'll be ten pence, if you please."

Henry drove slowly home to his empty Chelsea apartment. He had plenty to think about.

7

Jane Spence was pleased but puzzled when Henry telephoned on Tuesday morning and proposed himself as a house guest.

"Of course we'll be delighted, Henry. And Emmy will be tickled to death. But I thought you were terribly busy and couldn't take leave—"

"Well, I've been lucky," said Henry blandly. "I find I can take a few days off and combine them with a small piece of research. Do you think your friend Simon Yateley could spare me half an hour or so of his time this afternoon?"

"Simon? I expect so. This is all very mysterious. All right, all right, I wasn't intending to ask. Discretion personified. I'll ring Simon now and ask him round for a drink—"

"If it's possible," said Henry, "I'd rather visit him at his place. I want to—to pick his brains professionally. Can you fix that for me?"

"I'll certainly try. Anything to set the majesty of the law rolling."

"You're laughing at me," said Henry, resignedly.

"Not really—but you are being a bit cloak-and-dagger. D'you want to speak to Emmy? She's out in the garden, playing with Ginger."

"Not specially. Just give her my love and tell her I'm arriving."

"OK. See you at the station at a quarter to twelve."

Emmy received the news of Henry's impending return with less enthusiasm than Jane had predicted. In fact, she threw a stick for Ginger with unaccustomed ferocity, and said gloomily, "Oh, Lord."

"Hardly the right note, darling," Jane remarked. "Where's your wifely devotion?"

"Oh, it's not that I mind Henry coming down here. I mean, I'll be glad to see him. It's just that . . . I know the signs."

"The signs of what?"

"His bloody nose," said Emmy. Ginger, who had retrieved the stick from the depths of the shrubbery, returned in triumph and dropped his trophy at Emmy's feet, but she ignored him. "I could tell something was up when he and Bill came back from the pub on Friday night. I just hope he's not going to stir up trouble for you here in the village."

"For us?" Jane's eyebrows went up. "How could he possibly do that?"

"You'd be surprised," remarked her sister ominously.

"Anyhow," said Jane, "I'd better go and ring Simon Yateley. Henry wants to see him this afternoon."

"What about?" Emmy's voice was sharp.

"Haven't the faintest. To pick his brains, he said."

"Oh." Emmy sounded mollified. "Well, let's hope it's no more than that."

A few moments later, Emmy heard Jane telephoning to the Hilltop Kennels.

"Bella? Jane Spence here. What . . . ? Oh, no. No, I'm afraid I haven't . . . not a word. Sorry if I raised your hopes . . . still, she's sure to be found. P.C. Denning will let me know at once . . . Actually, it was Simon I wanted . . . yes, I'll hang on." There was a rather lengthy pause, and then, "Simon? Did I get you from the kennels? . . . So sorry . . . Look Simon, you remember my brother-in-law, Henry Tibbett? . . . That's right, on Saturday . . . Well, he's coming down to Gorsemere again this afternoon, for a few days' holiday, and he wondered if he could come and see you . . . some sort of professional advice, I think . . . No, he's not thinking of buying one, not that I know of . . . that's sweet of you, Simon. Three o'clock . . . I'll tell him . . ."

Henry was met at Gorsemere Halt by Emmy, accompanied by Ginger, who greeted Henry with yelps of welcome.

"I hope," said Henry with some severity, "that you're not getting too attached to that dog."

"Who? Me?" Emmy's voice was too innocent to be true. "Of course not. He just came along for the ride."

"We can't possibly keep a dog in London. You must see that."

"Of course I see it," said Emmy lightly. "Now, get into the car and tell me what this is all about. Not that we're not pleased to see you, but . . ."

Henry looked at her, sighed, and then grinned. "There's probably nothing in it," he said.

"But—" Emmy prompted.

"But it's just possible that a case I'm working on in London may have ramifications in this part of the world. In any case, I want to find out more about greyhound racing."

At three o'clock promptly, Henry was ringing the bell on the fortified iron gate which led to Hilltop Kennels. As on the previous occasion, this move was greeted by an excited outburst of barking and yapping from the row of whitewashed pens, and soon Simon Yateley appeared, smiling and tousle-headed in mud-stained brown corduroys and gumboots. He unlocked the gate and held it open, saying, "Come in, my dear fellow. Jane said you wanted to see me."

"That's right," said Henry. "Sorry to take up your valuable time, but I'd like to ask a few questions."

"That sounds very alarming, old man," said Simon, but he did not seem to be alarmed. "What's it all about, then? A crime wave in Gorsemere?"

Henry's heart sank. "I gather from that remark," he said, "that you know who I am?"

Yateley laughed. "You didn't think you could keep it secret in a village like this, did you? Chief Superintendent of the C.I.D.—the saloon bar of the Bull has talked of nothing else since your visit. Nor, I suspect, has the Women's Institute. You're quite a celebrity, you know." He looked sharply at Henry. "There's no secret about your profession, anyhow, is there? I mean, I've seen your picture in the papers. No good trying to hide your light under a bushel." He laughed with the satisfaction of one who has just composed an epigram.

"No," Henry agreed gloomily. "No secret at all."

"Well now," Yateley went on briskly, "what are these mysterious questions?"

"I'm trying to find out all I can about breeding, training, and racing greyhounds," said Henry.

Yateley brightened. "Thinking of buying, are you? I've a couple of good litters that might interest you—"

"No, no. I don't want to buy one."

"So Jane said. Pity. It's a fascinating hobby, y'know, and can be very lucrative—if you pick the right dog."

"But my dear man," Henry protested, "I live in the middle of London in a small flat, and I know absolutely nothing about—"

Yateley looked at him pityingly, unable to credit such ignorance. "You wouldn't keep the pup yourself," he explained, as if to a retarded child. "Oh, no. You choose it, pay for it, and leave it here with me. Visit it whenever you like, of course. Get to know your own animal. I rear it, register it, train it—all the donkey work. As owner, all you have to do is swan around the stadium watching your entry run—and you don't even have to do that if you don't want to—and pick up the kudos and prize money afterwards. Money for jam."

"If my dog wins," said Henry.

"Ah, well, there's an element of risk in everything, isn't there?"

"In any case," said Henry firmly, "I'm not interested in buying a greyhound. I just want to learn about the technicalities of training and racing."

"In that case," said Yateley, "I suggest we go indoors where we can talk in comfort. Later on, I'll show you round."

Soon they were installed in deep armchairs in the untidy, comfortable drawing room of the red brick house. Simon Yateley accepted a pipeful of tobacco from Henry, leaned back in his chair, and said, "Right. Fire away, sir."

"I hardly know where to start," Henry admitted. "I'm afraid I'm abysmally ignorant. All I've gathered so far is that you both

breed and race your own dogs, and also train other people's."
"That's right."
"How many dogs do you keep here at any one time?"
Simon Yateley considered. "Counting puppies, about fifty. Roughly half our own, and half boarders. We've room for more, but I don't use the old kennels any more. They were getting leaky and drafty, and greyhounds need good dry, warm quarters."
"And how old are the puppies before you begin their training?"
Yateley shrugged. "Around twelve months, as a general rule," he said. "No sense in starting too young. Under NGRC rules, a dog can't be entered for a race under fifteen months."
"NGRC?"
"National Greyhound Racing Club. All our dogs are registered with them—so are we, come to that. Otherwise we wouldn't be allowed to race our dogs on NGRC tracks—which means all the finest stadiums in the country."
"Presumably," Henry said, "not all your puppies will turn out to be champion racers."
Yateley laughed. "You can say that again," he remarked. "If they did, I'd be a rich man. No—I count myself lucky to get a couple of promising runners out of a litter of five or six."
"How soon can you tell which dogs are going to be good?" Henry asked.
"Quite early on, as a rule. Apart from pups which aren't up to standard physically, it's a question of temperament more than anything. Some of them shape well on their own, but can't get used to racing with other dogs—start fighting on the track. That can sometimes be trained out of them, sometimes not. What's more serious, and less easy to cure, is sheer lack of enthusiasm. Like that bitch Bella was talking about—Lady Griselda. A case in point. Just wouldn't put her heart into the job."
"I was going to ask you," Henry said. "What happens to the dogs who don't make the grade?"
"The youngsters are sold cheap or given away as pets," said Simon. "As for the old dogs—the best are kept for breeding.

The others—well, I know some trainers who have them put to sleep. But Bella and I are sentimental, I suppose. We keep them until they die of old age, if we can't find good homes for them. I've got half a dozen pensioners on my books at the moment." He grinned. "You're not in the market for a pet, I suppose? Wonderfully intelligent and affectionate, they are."

"I most certainly am not," said Henry, with undue vehemence.

"Ah, well—no harm in trying. Any more you want to know before we start the conducted tour?"

"Quite a lot, I'm afraid," said Henry. "There's a lot of money in greyhound racing, isn't there?"

"Well, that depends. Prize money is pretty good at big meetings, not so interesting at the smaller tracks, inevitably. A champion can win thousands of pounds during his racing career."

"I was thinking more," said Henry, "of the betting side of it."

"Oh, that." Yateley did not sound interested. "Yes, of course—enormous sums are wagered. I don't go in for it myself—not a gambling man. I haven't got a crusade on about it, like Sir Arthur Bratt-Cunningham—if I think one of my dogs has a real chance, I'll put a bit on him. But you'll find the hard betting done by characters who wouldn't know a hare from a harrier."

"I'm only too well aware of that," said Henry feelingly. "I come across a lot of them in my job, I'm afraid. And it's not just gambling, either. I imagine there's a fair amount of underhand business—doping, substitution, and so on."

Yateley said, "No, I wouldn't say that. The rules are too strict—the NGRC sees to that."

"I'm not very well up on the greyhound scene," Henry admitted, "but there have been several bad scandals recently over racehorses—"

"Ah, yes. That's a bit different." Yateley puffed at his pipe. "Think of it this way. In horse racing, you've got more of the human element."

"The human element?"

"The jockey. He's in control of the horse actually during the race. He can throw the race, if he's paid enough and is so inclined anyhow. Not that I'm saying many of them are, but the possibility's there. Now, with your greyhound, he's on his own. Once that trap is open, unless he's been doped, nothing and nobody can influence his performance. See what I mean?"

"Yes," said Henry. "But—"

"And under NGRC rules, it's virtually impossible for anybody to interfere with the dog once he's been delivered to the stadium for a race."

"Tell me about it," Henry said.

"Well, for a start, the dog must be delivered by a registered trainer, even if the owner has done most of the training himself. That's a guarantee, because none of us wants to be struck off by the club. Then, the track has its own vets, who examine the dogs and test them for dope. After that, until the actual race, the dogs are kept in the stadium's own kennels—and if you can break in there, you can steal the Crown Jewels."

"Supposing," said Henry slowly, "that the wrong dog is delivered? I mean, a substitute runner, of approximately the same size and coloring?"

Yateley laughed. "I may say, sir," he said, "that you're not the first person to have thought of that little dodge. That's why one of the first things the NGRC did was to institute identity cards for all registered dogs."

"With their signatures, I suppose?"

"As good as." Yateley got up and walked over to a big, old-fashioned desk. He opened a drawer, rummaged about for a moment, and pulled out a slim white booklet. "Take a look at this. It's a specimen identity card. You'll see what I mean."

He handed Henry the folder. The words "Greyhound Identity and Race Record Book" were printed on the front cover, with a space for the name of the dog to be entered. It was heavily overprinted with the word "Specimen" on each page. Inside were four outline drawings of a greyhound—back, front, and two side views—and on these were indicated coloring and exact markings; alongside was a column for recording sex, eye color, length of tail, ear mark, and other details. On the facing page were no less than five outline drawings of a greyhound's paw, which again were meticulously marked to identify the toes and nails.

"As good as fingerprints," Yateley remarked, as Henry turned the page. "The rest of the book is a record of all the races the dog runs, with full details of weight, distance, trap number, and result. The lot."

"The trainer keeps one of these for each dog, does he?" Henry asked.

"Not likely, old man. The NGRC itself keeps the cards under lock and key. When a dog is entered for a race, the NGRC sends the card to the racetrack manager so that he can check the creature's identity. Afterwards, the card must be returned to the NGRC, unless the dog is due to race again within forty-eight hours. Then it can be sent direct to the manager of the next racetrack. It's foolproof, old man."

Henry sighed. "A pity," he said. "I'll have to abandon my theory."

"What theory would that be?"

"Oh . . . just an idea. About the possibility of substituting an inferior runner for a champion."

Simon Yateley smiled. "I know of quite a few characters," he said, "who'd give a small fortune if you could show them how it could be done. One of the oldest tricks, before things tightened up." He stood up. "Well, come and have a look around."

Henry followed Simon out of the house to the long row of brick-built kennels. Wherever they went, they were followed by affectionate yapping—and Henry was introduced to the inmates of Hilltop. Two kennelsful of leaping puppies, nuzzling at the wire to lick Simon's hand; a sleek, beautiful bitch suckling her young family; several comfortable residences each occupied by two "old-age pensioners"—"They like to have company," Yateley explained; and finally the enclosures housing the current racers, the white hopes of the kennels. Several of these were empty, and Yateley explained that their occupants were still out, being schooled.

"I don't believe in very intensive training," he said. "It's mostly walking, with a few sprints. And then, of course, they have to get used to the track."

"The track?" Henry was surprised. "You mean, you have a track here?"

"Indeed we do. Oh, don't expect the White City. Ours is just an open-air practice track—but it's the same shape and size as a regular stadium course, and the dogs get used to it. This way."

Yateley led the way to a stretch of open moorland. As they approached it, Henry could see the oval racecourse, bordered by white fencing, its grassy surface worn by the procession of pounding feet, both canine and human. As Henry and Simon walked up to the fence, there was a call from somewhere out of sight, and the next moment a black form flashed like greased lightning down the track past them. Yateley laughed.

"You can have a demonstration," he said. "Bella and Tom are putting Black Prince through his paces. He's running at Wembley on Saturday. Got a good chance, too."

A moment later, Henry saw Bella Yateley. She made an attractive sight, in her beige breeches and Wellington boots, her face sunburned and her brown hair tousled in the fresh wind. She was leading the beautiful black dog—now panting in happy exhaustion—and she held a stopwatch in her hand. She greeted Henry and her husband with a wide smile.

"Thirty-two twenty, Simon," she said cryptically. She patted the dog's sleek head. "You're a clever boy. We'll show them on Saturday." She turned to a diminutive youngster in gumboots and a cloth cap several sizes too large for him. "Take Prince back to his kennels, will you, Tommy? And give him a good meal—he's earned it." She bent to pat the dog again, and he licked her hand affectionately before the kennel lad led him off toward the row of whitewashed huts.

Bella smiled at Henry. "Simon told me you were coming," she said. "Why the sudden interest in greyhounds?"

"Nothing, really. Just curiosity. I wanted a good look round."

"Well," said Bella, "I hope you're admiring our pride and joy."

"Black Prince, you mean?"

"No, the practice track. There aren't many trainers that have one, though I say it myself. It may not be very grand, but it's as good as some of the flapping tracks."

"Flapping tracks?" Henry repeated.

"Oh, come on back to the house, Bella," said Yateley. "Henry's had enough of tracks and dogs for one afternoon."

"I've certainly learnt a lot," said Henry. The three of them began to walk back toward the house. "Tell me more about flapping tracks."

"That's what we call them," Bella said. "They're small tracks, not under NGRC management. Oh, some of them are quite grand—proper enclosed stadiums and everything—but others are just open tracks like ours. Anybody can enter his own dog—it's all much less formal than the NGRC races."

"So all this identity card business you were telling me about wouldn't apply to a flapping track?" Henry asked, turning to Yateley.

"Well . . . I wouldn't say it doesn't apply . . . certainly the rules are less rigid . . ."

"Much less," Bella put in. "Of course, you don't get really top quality dogs entering."

"But you still get betting, I suppose," Henry said.

"My dear Henry," said Simon, "wherever you get two gamblers together, you'll get betting. I've known men bet on how many minutes late a train will be, or the color of the hair of the next man to walk into a bar. It's human nature, that's all."

Henry said good-bye to the Yateleys at the door of their house. They did not invite him in, and he saw no reason why they should. He thanked them for their help, and was turning to go, when Bella said, "But of course, you can't get out. The gate's locked. No, don't bother, Simon. I'll walk down with Henry."

As they walked, Bella suddenly said, "Oh, I meant to ask you. There's no news of Griselda, I suppose? The bitch I gave to Harry Heathfield. The police ought to have found her by now if she's running loose in the district."

"I'll ask Jane when I get back," Henry promised. "She didn't say anything."

Bella's eyes clouded. "I expect she's been picked up and is being cared for by somebody," she said, "but one always thinks of those ghouls who go round pinching stray dogs and selling them for vivisection." She paused, and then said, "Griselda's such a friendly, trusting creature. She'd go to anybody. You're a high-powered policeman, Henry. Can't you help? Poor little P.C. Denning does his best—but you could do much more, I'm sure."

Henry smiled. "It's hardly up my street, looking for stray dogs," he said, "but—well, yes, of course I'll help if I can. By the way, does your Lady Griselda have one of those identity cards that Simon was showing me?"

"Oh, yes. We registered her before we realized we'd never make a runner of her. And then Harry was so thrilled to think he owned a real racing greyhound that we went through all the correct procedure—had the change of ownership notified to the club and entered on the card and everything. In theory, he could enter her for a race anytime. Of course, that's only a pipe dream, but it made him so happy. Poor Harry."

"If I could get hold of that card," said Henry, "it would make it easier to identify her."

Bella laughed. "That's impossible, I'm afraid. The club will only part with the card to send it to the racetrack manager if a dog is entered in a race. The only other way to get hold of it would be for Harry himself to request to have it canceled and returned—and in that case, the pipe dream would be gone. She'd never be able to race again, even in theory."

"Oh, well," said Henry. "It was just an idea. Anyhow, I'll see what I can do."

They had reached the gate. Bella unlocked it, and smiled at Henry.

"I'd be so very grateful," she said.

8

Nobody would expect a prison to be a particularly cheerful place, but Middingfield Jail, Henry reflected, was even grimmer and more dismal than most. A gaunt, smoke-blackened Victorian building, it reared its grim façade among the mean, dark streets surrounding Middingfield's railway junction, and its small, barred windows scowled at the world like hostile, myopic eyes.

Henry parked Bill Spence's car, which he had borrowed for the trip, and rang the bell outside the forbidding black iron gate. An inspection grill shot open, enabling him to identify himself. At once, a heavy key turned in the lock, and the big gate swung open.

"Well, well, Chief Superintendent Tibbett. Come in, sir, come in. The governor is expecting you." The duty prison officer who greeted Henry could hardly have presented a greater contrast to his stark surroundings. He was a plump, jolly man in early middle age, with twinkling blue eyes and a smile like Santa Claus. Henry's heart rose, despite the familiar, nauseating prison smell which was already assailing his nostrils.

The prison officer relocked the gate carefully, and led the way across a bare courtyard to the administrative wing. He chatted garrulously as he walked. "It's 657 Heathfield you're interested in, I believe, sir? He's settling down surprisingly well, considering. We had a bit of trouble with him at first—always happens when a man's inside for the first time, and feels he's been hard done by. Your old lag, now, he takes it in his stride, philosophical-like. Quite glad to be back, sometimes. They feel secure in here, you see," added the officer, with perfect seriousness. "And then there's this business of his dogs. Well, you can understand it, can't you, sir? Some of the men here make pets of sparrows or rats—any animal they can find. Save bits of food for them. Yes, I've seen a Grievous Bodily Harm break down and cry when his release day came up, because he had to leave his tame sparrow behind and he didn't think his cellmate would feed it proper." The officer walked on in silence for a moment, and then said, diffidently, "I hope—that is, you'll forgive me for asking, sir—but I hope your coming here doesn't mean more trouble for 657. Like I said, I think we're beginning to make headway with him, and I wouldn't like to think—"

Henry hastened to reassure him. "No, no. It's just that he may be able to help in another enquiry I'm making—"

"That's what I was afraid of, sir," remarked the officer gloomily. "Being a first offender doesn't always mean it's a first offense, does it? Only the first that's been found out. Well, I'm really sorry about that. I was hoping 657 would be transferred to an open prison—seemed a suitable type to me. Just shows how wrong one can be."

"Heathfield isn't under any suspicion, officer," said Henry. "On the contrary. As a matter of fact, what I'm interested in is trying to trace that missing dog of his."

The officer brightened at once. "Well, that's good news and no mistake. Buck him up like a weekend at Brighton, that will. Ah, here we are, sir. I'll just tell the governor you're here."

The governor was a bluff, upright, ex-military man, with a bristling mustache. He was clearly a just and efficient administrator—but, listening to him talk, Henry was aware of a sense of chill. When the portly prison officer had spoken about "men," it seemed to underline the common humanity of the inmates and their guards; when the governor used the same word, it conjured up ranks of faceless units on a parade ground. As far as the governor was concerned, Harry Heathfield had been fitted neatly into a slot which read, "First Offender, not an habitual criminal, recommended as suitable for open prison." Not a very interesting character. The governor could not imagine why Chief Superintendent Tibbett should wish to talk to the man, although naturally he had arranged it as requested.

"As a matter of fact," said Henry, "it's about his dog."

"His *dog?*" repeated the governor, incredulously. He himself, with his aromatic tweeds and aura of grouse-moors, was obviously a dog enthusiast, if not exactly a lover; but it had never crossed his mind that an inmate of his prison could fall into the same category. Henry was glad when their short chat came to an end, and his friend the prison officer led him to a small, bleak room which had been set aside for his interview with Harry Heathfield.

Heathfield, in spite of his drab prison overalls, looked very much as Henry had expected from Jane's description. His weather-beaten face had not yet had time to acquire a prison pallor, and his brown eyes retained their sparkle; but he looked like a man still suffering from the effects of a severe shock—which, indeed, he was. It crossed Henry's mind that he must have had a deep, if misguided, conviction that he was innocent and would be acquitted.

"It's kind of you to visit me, sir," Heathfield said. He did not appear in the least overawed by Henry's rank. "You'll be a colleague of P.C. Denning's, I wouldn't wonder. There's a fine man for you. It's not his fault I find myself where I am, and that's the truth. I daresay you'll be setting about getting justice done."

"Justice?"

"Getting me out of here," said Harry Heathfield succinctly.

"I'm very much afraid—" Henry began.

Heathfield went on, unperturbed, "I have to get out, you see, because of the hound. You haven't come with news of her? No, or you'd have said so right away. I can't make the people here understand, sir, and that's the truth. She's not only a valuable racing dog, but she's a gentle creature and always been used to the best. She couldn't fend for herself, Griselda couldn't. I've just got to get out and find her."

Henry said, "I'm afraid it's not as simple as that, Mr. Heathfield. You've been convicted of a serious crime."

"Don't see how folks can say a man's committed a crime when he can't remember a blind thing about it," muttered Harry, stubbornly.

"But it's Griselda I want to talk to you about," Henry said.

Heathfield leaned forward eagerly, his eyes sparkling. "You've news of her, then? She's been found?"

Henry shook his head. "I'm afraid not," he said, "but I think I may have a lead on where she is. Tell me about her. How old is she, what's her coloring?"

"She'll be twenty-six months next week," Heathfield said. "Beautiful coloring. A lovely pale sort of beige, except for a white star on her forehead and white forefeet."

"I believe she has a proper NGRC identity card?"

"That she does." There was no mistaking the pride in Harry's voice. "Owner, Mr. Henry Heathfield, trained by Mrs. Bella Yateley. It's all there, official."

"But she hadn't actually raced, had she?"

"Well—only the once."

"I thought—"

"It was like this, you see, sir." Heathfield settled more comfortably into his hard chair. His hand went automatically to his pocket for his pipe, before he remembered and grinned ruefully. He went on, "Mrs. Yateley explained it all to me. The pups start their training at twelve months, and they can race for the first time at fifteen months. Well, she thought she had a proper winner in Griselda, so as soon as the bitch passed the fifteen-month mark, she entered her for a small race—some little track up north, it was."

"A flapping track?" Henry asked.

"A what, sir?"

"Never mind. So Mrs. Yateley registered Griselda and entered her for a small race."

"That's right, sir. And Griselda was a big disappointment, it seems. She'd looked like a champion on the Hilltop track, but she hadn't the . . . what Mrs. Yateley called the heart for racing. She's an affectionate creature, and she'd do her best on the practice track, because Mrs. Yateley herself was there to encourage her. But at the meeting, with the other dogs and just chasing an electric hare—well, Griselda couldn't see the point of it, and I must say I don't altogether blame her. No competitive spirit, that's what Mrs. Yateley said. Well, of course, Hilltop's a commercial kennel, and they couldn't keep a young dog that wouldn't never do any good for them. They'd never turn out an old one, of course—not the Yateleys—but what it come down to was they had to find a home for Griselda, and that's how I come to have her."

"And to be her registered owner?"

"That's it. To tell you the truth, sir, I've got plans for Griselda. Call it castles in the air, if you like—but once I get out of here and get Griselda back—well, why shouldn't she race again? Not in the big league, White City and all that—but at some of the little meetings. It's always been my ambition, see?" Harry shut his eyes, and dreamed. "The winner was Mr. Henry Heathfield's Lady Griselda, trained by Mrs. Bella Yateley . . . Sounds good, don't it?" He opened his eyes. "That's why I've got to get out of here and find her. She'd never have run off. The other two was there, weren't they, when Mrs. Spence went round? Tess and Ginger. So why wouldn't Griselda be? I'll tell you why. She's been nicked, that's what. I suppose you don't believe me, like all the rest."

"On the contrary, Mr. Heathfield," said Henry, "I think you are probably quite right. I'd like to try to find Griselda for you. Will you help me?"

"Help you? You're darn right, I'll help you, sir. But what can I do, stuck in here?"

Ignoring this, Henry said, "Since your take-over of Lady Griselda was so formal, did you get any sort of a paper from Hilltop Kennels—a receipt, as it were?"

"Oh, yes, sir. All written out proper. I had to send it to the NGRC, and they returned it to me after they'd altered the identity card."

"And where's this paper now?"

"Back at my place, of course. In the kitchen drawer, I kept it, along with my pension book and suchlike."

"It would still be there?"

"Far as I know. My married daughter's keeping up the rent for me, and Mrs. Donovan—that's the widow lady next door—she's got the key and is goin' in for a bit of a sweep-round once a week."

Henry took his notebook out of his pocket, tore a couple of pages out of it and passed them across the table to Heathfield, together with a pen. "Will you write there that you authorize me, Chief Superintendent Henry Tibbett, to enter your home and take away the receipt for the greyhound?"

"You bet I will, sir." Heathfield was already scribbling busily.

"And on the other page," Henry added, "you might write that you, as owner, authorize me as your agent to take possession of Lady Griselda at any time."

Heathfield wrote on the second sheet, and handed the two papers back to Henry. "There. I can't tell you how grateful I am, sir. It was real good of P.C. Denning to send you along."

Henry let this pass. He said, "Now, that evening in the White Bull—"

"I don't remember—"

"I know you don't remember the accident," Henry said, "but before that, in the bar . . . you'd never met either of the two gentlemen from London before?"

"Never set eyes on them in my life, cross my heart, sir. Like I told the judge."

"And they deliberately sought you out?"

"Well, I don't know as you'd say sought out, sir. I was in my usual place near the fire, and they comes and sits down by me, and we gets into conversation."

"You'd been telling stories and singing songs before they came and sat with you, hadn't you?" said Henry.

Heathfield looked puzzled. "After they came over, yes, sir. They egged me on, like. Before, I was on my own."

"And you visited the White Bull regularly, and always sat in the same place?"

"Well—yes, sir. I'd look in every evening for a pint or so after supper."

"So that anybody who wanted to find you of an evening would know when and where to look?" Henry persisted.

Harry looked surprised. "Well . . . anybody from Gorsemere way, yes, sir. But these two was strangers, from London. Never visited Gorsemere before—they said as much."

"Do you drink a lot normally, Mr. Heathfield?"

"That I do not." Harry was indignant. "Anyone will tell you."

"Then perhaps you have a weak head for liquor?"

Harry considered this seriously. "I'd say no, sir," he pronounced at last. "I pride myself on knowing when I've had enough."

"And yet, on that evening, you passed out completely—having first stolen and driven away someone else's car?"

Harry shook his head, as if trying to free it from a swarm of bees. "That's what they say, sir—so that must be the fact, mustn't it? But . . . well . . . I can't believe it myself, and that's the truth. I just can't believe it."

Henry smiled at him. "Well," he said, "don't be too downhearted. There may be an explanation, and if there is, I'll try to find it. Meanwhile, there's something more important to find."

"You mean Griselda, sir?"

"That's exactly what I mean."

It was nearly half-past six when Henry left the prison, but since his route took him past Harry Heathfield's house, he decided to pay a call on Mrs. Donovan and, if possible, collect the receipt for Lady Griselda. Just before seven o'clock he parked the station wagon outside the pair of gaunt semidetached houses on the Middingfield road, and rang Mrs. Donovan's doorbell. He saw the corner of a white lace curtain flick quickly back as he was inspected from the inside, and a moment later the door was opened.

"Yes?" said Mrs. Donovan. She stood on the threshold of her house, square and suspicious, wearing a grubby flowered apron over a shapeless brown skirt and blouse, no stockings, and ancient bedroom slippers. She added, "I was just having my supper."

"I'm sorry to disturb you, Mrs. Donovan," said Henry. "I've brought you a note from Mr. Heathfield."

At once, Mrs. Donovan's face broke into a wide, friendly smile. "Mr. Heathfield? You've seen him?"

"Yes. I've just come from the prison."

"You'll be from the Welfare, I daresay?"

"No. No, as a matter of fact, I'm a policeman."

"Oh, you are, are you?" Mrs. Donovan's attitude changed abruptly. "Well, I hope you're proud of yourself, after what you done to poor Mr. Heathfield. A real gentleman. It's a shame, that's what it is."

"I do assure you, Mrs. Donovan," said Henry, "that I had nothing at all to do with Mr. Heathfield's arrest or trial. I'm trying to help him."

Mrs. Donovan sniffed unbelievingly, but she said, "Well, I suppose you'd better come in." She led the way into a dark hallway, and from there to a cheerless, seldom-used front room. "What's all this about a note, then?"

Henry produced Heathfield's note from his pocket and handed it to Mrs. Donovan. She read it in silence, and then said, "Well, I suppose it's all right. It's certainly his writing. It's true enough I've got the key, though I've not been able to get in to have much of a dust around. I'm out at work all day, you see, up the biscuit factory in Middingfield. You'll have to take the house as you find it."

"Please don't worry about that, Mrs. Donovan. I only want to collect a paper about the dog, as Mr. Heathfield says in his note."

"The key's in here somewhere." Mrs. Donovan pulled open a drawer in a hideously ornate dresser, and began rummaging in its recesses. "So they never found the poor dog? A shame, I call it."

"No—she hasn't been found yet," said Henry. He added, "When did you last see her—the greyhound?"

"Let's see—ah, here's the key, like I said—yes, it would have been the morning poor Mr. Heathfield went off to the police court and never come back. He was feeding the dogs in the backyard like he always did, and I had a word with him over the fence, 'Best of luck, Mr. Heathfield,' I said. 'I'm ever so sorry I have to give evidence,' I said, 'but I'll do my best for you.' 'Don't you worry, Mrs. Donovan,' he said. 'I'll see you back here this evening.' And then they sent him to prison. I had to go straight to work from the court, but I knew something was wrong when I got back here, and all the dogs was barking and yelping, poor dumb creatures, and no sign of Mr. Heathfield. So I telephoned P.C. Denning, and he told me what happened."

"And you didn't see the greyhound that evening?"

"No. I mean, I thought she'd be in the shed, like he always left her if he had to go out. And then the Cruelty ladies came, and said there was just the two dogs. The poor thing must have escaped and run off."

"Well, we're hoping to trace her," Henry said cheerfully. "Thanks for the key, Mrs. Donovan. I'll let you have it back in a few minutes."

As it turned out, Henry need hardly have bothered Mrs. Donovan for the key. Harry Heathfield's front door was secured by the flimsiest sort of lock, which any enterprising amateur housebreaker could have opened, given two minutes and a sheet of Perspex. Inside, the house was depressing. It was immediately obvious that Mrs. Donovan's good intentions had not been translated into action. The place was exactly as Heathfield had left it the previous week, sublimely confident of being back by the evening. Unwashed crockery in the kitchen sink showed that he had eaten a good breakfast before going off to court. A pair of comfortably worn slippers waited, somehow pathetically, beside the deep, tattered armchair in front of the cold gray ashes in the fireplace.

Henry did a quick tour of the little house. Upstairs was a

small bedroom with an unmade bed, and a scatter of clean but threadbare clothes; a cluttered bathroom with worn linoleum on the floor and an old-fashioned gas geyser above the stained enamel bath; and, at the back overlooking the yard, a bleak little room which must have been intended as a second bedroom, but was full of the junk of an attic. Downstairs, the sitting room, a cramped cloakroom, and a good-sized kitchen completed the accommodation.

In the drawer of the scrubbed kitchen table, Henry found the most precious documents in Harry Heathfield's life. His old-age pension book; discharge papers from the Pioneer Corps in 1946; a tattered certificate, dated 1931, which showed that Henry Albert Heathfield had married Elsie Phyllis Baker. Pinned to this was another certificate stating that Mrs. Elsie Phyllis Heathfield had died of bronchial pneumonia in 1962. There was a sort of scroll proclaiming that Henry Heathfield had taken second prize for tomatoes at the county Horticultural Show in 1965; and a Post Office savings book showing a balance of some ten pounds. There were no other documents of any sort whatsoever. Henry sighed, and went downstairs and out of the house. He locked the front door behind him, and walked around to the backyard.

The shed in which Harry Heathfield had housed Lady Griselda was not a particularly attractive place, but it was functional and well built. The concrete floor ensured dryness, and Henry noticed that Heathfield had installed a broad wooden bench, raised off the floor, similar to those in Simon Yateley's kennels and clearly intended as a dog bed. There were, however, several things that struck Henry as curious. For one, although there were traces of straw on the bench, the major part of the dog's bedding had disappeared. For another, the bench was littered with miscellaneous items like flowerpots and garden implements, which appeared to have been taken from a pile of such things stacked in a corner of the shed, and carefully strewn about the bench. It was as though somebody had made a hasty attempt to obscure the fact that there had ever been a dog in the shed.

One piece of evidence, however, had proved impossible to remove. This was a long, lightweight and new-looking chain, which was bolted securely onto an iron ring in the wall above the bench. The ring was slightly askew, and it looked very much to Henry as though somebody had attempted to wrench it out of the wall and failed. The other end of the chain terminated in a springhook of the sort usually found on dog leads, and intended to clip onto the animal's collar. Here was definite proof that Lady Griselda had neither slipped her collar nor broken her chain. She had been deliberately released—by someone who had then tried to obliterate the traces of her occupancy of the shed, but had not had enough time to do the job properly.

Henry returned the house key to Mrs. Donovan, and drove slowly back to Cherry Tree Drive. As he went, he tried to reconstruct in his mind the movements of the unfortunate Lady Griselda. It seemed at least a possibility that Larry Lawson had been on his way to steal the greyhound when he met his death. Steal, or perhaps substitute. Heathfield had only recently acquired the bitch, and might not have noticed the difference, if the substitute had been sufficiently similar in appearance. Heathfield—who had been kept away from his home and plied with drinks by Major Weatherby and his friend, so as to leave the coast clear; Heathfield—who, by a nice piece of irony—had then driven drunkenly into the wall and killed Lawson.

Had Lawson already switched the greyhound for a substitute when he was killed? Had the real Lady Griselda fled, terrified, into the darkness after the accident—leaving Heathfield to cherish the substitute from that day until his imprisonment six weeks later? Whatever the truth, the fact remained that the greyhound bitch, fawn with a white star and forefeet, which Harry Heathfield had left in his shed when he went for trial, had been stolen. Stolen during the day of the trial, when Mrs. Donovan was either in court or, as she put it, up the biscuit factory.

It also seemed a reasonable assumption that one or the other of the dogs had been kept for a couple of days in the garden shed at 18 Sandown Avenue, disturbing Nanny's rest and causing her to complain to Mummy. It infuriated Henry to think that the bitch might well have been in the shed when he first visited the house, and had been whisked off in the blue van by Shorty Bates under Henry's very nose. Where was Lady Griselda now? How much did Marlene Lawson know? And who had shot Red Dicky Marsh? Questions buzzed like angry bees in Henry's head, and he did not know the answers.

It was shortly before eight that Henry arrived back at Cherry Tree Cottage, with a pre-prepared excuse for his lateness hovering on his lips. He need not have worried, however. The pale blue MG sports car parked outside the gate told him that the Spences had a visitor, and the latter's identity was made plain by the fact that Tess, Ginger, and the other dogs were accompanied—indeed, overshadowed—by the huge, leaping figure of Wotan when they rushed to the gate to greet him. Sure enough, Amanda Bratt-Cunningham was drinking sherry in the drawing room, talking earnestly to Jane about her home-grown produce stall for the village fête. Henry was duly introduced, and noticed with some gloom that Emmy was being drawn, inch by inch, into the discussion. Remembering an earlier and disastrous fête in East Anglia, he hoped that she might at least be spared the Fortune Teller's Tent and the Lucky Dip.

Bill Spence, Henry noticed with sympathy, had retired into the garden, where he was making a pretense of weeding an already immaculate flower bed.

"Sorry I'm a bit late, Jane," Henry remarked.

The three women barely looked up. "That's OK," said Jane. "Now, Amanda, the thing we've got to decide is whether you can combine your vegetable stall with Mrs. Pickworth's home-made jams, or whether she should go in with Lady Drake's cakes and pastries. I should have thought—"

Henry did not even bother to ask if he might use the telephone. He went into the hall and looked up the number of Hilltop Kennels in the telephone book. A moment later, he was talking to Bella Yateley.

"It's about Griselda," Henry said. "Can you tell me the name of the track where she ran her one and only race?"

"Of course." Bella sounded surprised. "Doblington. In Yorkshire."

"It's what you call a flapping track, is it?"

"Oh, no. It's under NGRC management. Quite a swish affair."

"You mean it's a proper stadium?"

"Oh, very much so. There's a lot of brass about up there, as the natives say. I can remember Doblington ten years ago," Bella added, "when it wasn't much different from our open-air track at Hilltop. But now—NGRC recognition, a new stadium, a restaurant, two bars. They do themselves well up there."

"Which means," said Henry, "important races and important bets."

"I told you, there's a lot of money about. Why are you so interested, anyway?" Henry thought he could detect a slight tinge of anxiety in Bella's voice.

He said, "Oh, it's just an idea. I'm trying to find Griselda, you see."

"In that case, more power to your arm. But I can't imagine you'll find her in Doblington. We only took her up there once, for the race. She must surely be somewhere in the Gorsemere district."

"I wonder," said Henry. "Anyhow, can you give me all the details—the date and time of the race, and which dog won, and so on?"

Bella laughed. "That's a bit of a tall order, after all this time. The best thing you can do is call Doblington."

"I still need to know at least the date of the race. Mrs. Yateley—"

"Bella, please."

"Bella, can't you find me that information from your own records?"

There was a perceptible hesitation from the other end of the line. Then Bella Yateley said, "I don't think Tommy's gone home yet. He might remember. Hold on."

Henry held on. From the drawing room, Jane's voice floated out, serene and confident, telling Amanda not to pay the slightest attention to what the Reverend Mr. Thacker had said.

There were going to be *two* home produce stalls. From the garden, the gentle whirring of the lawn mower indicated that Bill Spence had grown tired of pretending to weed, and was now pretending to cut the grass instead. At last, Bella's voice came on the line again. "Sorry to keep you waiting."

"Not at all," said Henry politely. "I thought you were remarkably quick."

"Well, luckily Tommy happened to remember. She ran at Doblington in the 2:30 race on June 18th last—that's almost a year ago. They call it the Novices' Silver Collar—a sort of imitation of the Catford Gold Collar, I suppose, and run over the same distance, 440 yards flat. Open only to dogs who haven't raced before, as the name suggests. Poor Griselda came last—I can remember that for myself. As to which dog won, I can't help you, but Doblington should have it on record."

Amanda Bratt-Cunningham departed at half-past eight, accompanied by Wotan, who sat beside her in the passenger seat of the tiny car, looking like Falstaff riding in a perambulator. Jane and Emmy promptly fled to the kitchen, and a quarter of an hour later a very creditable supper was ready. Afterward, over coffee, Jane said, "I heard you calling Bella Yateley. Any news of Griselda?"

"Not for the moment, I'm afraid," Henry said, "but I've a great favor to ask of you, Jane. May I use your telephone?"

Jane's eyebrows went up. "Of course. You've been using it all day."

"I know. But this time I want to make a long-distance call. To Doblington in Yorkshire."

Henry was in luck. There was a race meeting at Doblington Greyhound Stadium that evening, and a helpful girl from Directory Enquiries soon had Henry connected with the Racecourse Manager's office. After a certain amount of secretarial stalling, Henry at last found himself speaking to the Manager himself—a Mr. Pomfret, whose rich Yorkshire accent came rolling down the wire.

"Last June? Novices' Silver Collar? Ay, so 'appen I do remember. Well, 'twere the first race she wun. Marleen's Fancy.

Proper little champion, that bitch. Gone on to great things, as yew'll know. 'Oo owned 'er? 'Ang on a tic, I'll luke it oop. 'Ere we are. Winner, Mrs. Rose Bertini's Marleen's Fancy, ten to wun. Thank *you*, sir. Glad to 'ave bin of assistance."

The following morning, Henry contacted the headquarters of the National Greyhound Racing Club in London, where the helpful staff were able to verify the identifying details of Marlene's Fancy. She was a bitch, now two years and two months old. She was registered as belonging to Mrs. Rose Bertini of Nelson's Buildings, Battersea, London. Since her original success in the Novices' Silver Collar race at Doblington, she had shown a remarkable record of success, winning races at NGRC stadiums all over the north of England. She had not yet raced in the south or the London area. She was described as being of an overall beige color, with a white star on her forehead and white forefeet. The last race which she had run—and won—had again been at Doblington three weeks ago. That was all the available information, and the charming young lady hoped she had been able to help Henry.

Henry thanked her, and hung up. Whether or not he had been helped, he felt, was a moot point. The description of Marlene's Fancy tallied exactly with that of Lady Griselda. But Marlene's Fancy was clearly a potential champion, whereas Lady Griselda had been—allegedly—given away to Harry Heathfield because she was hopeless on the racetrack. Had there been a substitution—and if so, how had it been arranged? Where were Marlene's Fancy and Lady Griselda now? Above all, it was clear to Henry that his first move must be another interview with Mrs. Bertini and her daughter, the recently widowed Marlene Lawson. And another London visit which was, Henry realized, long overdue.

9

"But Henry," Jane protested, "I thought you were going to stay a few more days with us."

"My dear Jane, I am going to stay, if you'll have me. It's just that I have to go up to London today. I'll be back around suppertime, with any luck. Don't bother to meet me. I'll walk from the station."

"But Emmy said . . ."

Henry said, "I'm not on holiday, you know."

"Aren't you?" Jane sounded surprised. "Well, you're not exactly working either, are you? Down here in Gorsemere?"

"Yes and no. Anyhow, I shall be working in London today. So be an angel and find out when the next suitable train leaves."

"I do wish all you men didn't feel such a need to be mysterious." Jane was running her thumb down a column of the railway timetable. "Amanda was saying last night . . . here we are, Gorsemere Halt 10:45, Waterloo 12 o'clock. That means you needn't hurry—it's only ten now, and I can run you to the station in five minutes."

"What was Amanda saying?" Henry asked. He was not in the least interested in what Amanda had said, but he thought it prudent to divert Jane's probing enquiries from his present activities. Gossip runs fast in a village, and he was anxious that Gorsemere should consider him to be on holiday.

"Oh . . . just wondering what you were doing down here, and why you were taking such an interest in Lady Griselda . . ."

"Blast," said Henry. "Is she the only one who's saying that?"

"I shouldn't think so," said Jane cheerfully. "We don't get many sensations in the village, and the Harry Heathfield case was beginning to die of exhaustion as a topic of conversation. Now, you've revived it."

"Look here, Jane," Henry said, "will you please do something for me?"

"If I can. What?"

"Take every opportunity you can to drop into the conversation the fact that I'm taking a few days' holiday down here, and that my only interest in Lady Griselda is that I'm tremendously keen on animal welfare."

Jane's eyebrows went up. "You are? To think I never noticed!"

"Tell them I'm a governor of the Battersea Dogs' Home. Tell them anything you like—but do your best to deflate these rumors."

Jane smiled. "So there really *is* a mystery," she remarked. "OK, don't look so suspicious. My lips are sealed, and I'll tell everybody you're just a holiday-making dog-lover. Only don't blame me if they don't believe me."

In London, Henry went first to his office at Scotland Yard, and conferred with Sergeant Reynolds. The sergeant was able to come up with some interesting information, illustrated by photographs from the Criminal Record Office.

It appeared that Larry Lawson's chief lieutenant had been Shorty Bates, the pseudo-house agent and driver of the blue van. The other members of the mob had been insignificant characters who had drifted off to attach themselves to new leaders after Lawson's death. As for Bates, apart from the fact that he had a bad record, lived by gambling, hung around dogtracks, and kept dubious company, the police had no definite charges outstanding against him. He had naturally been a suspect in the shooting of Marsh, but had been able to produce a cast-iron alibi for the crucial time. He had, of all unlikely things, been at an evening session of a Blood Transfusion Center, donating blood.

"I know it sounds too good to be true," Sergeant Reynolds commented, "but the fact remains that that's where he was, and he couldn't have been at Runworth shooting Red Dicky at the same time. It does make one think that he might have known what was going to happen, and made sure of covering himself —but try proving that one."

Red Dicky Marsh, currently hovering between life and death in the hospital, also had a henchman and confidant—an enormous West Indian called Robert Smith, commonly referred to as Calypso, or Cal. It was he who had been with Red Dicky at the time of the shooting. As his chief fell wounded, Cal had whipped out a gun and fired wildly at the attacker—only succeeding in winging the ultrarespectable Mr. Hudson, bank cashier from Runworth Common, who was treating his wife to an evening at the dogs. This had enabled the police to hold Calypso—much to his disgust—on charges of unlawful wounding and unlawful possession of a firearm.

"He may get off the wounding charge by pleading self-defense," Reynolds said, "but I'm damned if I'm going to let him wriggle out of the unlawful possession. I've been after him for a long time."

"You sound as though you don't like the gentleman," Henry remarked. "I never suspected you of color prejudice, Sergeant."

For a moment, it looked as though Sergeant Reynolds might explode. Then he grinned. "I'll take that sort of joke from you, sir," he said, "but from nobody else. No, it's the very opposite. If these small-time villains cheat and trick each other, and shoot each other, come to that, it's no skin off my nose. But this Cal Smith—he's mixed up in some very nasty rent and lodging rackets that hit his own people. They come over to this country, they're honest, hard-working folk who just want a place to live—but they're confused, they don't understand our ways. So of course they're delighted to find a fellow-countryman who'll help solve their problems." Reynolds laughed, bitterly. "Solve? He fleeces them of everything they've got, and then throws them out of even the miserable, dirty, overcrowded rooms he's put them into. And so far, he's skated through so many legal loopholes that we've never been able to nail him. Well, I've got him inside now—bail refused—and I intend to keep him."

"So," Henry said, "what it boils down to is that for the last couple of days, the remnants of Larry Lawson's mob have been at large and free to operate, while the Marsh gang is to all intents and purposes under lock and key."

"That's about it, sir," Reynolds agreed. "There's none of Marsh's small fry would make a move without Dicky or Cal."

"And Weatherby? Was he friendly with Marsh? Does he know Smith?"

Reynolds shrugged. "You know the setup, sir. They all drink in his pub. He *knows* them all. Strictly as patrons of his Private Bar. If you ask me, Weatherby's got no friends. He's just a useful sort of character, available to anybody if the money is right and the risk minimal. The Byers case shook him badly. He must have thought this was a foolproof assignment—if it was an assignment. Supposing that drunk really did steal his car?"

Henry sighed. "I know. That thought keeps occurring to me, but I simply don't believe it. Now, you've already told me there's nothing in CRO on Mrs. Lawson or Mrs. Bertini. Is there anything else at all that might tie in with the case? There's a link missing somewhere, you see. Frankly, I don't believe in small-time villains who are so sentimental that they'd risk a murder rap just to avenge a dead leader—especially when there's so little evidence that Marsh had anything to do with Lawson's death. I want to know *why* Marsh was shot, Sergeant."

Sergeant Reynolds shook his head. "I can't think of anything, sir. Anything at all. All we know, it's there on the file."

"Where does Marsh live, when he's at home?"

Reynolds consulted the dossier. "Wimbledon, sir. 128 Parson's Drive. Very respectable neighborhood."

"Married?"

"No, sir. He shares the house with Cal Smith—trust *him* to live in luxury."

"So the house is empty at the moment, with Marsh in the hospital and Smith in prison?"

"I imagine so, sir." Reynolds sounded puzzled.

Henry said, "It's a long shot, but it might produce something. I'll just have a word with the Wimbledon Police." He reached for the telephone. A few moments later, he was speaking to a polite young duty constable at Wimbledon Police Station.

"Yes, Chief Superintendent. Certainly, Chief Superintendent. Right away, Chief Superintendent." The young man, whose name was Hawthorn, was obviously overwhelmed by Henry's rank. A minute later he was back on the line. "Nothing very interesting, I'm afraid, Chief Superintendent. Parson's Drive, you said? No, nothing . . . oh, here's a . . . no. That wouldn't interest you, sir."

"That's for me to say," said Henry. "I'm interested in anything that happened in Parson's Drive last Thursday night."

"But this is only old mother—I mean, Mrs. Rundle-Webster, sir."

"Who's she?"

"She's the old lady who lives in 131. Over the street from 128. She's always making complaints to us, sir. You know the type. Neighbors' radios playing too late, parties going on after eleven, dogs barking—"

"Dogs barking?" Henry asked sharply.

"Well, sir . . ." The young constable's embarrassment came clearly down the line. "I was speaking figuratively, like. She *has* complained about dogs barking, that's for sure, but that particular night it was suspicious personages."

"Suspicious personages?" Henry echoed.

"Yes, sir. Seems she woke up in the night and saw a car parked on the opposite side of the street—which is perfectly legal, incidentally. This was pointed out to her by the duty sergeant, whereupon she went on to say that this was a suspicious vehicle. The sarge asked what she meant by that, and she said she had seen a figure lurking in the garden of No. 128. Well, I'm sorry, sir, but we've had so much of this sort of thing from her, we really didn't pay any attention. The news of the shooting hadn't come in then, of course. However, we obeyed regulations. We sent a car round to investigate. Nothing, of course. Number 128 was quite dark and deserted. No suspicious characters hanging about. No parked van."

Henry sat up straight. "I thought you said a car."

"Not actually a car, sir, no. It was a van, she said. A small, dark-colored van."

It did not take Henry long to locate No. 14 Tyson Place, Chelsea—the residence, if the court records were to be believed, of Mr. Albert Pennington, Company Director. Of all the characters directly involved in the death of Larry Lawson and the arrest of Henry Heathfield, Pennington was the unknown quantity. Unknown to the police, unknown to the village of Gorsemere. The one fact that was known about him was that he must be an acquaintance of Major George Weatherby; otherwise he would not have accompanied him on that fateful pub crawl. He had almost certainly been taken along to add respectability and credibility to Weatherby's story, but he had to be checked in any case.

As a local resident himself—though of a less affluent area—Henry knew that Tyson Place was one of the pretty little tree-lined streets which ran parallel to the bustle of the King's Road. The small Regency houses, each with its own garden or patio, were currently changing hands at prices out of all proportion to the accommodation they offered. Henry could not imagine what attraction a resident of Tyson Place could possibly find in Major Weatherby and his seedy North London pub. Could this be the small incongruity which would lead to the unraveling of the whole story? Henry doubted it.

Number 14 was an early Victorian brick townhouse, tall and narrow, which had been painted white and expensively restored. A brass knocker in the shape of a clenched fist gleamed on the sky-blue front door, and a flowering cherry tree in the tiny front garden shaded the muslin-curtained windows from prying eyes. On the surface, at least, Mr. Pennington was rich, respectable, and upper-class—or a combination of at least two of those attributes. Henry pressed the doorbell (the knocker was purely decorative) and waited with interest.

The door was opened almost immediately. Before Henry could make out the appearance of his host in the dark hallway, a low-pitched but pettish masculine voice said, "At last! *Where* have you been? I thought—" The voice broke off into a dismayed choke as its owner digested the fact that Henry was not his expected visitor.

"Mr. Albert Pennington?" Henry asked politely. He could now see that the other was a thin, willowy young man with straight fair hair which—while not exactly short—was neatly barbered and a far cry from the Jesus Christ–Chelsea school of thought, as was his neatly clipped mustache. He wore an impeccably tailored dark gray suit with very narrow trousers, and a spotless white shirt. The epitome of a well-to-do, rapidly rising young executive.

He did not reply to Henry's query, but began to close the door. With a skill born of years of experience, Henry inserted a wedging foot. He said again, "Mr. Albert Pennington?"

"Yes." The young man sounded defiant, as if proving a point. "What's more important is—who are you?"

Henry had his official card in his hand. He displayed it briefly. "Chief Superintendent Tibbett, C.I.D.," he said.

Mr. Pennington paled. "But they can't . . . I mean, what do you want?"

"Just a word with you, if you don't mind."

"What about?"

"If I may come in and sit down," said Henry, I'll explain."

Albert Pennington hesitated. Then he said, "Oh, all *right*. But I warn you, I'm saying nothing without my lawyer present. This way."

The drawing room was elegantly furnished with small, breakable-looking antiques and Regency-striped silk brocade. Glazed doors gave onto a sunny little garden. It was all very cosy and very expensive. Albert Pennington motioned Henry to a spindle-legged sofa, sat down himself on one of the solider chairs, and said, "Well? What's all this about?" His voice was hard and had lost its slight simper.

Henry said carefully, "I'm making further enquiries into a case in which you were involved a couple of months ago, Mr. Pennington. I'm sure you recall it. The evening when you drove to Gorsemere with Major George Weatherby."

Pennington, who had been about to light a cigarette, suddenly sat perfectly still, as if turned to stone. His face showed no expression whatsoever—Henry could not judge whether he was alarmed or relieved to be told the object of the visit. The immobility lasted only a split second. Then Pennington lit his cigarette, offered one to Henry, and said, "I thought I'd heard the last of that. Had to go down to Middingfield only last week to give evidence against the poor fellow. I understand he's in prison."

"That's right," said Henry. "Now, Mr. Pennington—how well do you know Major Weatherby?"

"Old George? Oh, known him on and off for years." Pennington sounded just a little uneasy. As if to forestall Henry's next move, he added, "Rough diamond, of course, old George. Splendid fellow when you get to know him, but I must admit that it was only a mutual interest in the turf that first brought us together."

Henry smiled. "You're interested in horse-racing, then?"

Pennington gave him a withering look. "My father," he said, "was Sir Humphrey Pennington." Henry regarded him with bright incomprehension. Irritated, Pennington said, "I suppose a person like you couldn't be expected to know it, but my father was a very big racehorse owner in the fifties. Very big indeed. One of the finest strings in the country."

"Ah," said Henry. "That would explain your interest, then."

"Naturally."

"And your friendship with Major Weatherby."

"Of course."

"Well now, Mr. Pennington, I wonder if you would just run over the events of that evening for me."

Pennington threw up his hands in a despairing gesture. "Great heavens, haven't we been over all that often enough? I tell you, the case is closed. The man's in jail."

"True. But complications have arisen concerning the unfortunate passerby who was killed. I'm afraid I have to make more enquiries."

Pennington shrugged. "Oh, very well. Go ahead. I can't tell you anything that I haven't already put in my statement. Weatherby and I bought a few drinks for this Heathfield character, because he seemed an amusing sort of local yokel. Then he suddenly got up and said he had to go. And he went. Next thing we knew, the pub closed and the car had gone. What else can I tell you?"

"Whose idea was the trip to the country? Yours or Weatherby's?"

"Oh, Weatherby's." Pennington was very definite on the point. "He called me up and suggested it. Said he had the chance of a rare evening off from the Parrot, and that he knew this charming old pub down in Hampshire—"

"That's funny," said Henry. "He told me you stumbled on the White Bull quite by chance, having visited several other inns on the road."

Pennington hesitated. Then he said, "That's right. Now I come to think of it, it was only when we were driving through Gorsemere that George remembered somebody had told him . . ." Under the steady scrutiny of Henry's blue eyes, Pennington faltered and then stopped. Then he giggled and said, "Oh, all right. I admit it. I've completely forgotten what he did say." Then, more aggressively, "Is there any reason why I should remember, after all this time?" And finally, passing to the attack, "What do all these questions mean, anyhow? Just because a drunkard stole George's car, it doesn't mean we had anything to do with the poor wretch he killed."

"No," said Henry. "No, Mr. Pennington, I hope it doesn't. I'm sorry I had to bother you with questions—but there's an element of mystery about the whole affair, and I'm trying to clear it up."

"Mystery?" Pennington repeated, offhandedly. "What sort of mystery, for heaven's sake? It all seemed straightforward enough to me."

Henry had no intention ot discussing with Albert Pennington the disappearance of Lady Griselda, or any other related problem. In fact, he did not consider it politic to mention dogs at all. So he simply said, as he stood up to leave, "Oh—just something that seems to be missing."

"Missing?"

"Let's say—out of a set of three, only two are accounted for. You remember 'The Third Man'?"

The effect of this remark on Albert Pennington was quite sensational. He, too, had risen to his feet, and he now turned a delicate shade of green and clutched at a fragile chairback for support. In a strangled, high-pitched voice, he said, "I'm saying no more without my solicitor present. Not another word. D'you hear me?"

Somewhat surprised, Henry said, "I heard you the first time, Mr. Pennington. But really, there's no need to call your solicitor. Nobody is accusing you of anything."

Pennington pulled himself together. "I'm sorry, Superintendent. I'm afraid I'm a little upset today—about something quite different. Something entirely private. Of course—nobody is accusing me of anything." He repeated Henry's words as if they had been some sort of talisman.

"Well, it was kind of you to see me," said Henry cheerfully. "Please don't bother—I'll let myself out."

He left Pennington standing in the improbably elegant little drawing room, and walked out under the cherry tree toward his car. And as he went, Henry was mentally kicking himself for his slowness. "You see?" remarked the voice in his head which he called his "nose." "I've been trying to tell you, but you wouldn't listen. Now do you believe me? There *was* a third man."

Henry arrived at Nelson's Buildings soon after four in the afternoon, having driven over the river from Chelsea after his talk with Albert Pennington. It was a warm day, and the insistent rhythms of pop music floated through open apartment windows onto the still air. It seemed a stiffer climb than last time to reach the second floor.

For some seconds, Henry's pressure on the bell-push went unanswered; at last, the door opened a crack to reveal Mrs. Bertini, very cross and bleary-eyed, wearing a flowered housecoat and with her brass-blonde hair screwed up in rollers.

"What is it now?" she demanded petulantly. "I was trying to get a bit of a zizz—" She broke off as she recognized Henry. "My God. You again. I thought you were going to leave us alone."

"I'm afraid not, Mrs. Bertini," said Henry pleasantly. "Just a few questions—"

"Marlene isn't home. You'd best come back later."

"It's not your daughter I want to see, Mrs. Bertini. It's you."

"Me? Whatever about?"

"About your greyhound."

For a moment, Henry thought that Mrs. Bertini was going to faint. Her face, which already looked sallow and unhealthy without its thick makeup, turned to whitish-green, and she put out a hand to steady herself against the door jamb. Then, recovering, she said in a whisper, "I don't know what you mean. I've got no greyhound."

"I think you know perfectly well what I mean, Mrs. Bertini. May I come in?"

Behind Henry, a door opened slightly. He needed no eyes in the back of his head to sense an inquisitive neighbor.

"Come on in then, if you must," said Mrs. Bertini. She almost dragged him into the apartment, and slammed the door behind him. In the narrow hallway, she confronted him. "I've never had a greyhound. You must be off your rocker."

"You're too modest, Mrs. Bertini," said Henry. "Marlene's Fancy is becoming quite a well-known racer. Since that first win of hers at Doblington last June, she's gone from strength to strength. A champion in the making, I'd say. You must be very proud of her."

Mrs. Bertini looked at him for a long moment, her face betraying a mixture of fear and hatred. Then she said, "Marlene's Fancy isn't mine. Never has been."

"How very strange," Henry said. "She's entered in the NGRC registration book as belonging to you."

"I don't know nothing about it. Larry brought some papers and said I should sign them. I've never even seen the wretched dog. You can't call that owning it."

"What you are saying, then, is that your late son-in-law, Larry Lawson, was the substantive owner of the bitch; and that he registered her in your name for some reason of his own. Is that right?"

"Cross my heart, I never set eyes on—"

"All right, Mrs. Bertini. I can well believe that. Could we perhaps go into the sitting room and talk about this?"

"I suppose so." Grudgingly, Mrs. Bertini led the way. From among the Chianti bottles and raffia fruit, her late husband surveyed the scene with Latin disdain, staring arrogantly from his silver photograph frame. The whole apartment was permeated by the delicious aroma of tomato, olive oil, and garlic that Henry remembered from his previous visit. He sat down on the sofa, and said, "And where is Marlene's Fancy now, Mrs. Bertini?"

"How should I know?"

"What happened to the greyhound after your son-in-law's death?"

Mrs. Bertini glanced nervously toward the door. "I don't know. Marlene's due home soon. Better ask her."

"Are you still the registered owner, Mrs. Bertini?"

"I tell you, I don't know. You'll have to ask Marlene."

"Has anybody brought you any forms or letters to sign—to do with the greyhound, that is—since Larry Lawson's death?" Henry persisted.

"No. That I do know." Mrs. Bertini seemed relieved to be able to answer at least one question positively. "I've signed nothing. You can't say I have."

"I'm not trying to, Mrs. Bertini." From the hall outside,

Henry heard a door open and close softly. He went on, "I'm simply trying to find out what happened to Marlene's Fancy —where she is and who owns her now."

Before Mrs. Bertini could answer—and indeed, she showed no signs of wanting to—the door of the sitting room was thrown open and Marlene Lawson walked in. "We sold her," she said, loudly.

Henry looked up, slowly. Marlene's handsome, tanned face was flushed, and her eyes sparkled—but whether from anger or excitement, Henry could not be sure. He said, "Good afternoon, Mrs. Lawson. I think you must have overheard my question to your mother."

"Yes, I did."

"By 'we,'" Henry went on, "you mean—?"

"Mum and me. We sold her. We didn't want nothing more to do with her."

"To whom did you sell her, Mrs. Lawson?"

Marlene hesitated. Then she said, "I don't know. I gave her to a friend to sell for me."

"For Mrs. Bertini, you mean."

"Comes to the same thing."

"Who was this friend?"

"None of your bloody business," Marlene snapped.

"Now, Marlene—" Mrs. Bertini, deeply distressed, tried to intervene, but Marlene cut her short.

"Leave this to me, Mum." She wheeled back to face Henry. "Now get this. I gave the bitch to a friend to sell, and I know he sold her, because he gave me the money."

"How much?"

"None of your business. That's all I'm telling you, because it's all I know."

"Has the change of ownership been registered with the NGRC?"

"You'd better ask them, hadn't you?"

"As a matter of fact, I have," said Henry.

"Then why ask me?"

"And when did this sale take place?"

"Weeks ago. Right after Larry was killed. What would Mum and me want with a greyhound? We'd never even seen it, had we, Mum?"

"No, we hadn't. I told the superintendent. It was nothing to do with us." Mrs. Bertini was vehement and near tears.

"Who trained Marlene's Fancy?"

"I haven't the foggiest."

"And where was the greyhound normally kept?"

A tiny hesitation. Then Marlene said, "Some friends of Larry's had a kennels. Up north. Don't even know their name."

"In that case," said Henry, "how did you manage to give the dog to this friend of yours, if you didn't even know where to find her?"

For a moment, Marlene seemed stumped for an answer. Then she said, "I simply gave him a letter saying he was authorized to take the dog and sell her. He knew where she was kept."

"A letter signed by Mrs. Bertini, of course, as the owner."

"That's right." Marlene glanced at her mother, who nodded vigorously.

"Mrs. Bertini," said Henry, "you told me just now that you'd signed nothing recently in connection with the greyhound."

"Well . . ." Mrs. Bertini was thoroughly confused. She shot a look of hopeless appeal at Marlene, who said briskly, "Mum must have thought you meant official forms. You haven't signed any official forms, Mum, have you?"

"I should hope not!" Mrs. Bertini, rescued from her dilemma, managed to sound outraged.

Henry said, "And that is all you can tell me, Mrs. Lawson?"

"Yes, it is." Marlene tossed her head, setting her long black hair swinging.

"Very well," Henry said. "Then I'll tell you what I think is the truth of the matter. Your late husband acquired Marlene's Fancy as a puppy, and registered her in Mrs. Bertini's name for —as I was saying—reasons of his own. I daresay both you and your mother had quite forgotten about the greyhound, until a few days ago, when you were approached by a Mr. Bates—

an associate of Mr. Lawson's." As Henry could easily have predicted, Marlene did not bat an eyelash; but Mrs. Bertini reacted with a sharp intake of breath, and was rewarded by a swift, steely glance from her daughter. Henry went on, "Bates demanded a letter authorizing him to take possession of the greyhound. He also made you ring the estate agent in Finchley to make sure that the Sandown Avenue house was still empty, and he took the spare key to the garden shed. The fact of the matter was that he had the bitch with him in his blue van, and he wanted to hide her for a few nights."

"Why would he want to do that, for God's sake?" Henry realized, with a sinking heart, that Marlene sounded positively amused. His random shot seemed to have fallen well wide of the mark. And yet . . . He said, "I'll be frank with you, Mrs. Lawson. Marlene's Fancy is a very valuable dog, you know. I think it is likely that, after your husband's death, she may have . . . disappeared . . . from her kennels. Some of Mr. Lawson's . . . er . . . competitors were undoubtedly anxious to get possession of the bitch, for reasons that we needn't go into now. My theory is that last Thursday evening Mr. Bates regained possession of Marlene's Fancy, and that he has been hiding her even since, with your collaboration. Not because he has stolen her—I am sure he has Mrs. Bertini's permission to keep her. On the contrary, I think he is afraid that she may be stolen from you, for the second time."

"Quite the little storyteller, aren't you?" said Marlene. "You ought to be on the telly. And why are all these people supposed to be going round stealing the poor dog, may I ask?"

"To race her and win the prize money, of course," said Henry shortly. He did not intend to mention Lady Griselda or the possibility of substitution.

"Well, I'm sorry to disappoint you, Mister Chief Superintendent, but you're wrong!" Marlene was a picture of smug triumph. "Marlene's Fancy hasn't raced for weeks, and nor will she. Look at this!"

She stood up, walked over to the table, and picked up a

magazine which she tossed carelessly to Henry. It was called *Greyhound Express,* and carried a cover photograph in color of several elongated, streaking animals racing *ventre à terre* against a background of green turf. Marlene said, "Inside. Page 10."

Henry turned to page 10, which was a sort of greyhound's social gossip column, entitled "Kennel Whispers." The very first item read as follows:

> Reliable sources inform us that Mrs. Rose Bertini's promising bitch, Marlene's Fancy, will not be seen on the tracks for some time to come. The reason? A happy event in the offing. A spokesman for Mrs. Bertini told me, "Marlene's Fancy was mated several weeks ago, and is definitely in whelp." The sire? For the time being, his identity is being kept secret.

As Henry looked up from the magazine, Marlene said smugly, "See? Should have done your homework, shouldn't you? That's why I sold her and that's why I got a good price . . . the puppies go with her. I didn't want a whole litter to bring up and be responsible for, I can tell you."

"And where is she now? You must know."

"I told you, I don't. Some kennels in Surrey or Sussex or somewhere, I think. Wherever she is, she'll be staying there till the pups are born, that I can tell you. I may not know much about dogs, but I do know that nobody who intended to make money out of her or the pups would go carting her around in vans in her condition. They'd as like as not lose the lot."

It struck Henry that Marlene Lawson knew rather more about greyhounds than she cared to admit. However, for the moment it seemed that she had played a trump card, and there was little to be gained by staying in Nelson's Buildings any longer. He stood up.

"Take the magazine, if you want," Marlene added, with a positively insulting grin. "Give you something to read on the bus. I've got plenty more copies."

As Henry went out into the corridor of Nelson's Buildings, he was thinking that Marlene Lawson most certainly did know where Marlene's Fancy was currently quartered; and this conviction was confirmed by a remark made by Mrs. Bertini just as the front door was closing behind him.

"Oh, Marlene, I thought you were splendid." And then, urgently, "You'd better ring her right away, hadn't you, dear?"

10

Henry arrived back at Scotland Yard deep in thought. The jigsaw puzzle was at last beginning to take shape, and with every new piece that fitted, the pattern became clearer; but there were still gaps.

He found Sergeant Reynolds in a very bad humor indeed. It appeared that, a few minutes earlier, the Runworth magistrates—needled, no doubt, by press allegation of bias in favor of the police—had turned down the prosecution's continued objection to bail in the case of Robert "Calypso" Smith. Smith's persuasive and expensive advocate had found it easy to convince the bench that the charge of unlawful wounding might well be dismissed as self-defense, and that the mere possession of a firearm was no reason to incarcerate a citizen still presumed innocent under the law. The subtle hint that a white man would not have been so persecuted had been enough to tip the balance. Accordingly, Cal Smith was free to return to the splendors of Parson's Drive—at least for the time being—and Sergeant Reynolds was very cross.

He found a somewhat unsympathetic audience in Henry, who was too preoccupied with his own problems to pay much attention to the sergeant's tale of woe. It was almost as an afterthought that Reynolds imparted a much more important item of news: that Red Dicky Marsh had died in the hospital at five o'clock, still without giving the authorities any useful information about his attacker. The case was now classified as murder.

Henry issued certain instructions, asked Sergeant Reynolds to check certain facts, and then, just before six o'clock, left Scotland Yard and took a taxi to Waterloo Station.

It was a slow journey, in the evening rush hour, and Henry whiled away the traffic jams by studying the *Greyhound Express*. What he read, combined with his recent visit to Hilltop Kennels, had the effect of quickening his interest in greyhounds—their breeding, training, and qualities. He realized that, up to now, he had been associated only with the seamier side of the sport—the gamblers and crooks and touts who were attracted to the tracks solely by the idea of making money. Reading the magazine opened up a whole new aspect of the subject, which was fascinating as well as potentially useful to his present investigation.

At Waterloo, Henry paused at a newsstand and thumbed through a rack of sporting periodicals in search of more greyhound literature, but he could find nothing. The only publication available was a cheaply printed sporting daily, which concerned itself mainly with race results, including those from the smaller tracks. Still, it had a few editorial articles. Henry bought it.

In the six-thirty-two train for Gorsemere, Henry settled into his corner seat and began to turn the pages of the paper. No, he decided, it was really very tatty and bad. Nothing to interest the serious enthusiast. And then, suddenly, a stop-press paragraph caught his eye. SURPRISE WIN FOR OUTSIDER, the headline ran. And underneath:

> The form book was upset at Kevingfield, Northants, this afternoon when a 100-to-1 outsider romped home in the 1:30 race to beat the 2-to-1 favorite. The surprise winner was Mr. Henry Heathfield's Lady Griselda, trained by Mrs. Bella Yateley.

Henry's first thought was of Harry Heathfield, sitting in the bleak visiting room at Middingfield Jail, and putting his impossible daydream into those exact words. Then he pulled himself together and began to consider the implications of what he had read.

He was still deep in thought when he became aware that the train had stopped, and that a bored, raucous voice was shouting, "Gorsemere Halt!" Quickly, he folded the newspaper, put it into his raincoat pocket with Marlene's magazine, and stepped out onto the platform.

The train, while too late to be a real commuter special, was nevertheless well patronized by businessmen who had been kept late at the office—or who had slipped out to a city pub to slake their thirst after a hard day's work. Some twenty or so dark-suited executives joined Henry on the platform, and, as the train moved off toward the south, made their collective way toward the car park, where a selection of vehicles awaited them, each with a wife in the driver's seat, some complete with dogs and children. Only Henry, it seemed, had nobody to meet him—and he directed his footsteps in the opposite direction, to the road.

As he walked down the lane which led from the station to the village, Henry was passed by a succession of homeward-bound cars. Had he bothered to look back toward the parking lot after the last commuter had sped past, he would have noticed that one vehicle, with its driver, still remained behind; but he did not bother. Nor did he even look around when he heard the whisper of tires coming up the lane behind him; he simply stepped a little closer to the hedge to allow the vehicle plenty of room to pass him. And then, without warning, the sky fell, the world spun dizzily, and everything went black.

Jane glanced at her watch. "He can't have been on the seven-thirty-two, or he'd be home by now."

"I wouldn't worry," Emmy said. "I'm most terribly sorry, Jane. It's absolutely inexcusable, and I'll tear him to pieces when he does arrive. Is it ruined?"

"Not quite," said Jane Spence, with commendable restraint. "But I suggest we eat it now. I can do an omelet or something for Henry when he finally turns up." She hesitated. "You don't think we ought to telephone and make sure he's all right?"

Emmy shrugged hopelessly. "Telephone who?" she asked,

ungrammatically. "We know he left the Yard hours ago, because of Sergeant Reynolds' call." The sergeant had telephoned at eight o'clock to leave the cryptic message that the answer was "yes," and that Henry would understand what he meant.

"That's what worries me," said Jane. "Surely he ought to be back by now."

"You don't know Henry," said Emmy gloomily. "He's onto something—I'm certain of that. And once he gets his teeth into a case, he's absolutely impossible. If you ask me, he's probably either having dinner with one of his barrister friends, like Michael Barker, picking his legal brains; or he's on a train to Manchester because the man he's following is on it too; or he's visiting every pub south of the river looking for somebody. Whatever he's doing, you can be sure of two things—he's completely forgotten that he said he'd be back for supper, and he's thoroughly enjoying himself."

Emmy could hardly have been more wrong. When Henry recovered consciousness, the first thing he was aware of was a super-headache made in hell—as though an exceptionally well-nourished torturer were driving iron spikes through his cranium with a mallet. It took him a minute or so to sort out that there were two separate and distinct causes for his agony: the first, a simple and skull-splitting headache, caused by a blow or buffet with a blunt instrument; and the second, the fact that he was lying on his back, his hands and feet pinioned, on the corrugated iron floor of a small, vibrating cell—which every second or so lifted his aching head and threw it down again to clatter against the adamant irregularities of the floor. Another few seconds, and he had identified his prison. He was in the back of a small closed van, which was traveling at considerable speed.

With a great effort, Henry managed to roll over onto his side, so that he could vary his original viewpoint, which was a monotonous panorama of the ridged metal roof of the van. The new position afforded little improvement. From here, he could see that the vehicle had been firmly departmentalized, and that his only possible contact with the driver and passenger seats was through a small barred window behind the driver's left ear. Very much, in fact, like a police van, or Black Maria—but on a smaller scale.

Henry was still contemplating his next move—purely as a matter of form, because as far as he could see no move in any direction was possible—when the van slowed down and began to move tentatively, as though the driver were unsure of his way. From the darkness inside the van, and the occasional flickers of light through the barred window, Henry judged that it was deep twilight outside, and that the van was being driven along lamplit streets—although the absence of traffic roar indicated that they were not on a main road.

At last, the van slowed to near-stationary, and then swung to the right, as if into a narrow alley or driveway. With his hands tied behind him, Henry was incapable of bracing himself against the turn, and rolled helplessly over the hard metal floor. Then the van turned right again, and finally stopped. There was a double slamming of doors as the driver and passenger alighted. Then Henry heard footsteps approaching the double doors at the back of the van.

It was no moment for heroics. He was outnumbered by two to one, he was securely trussed hand and foot, and the twofold right turn had undoubtedly brought the van to a secluded back alley, well hidden even from the small street on which it had been traveling. Henry slumped onto the floor of the van, muscles relaxed, eyes closed; as far as his captors were concerned, he decided, he had not yet recovered consciousness.

The back doors of the van swung open, and Henry was aware, through closed eyelids, of the momentary brightness of a torch beam as it flickered over him. Then a voice said, "Still out cold. Just as well. Don't want any trouble." Without either difficulty or surprise, he identified the speaker as Harold "Shorty" Bates. The voice continued. "All right. You take his shoulders and I'll take his legs. That way, if he does come round, he won't see your ugly mug. And whatever happens, keep your trap shut."

With a certain amount of grunting and groaning, Bates and his companion lugged Henry's inert body across the floor of the van to the open doors, and finally hoisted it outside. Henry felt himself being carried a short distance—not more than a few feet—and then there was a pause and more grunting as Bates evidently succeeded in opening a door or gate of some sort. A few more feet—another door or gate—and Henry was flung down unceremoniously into what felt like a concrete floor, in pitch darkness.

"Right," said Bates. "Now let's get the hell out of here." A door slammed, making the darkness even more impenetrable, and a key turned in a lock. Henry was left alone. As he began to work, slowly and painfully, to free his hands from the rope that bound them, he meditated on a curious fact. Whoever had been carrying him by the shoulders had certainly been no taller than Bates, and probably shorter; moreover, the hands which had momentarily touched his neck as they grabbed the back of his collar were small and reasonably soft; and Bates had been the brawnier of the two, taking most of the weight of the shared burden. Also, Bates' injunction that the other should "keep your trap shut" indicated that his voice was probably known to Henry. "His?" Or could it be "hers?"

At a quarter past nine, the Reverend Mr. Thacker arrived at Cherry Tree Cottage, unannounced as usual. Supper had been eaten and cleared away, and Jane, Emmy, and Bill were beginning to feel distinctly uneasy about Henry. They could have done without their unexpected caller, but Jane was too polite to snub him, and soon he was settled in an armchair with a cup of coffee, and in full spate.

"So very glad I caught you at home, Mrs. Spence . . . no luck with my other visits this evening . . . bicycled all the way up to Hilltop for a talk with Mrs. Yateley, only to find nobody at home . . . whole place dark and locked up, and the noise those dogs made when I rattled the gate! Goodness me, you'd have thought I was a burglar! Then I thought I'd have a word with young Amanda Bratt-Cunningham about her vegetable stall, but Sir Arthur tells me she's up in town this evening . . . gone to the theatre . . . no harm in that, I suppose, although some of the things they put on the stage these days . . . well, I don't know how the Archbishop can just sit there in the House of Lords, prancing around with no clothes on . . . not the Archbishop, don't misunderstand me, but so-called entertainments like . . . what is it? . . . 'Oh, Bombay!'—curious title; I understand the show has no connection with India . . . where was I?"

"You were saying that Amanda was in London," said Jane.

"That's right. I fear I'm boring you with my tale of woe. However, I am most delighted to find you at home. You see," added Mr. Thacker, with a grisly eccesiastical ogle, "I have *designs* on your sister."

Bill Spence let out a snort of involuntary laughter which he quickly turned into a cough, and Emmy suppressed an hysterical desire to giggle. Mr. Thacker went on, waggishly, "Don't get me wrong, dear ladies. My motives are pure as driven snow. Nothing that the good superintendent could object to. Where is Mr. Tibbett, by the way? Not with you? I understood that he was spending a few more days down here. He has been taking such a kind interest in poor Heathfield and his dogs. Or so I hear."

Emmy flashed a quick glance of warning to Jane, who said easily, "Oh, he had to go up to town for an Old Boys' Dinner. He'll be back tomorrow to finish his holiday."

"A little bird has been whispering," said Mr. Thacker, rather grimly, "that his stay here is not *all* pleasure. I understand just a little work is also involved?" He ended on a note of interrogation.

"I'm afraid your little bird is twittering up the wrong tree, Mr. Thacker," said Jane firmly.

"People have been saying," Thacker went on, undeterred, "that the unfortunate fellow Heathfield ran over was a *well-known figure* in the *underworld.* A notorious gambler on the *dogs.* And of course, now that a greyhound is missing—"

"Mr. Thacker," said Jane, "I can't imagine who has been pulling your leg like that."

"My leg?" Thacker's hand tightened its grip on his knee, as

if to assure himself that the limb in question was still intact.

"All this talk about gamblers and greyhound races," Jane went on, serenely. "You surely must know that Bella Yateley only gave the dog to Harry because it was no good at all for racing—and my brother-in-law is interested simply because he shares my concern for lost animals. He is an official of the RSPCA, you know."

Mr. Thacker gasped a little. "I understood he was an officer of the C.I.D."

Jane gave him a withering look. "It is possible to be both," she said. "As to the poor man who was killed, I believe he was a junior clerk in the Inland Revenue service. Who on earth has been fooling you with all these stories, Mr. Thacker?"

The clergyman had the grace to smile sheepishly and hang his head. "Oh dear, oh dear," he said. "I suppose I *am* somewhat gullible and she always had a mischievous sense of humor. I fear I—"

"Who?" Jane's question was so brisk and businesslike that Mr. Thacker apparently found nothing strange in it.

"Why, Amanda, of course. The naughty little miss. I can see now that she was twitting me."

"Well, I hope you haven't been repeating this talk all over the village, Mr. Thacker," said Jane, "because if you have, I'm afraid you're going to look very foolish indeed."

"Yes, yes, I quite see that . . . if I have given any misleading impressions . . . correct any misapprehensions at once . . . most grateful to you, Mrs. Spence . . ." The Reverend Mr. Thacker cleared his throat loudly, and emerged from his confusion in good order. "And now, my dear Mrs. Tibbett, may I come to the point of my visit here this evening? A little bird . . . that is, I feel sure that you would not deprive us of your talents when it comes to a matter of deathwatch beetles."

"I'm sorry," said Emmy, bewildered. "I'm afraid I don't—"

"The fête," said Mr. Thacker, snappishly. "Surely your sister must have told you that our object is to raise money to eradicate deathwatch beetles from the chancel beams?"

"Well, no. Actually, we haven't discussed—"

"And so, Mrs. Tibbett, I feel absolutely confident that you will not turn down my heartfelt appeal to you to preside over the Hoop-La stall next Saturday. Every hoop cast will spell destruction for another beetle, and a square inch of our English heritage preserved for future generations. Now, first you should contact Mrs. Claverton at the White Bull . . ."

Emmy wriggled feebly in an attempt at escape, but she knew that she was well and truly corralled and might as well submit with a good grace. Anyhow, Hoop-La didn't sound too bad, and for the moment she was far more concerned with what had happened to Henry.

The darkness retreated minimally as Henry's eyes grew accustomed to the gloom. He could now make out enough of his surroundings to see that he was in some sort of windowless shed. Around the edges of the locked door crept a faint, pinkish glow, as if the lights of a town were being filtered into his prison, and from some way away he could hear the distant rumble of traffic and the occasional car horn. Henry tried to recall the details of his visit to Sandown Avenue, and the interior of the garden shed. He could not be sure that he was in the same place, but the size and general layout seemed to be the same, and after all, it had been used before by Shorty Bates as a temporary dumping point for livestock. Henry hoped that Nanny was alert and awake next door, and wondered how he could best attract her attention.

Meanwhile, the important thing was to free his hands. After an agonizingly slow wriggle across the hard floor, he reached the far wall of the shed, where a selection of garden implements stood haphazardly in the corner. It was too dark to identify them, and it seemed an age before Henry located a reasonably sharp edge—apparently the tine of a garden fork. It took the best part of another half hour to maneuver the implement to such a position that it was wedged firmly against the wall, and he was able to chafe the cords on his wrists by rubbing them up and down on the metal edge.

He was still busily engaged on this task, and had had the

gratification of feeling two of the three strands of rope parting, when the key turned in the lock and the door of his prison opened. Instantly, Henry resumed his sack-of-coals impersonation—a procedure which involved slumping forward with his head on the floor, so that he was not able to get any idea of who it was who had opened the door. A feeble ray of light from outside penetrated the shed—and was instantly cut off, as the newcomer slammed the door behind him. Henry, lying still and holding his breath, was surprised. Coming in from the relative lightness of the garden outside, the intruder must now be totally blind inside the darkness of the shed. Why had he slammed the door?

Henry heard somebody moving around the dark shed, stumbling, feeling his way. Then a man's voice said, "All right. Where are you? Come on, you ugly brute, I know you're there. Come on out this minute!"

With infinite caution, Henry moved his head so that he could look in the newcomer's direction. His eyes were well accustomed to the darkness, and he made out the man's figure at once—a tall, lanky fellow wearing a light-colored suit. But . . . there was something strange. Something wrong. The man had no face, no hands . . . it was just the glimmering, pale suit which Henry could see groping uncertainly in the gloom. Where the man's face should have been . . . And then, suddenly, he realized the explanation. The man's face and hands were invisible because he was a black man. Henry was not in the garden shed at Sandown Avenue. He was at Parson's Drive, Wimbledon, and his companion was Cal Smith.

Henry grinned wryly to himself in the darkness. He had to admire the tactics of Shorty Bates, in dumping a kidnapped police officer on his deadliest rival and enemy. If Henry had indeed been unconscious on his arrival at Parson's Drive, it would never have occurred to him or to anybody else that he had not been abducted by Cal Smith and the Marsh gang. As he strained desperately to break the last strand of rope binding his hands, it also occurred to him to wonder what had made Cal Smith come out to the shed, and how he could know that somebody was in there. All in all, the man's behavior was very strange. He was moving round the shed now, feeling the walls, bent low with his questing hands not more than a couple of feet from the ground. Soon, he must inevitably come to the corner where Henry lay.

At last, the final strand of rope gave way with a small, snapping sound, and Henry rolled over, his hands now free although his feet were still pinioned. The noise attracted Smith's attention at once. He stiffened, straightened up, and turned toward the source of the sound.

"All right, all right," he said. "Come here. I won't hurt you. Come here, you silly bitch."

And Henry understood. He had been mistaken for Lady Griselda.

Mr. Thacker drained the last drops of coffee from his cup, wiped the cake crumbs from his lips with a white linen handkerchief, and said, "That was really delicious, Mrs. Spence. A most enjoyable way of combining business with pleasure. I can't tell you how relieved I am to think that the Hoop-La will be in such capable hands." He beamed at Emmy. "Well, I really must be off now. It will take me at least ten minutes to bicycle back to the vicarage, and I always like to be safely at home before the Bull closes. Even if the drivers are not drunk, they tend to be careless late at night, and the recent sad accident is in all our minds . . . that poor fellow from the Income Tax, I think you said . . . ?"

"That's right," said Jane blandly. Mr. Thacker's eyes strayed wistfully toward the coffee tray, but Jane did not take the hint. She stood up.

"I think you're very wise, Mr. Thacker," she said. "If you start now, you should be home before half-past ten."

The front door had only just closed behind Mr. Thacker when the telephone rang.

"Thank God!" Emmy exclaimed. "That must be Henry. I'll take it." She made a dive for the instrument. "Hello! Yes . . . Oh . . ." Her voice fell. "Yes . . . just a moment, I'll get her

. . . no, this is her sister . . . I was expecting a call . . . hold on a moment . . ." She put the receiver down and came back into the drawing room. "For you, Jane. Amanda Bratt-Cunningham."

"Oh dear," said Jane. "I'm sorry, love. Don't worry, though, I'm sure he's all right." She went out into the hall.

"Jane?" Amanda's clear young voice floated down the wire. "Terribly sorry to disturb you at this hour . . . oh, has he? You poor things. Daddy says he was after me, too, but luckily I was out . . . just got back from town this minute . . . actually, I was ringing to ask if Simon and Bella were with you, by any chance? . . . Oh, well, never mind. It was just an idea. There's no reply from their place, and it seems the dogs have been making one hell of a noise. The neighbors have been ringing Daddy and complaining—nothing to do with him, of course, but people *will* . . . it's a bit odd, because the Yateleys don't usually go out on Tommy's night off . . . oh, well, of course, if old Thacker's been prowling around, rattling the gates, that's the explanation . . . no, I wouldn't worry, I expect they've calmed down by now." Amanda hesitated a moment, and then said, "Daddy was most frightfully interested to hear I'd met your brother-in-law. I'm afraid, when I first met Emmy, the penny didn't drop—I mean, that her husband was Chief Superintendent Tibbett of Scotland Yard. Of course, Daddy's terribly keen on police work, being a J.P. and everything, and he'd love to meet the superintendent. He's still staying with you, isn't he? Do you think you and Bill could persuade him to come over here for a drink at lunchtime tomorrow? With you and your sister, of course. Around twelve, say?"

It occurred to Jane that Amanda was—to her credit—a very bad liar. She was reasonably certain that Sir Arthur Bratt-Cunningham's interest in Henry Tibbett was minimal, and that he had expressed no desire to make his acquaintance. Either Amanda wanted to see Henry for purposes of her own, or else she was trying to establish his whereabouts—which, in the circumstances, was rather remarkable.

Jane said, "I think we'd all love to, Amanda, but I'll have to let you know tomorrow. Henry's stayed up in town for a reunion dinner, and we're not expecting him back till later on."

"Oh." Amanda sounded distinctly deflated. "Well . . . please do ask him and let me know in the morning. Tell him we'll give him the hair of the dog," she added, with a nervous little laugh.

"I expect he'll need it," said Jane.

Men in Henry Tibbett's position are supposed to think on their feet. This, Henry decided, was not easy when you were lying on your side in pitch darkness, and it was obvious that a dangerous and probably armed man was going to trip over you before you could free the hobbling cords around your ankles. Nevertheless, his brain was ticking over at full speed, assessing the situation.

First, did Bates and his accomplice know that Cal Smith had been released on bail? Almost certainly not, for the news had only been telephoned through to Sergeant Reynolds at the Yard a matter of minutes before Henry started his journey to Gorsemere—by which time, the ambush was already being prepared at Gorsemere Halt. Bates must have a key to the Parson's Drive garden shed—an interesting point—and he had decided to dump Henry into cold storage, because he imagined the property to be deserted. This gave rise to several unpleasant lines of thought.

Meanwhile, Cal Smith had left a greyhound bitch locked in his shed when he went to Runworth Stadium with his chief, Dicky Marsh, just a week ago. Granted that she had been left a good supply of food and water, Cal might reasonably expect to find her still alive, even if debilitated. That, of course, was why he had slammed the shed door behind him, and then proceeded to grope around near floor level. He wanted to stop her from escaping, but really expected to find her lying weak and exhausted on the floor.

So far, so good. Now, the crucial question. What would Cal's reaction be on discovering not a dog but a bound man in his shed? He did not know Henry personally, so it was unlikely that he would identify his unexpected visitor as a member of the C.I.D.; and a man who was trussed and thrown into a locked shed was hardly likely to be on an offensive mission. Fleetingly, Henry regretted having freed his hands. Conversely, on finding a man instead of a dog, Smith's reaction might well be to shoot first and ask questions afterward.

In this situation, with less than a couple of seconds to go, Henry made up his mind. He let out a low and—he hoped—painful groan.

The other man stopped dead and stood, like a statue. Henry moaned again. Smith was now so close that Henry could see the gleam of his eyes in the invisible blackness of his face. In a terrified whisper, and with a marked West Indian accent, Smith said, "Who's that? Whar are yo', man? Whad'yo doin' heah?"

Henry could have told him the answers to most of these questions, but instead he groaned again, this time making the sound more surely human. Then he muttered, "Where am I? What's happening?"

Cal Smith seemed no more inclined to answer questions than Henry was. In reply to these queries, he bolted out of the shed as if an army of demons had been at his heels, slamming and locking the door behind him.

Henry sat up, and began working on his ankle ropes again. At least Smith had not immediately fired in the direction of the voice—though whether from prudence, humanity, or the mere fact that he had no gun with him, it was impossible to say. His abrupt departure at least gave Henry time to rid himself of his final bonds—but he had to face the fact that he had no weapon handy except a garden fork—whereas Cal Smith would certainly return with a powerful flashlight and a gun.

On the other hand, the West Indian would have to unlock and open the door, thus presenting himself as a good target. Henry was reminded of the contest between the gladiator and the retiarius. Who had the greater advantage—the man with the conventional weapon, or the man with the net and trident? For his trident, Henry had the garden fork, which he held hidden behind his back, grasped firmly in his right hand; for his net—nothing but an insubstantial mesh of honeyed words, which he might never even get the chance to throw out. In the silence of the dark shed, Henry waited.

11

It must have been about five minutes later that Henry saw, through the cracks around the shed door, the beam of the powerful torch approaching from the direction of the house. Then he caught the sound of footsteps on a graveled path. He braced himself, waiting for the next expected sound—the turning of the key in the lock. This did not come. Instead, there was a moment of absolute silence, and then a shocking, deafening report as a gun went off. The door flew open, and Henry found himself facing a dazzling spotlight, whose brilliance quite obliterated the figure behind it. Then another shot tore up the packed earth floor in front of Henry's feet, and the bullet ricocheted off to rip a hole in the wooden sidewall of the shed.

From behind the light, a soft voice said, "That was jus' to show yo' I'm serious. Whar's the dawg?"

In as light a tone as he could manage, Henry said, "Mr. Smith, I presume?"

"I don't want none of yo' talkin'. Whar's the dawg?"

"I imagine," said Henry, "that Mr. Bates has her."

"What you imagines or don't imagine don't rate. I want facts. Whar is she?"

Henry said, "Aren't you interested to know who I am?"

"Who yo' are don't rate neither. Yo'll tell me whar the hound is, and then—yo' won't be worryin' who yo' are, brother." Smith chuckled. "All I care is, yo'se a Lawson man. And there's only one good place fo' a Lawson man, and that's whar Lawson is."

"And Marsh," Henry said.

"What's that? What yo' said?"

"Marsh died in hospital this afternoon."

"Yo' liar!"

"It's perfectly true, I assure you. You're on your own now, Smith."

There was a tiny pause, and then Smith said contemptuously, "An' how come yo' know so much? If Red Dicky done died, the fuzz wouldn't go publicizing the fact to a small-time no-account dawg stealer."

"I'm glad that point occurred to you," Henry said, as cheerfully as he could, "because it so happens I'm not a dog stealer. I'm an officer of the C.I.D., and I'm conducting an investigation."

Smith laughed, without amusement. "And I'm the Queen of England. Yo' needn't think to save yo' dirty skin with that sort of story. Yo'se no busy."

"I can't stop you shooting me now," Henry agreed, "but I can assure you you'll regret it. My men know where I am, and they'll be arriving at any moment." If only that were true, he thought. In fact, only two people knew where he was—Shorty Bates and his small, lightweight companion; and they were certainly not going to come back and rescue him.

Smith stretched out a lanky leg behind him, and pulled the shed door shut. Both torch beam and gun remained trained on Henry. Smith leaned back against the door, apparently relaxed and yet as tense as a spring.

"OK," he said. "Let's have it. Whar's the hound? I'll count to ten, and then I shoot."

The duty sergeant at Wimbledon Police Station picked up the ringing telephone. "Police here . . . yes, madam, this is the duty officer . . . oh . . ." He looked at the young constable who sat at the other desk, winked, and gave a huge and fortunately inaudible shrug and sigh. Then he picked up a pencil and pulled a memo pad toward him. "Yes, Mrs. Rundle-Webster . . . no, Mrs. Rundle-Webster . . . how long ago, Mrs. Rundle-

Webster? . . . Just a few moments . . . I see . . . you don't think it could have been a car backfiring? . . . Well, cars do sometimes backfire twice, you know, madam . . . No, Mrs. Rundle-Webster, I didn't mean to imply . . . I'm sure you know the difference, but all the same . . . well, Parson's Drive is not exactly the sort of place . . . you've heard nothing since? No shouts or footsteps or . . . yes, yes, I'm sure you would, Mrs. Rundle-Webster . . . oh, really? How long ago was that? . . . About half an hour . . . You're sure it was the same one? . . . No, no, madam, I simply meant that there are a lot of small vans about . . . you didn't notice the registration number? . . . I see . . . A taxi? Just a few minutes ago? . . . well, that would probably be the owner returning . . . ah, you recognized him? . . . yes, I quite understand you are worried . . . naturally we'll make enquiries, madam . . . of course we take you seriously . . ." A long pause, during which the duty sergeant indulged in much eye rolling and sign talk with his companion. At length, seizing the opportunity of breaking the flow, he said, "Now, madam, please don't misunderstand . . . duty of every citizen, I quite agree . . . no, please don't hesitate . . . yes, we'll investigate right away . . . yes, I should do that, madam . . . yes, a hot water bottle is a great comfort . . . good night, Mrs. Rundle-Webster . . ."

He replaced the telephone and went into a great pantomime of mopping his brow.

"Old Mother R-W again, I gather," remarked the constable. "What's it this time, Sarge? Communists under the bed?"

"Just about as silly. Gunshots in Parson's Drive. Obviously a car backfiring, but you know the old biddy . . ." The sergeant shook his head.

"Where were these gunmen supposed to be operating—in her garden? Ah, hello, young Hawthorn," he added, as another young constable came into the office. "About time you showed up for duty, my wife's fair fed up with me being home late for supper." He stood up and began assembling the papers on his desk.

"Anything happening, sir?" Hawthorn asked the sergeant.

"Couple of minor traffic accidents—all under control. Details are on your desk. Nothing else interesting." Then, to the departing constable, he added, "No, not in her garden, funnily enough. She said they came from number 128, on the other side of the street."

Hawthorn, who had started to read the reports on his desk, looked up. "Sounds like Mother Rundle-Webster again," he said.

"That's right," said the sergeant. "Crime wave in Parson's Drive. Gunshots. Ye Gods, what'll she think of next?"

"Wait a minute," Hawthorn said. "Number 128, you said, sir?"

"I said nothing at all, boy. That's what the lady said."

"But that's where . . . I mean, Chief Superintendent Tibbett was—"

"Name-dropping will get you nowhere around here, young man." The sergeant, who was comfortably middle-aged, believed in putting young whippersnappers in their place. "Since when have you been hobnobbing with chief superintendents?"

"No, really, sir." Hawthorn was so obviously and desperately in earnest that the sergeant looked up from the report he was writing. "The chief superintendent called when I was on duty earlier. He wanted to know anything and everything about 128 Parson's Drive—however trivial. He said it was important. I really think we ought to investigate, sir."

The sergeant chewed the end of his ballpoint thoughtfully. He said, "She doesn't miss much, the old lady. Must spend all her time peeking round her lace curtains. According to her, about half an hour ago, a small blue van drove into the drive of number 128 and disappeared round to the back."

"A blue van!" Hawthorn's young voice was trembling with excitement. "She reported one in Parson's Drive before, and the chief superintendent said it was—"

"All right, all right. Then, she says, a minute or two later the van drove out again and away. Next thing, just a few minutes ago, a taxi drove up and a man got out whom she recognized as the owner of the house. Such a delightful gentleman, according to Mrs. R-W, even if he is colored. Nobody could accuse *her* of color prejudice, she said. He was charming."

Hawthorn laughed. "Little does she know."

"What do you mean?"

"Well, sir—that's Calypso Smith. Red Dicky Marsh's sidekick. They live in 128—didn't you know?"

The sergeant had gone pink. He said, "I'm not on visiting terms with every villain in the district." Then, with a double take, he added, "I thought Cal Smith was inside—refused bail."

"Doesn't sound like it, does it, sir?"

"Well, according to Mother Rundle-Webster, he didn't go in through the front door, but also went round the back. Next thing, a few minutes later, she swears she heard two shots. She's convinced the blue van deposited a desperate criminal in the garage, who was lying in wait for poor Mr. Smith and must have shot him. I put it down to a car backfiring, but . . . well, let's see . . . there's a squad car cruising in that neighborhood. Get Control to give it a buzz. No harm in taking a look . . ."

"Five . . . six . . ." Cal Smith was counting slowly, lazily. He had already spun his count out to cover a good five minutes. "C'mon, man. If yo' tells me whar *both* hounds is, I might even let yo' go."

"So you've lost them both, have you?" said Henry. "Very careless."

"No back talk," snapped Smith. "Seven . . . eight . . . only two more to go . . ."

"Even if I told you," Henry said, "what could you do about it? Marsh is dead, Weatherby's a broken reed, and Pennington's dead scared." He took a firmer grip on the garden fork.

"I'm askin' the questions around heah. Never mind what I'd do. Jus' tell me."

"How should I know? I'm a Police Officer."

"Oh, yeah? And whar's the fuzz in their squad cars, blowin' their sirens, comin' to fetch their buddy? Brother, you couldn't fool a newborn babe. Nine . . ."

At that moment, three things happened. Henry launched himself toward the blinding torch beam, striking out with the garden fork; Smith's gun went off with a shattering report; and the torch went out.

Smith let out a scream of mingled pain, surprise, and terror, and Henry knew the fork had found its mark. Unfortunately, however, Cal Smith's bullet had not been entirely wasted. Henry was aware of a sharp pain in his right shoulder. For the moment, he had some part of Smith or of his clothing pinned down by the garden fork—in the darkness, he could tell no more than that; but he knew that, with his injured shoulder rapidly weakening and the pain increasing, he could no longer exert sufficient pressure on the fork. Swiftly, he transferred the handle to his left hand—and was at once aware of a lessening of force, as his victim, grunting with exertion, fought back. He had lunged in the direction of Smith's right arm, and the fact that the West Indian had not fired again led him to believe that he had, indeed, immobilized the hand which held the gun. The darkness, too, was on Henry's side. But Smith could transfer the weapon to his other hand, and at this close range even a left-handed shot could hardly miss. It had been worth a try, Henry thought grimly, but a try was not good enough. Was it worth the agony of hanging on for the few seconds that remained to him? Yes . . . there's always the possibility of a miracle . . .

And the miracle happened. When Henry heard the scream of the siren and the squeal of brakes as the squad car roared up the drive and around the corner of the house, he imagined that delirium had set in, and that the longed-for sounds were no more than a delusion. Then came the slamming of car doors, the sound of running feet. Desperately, with the last remnants of strength and consciousness, Henry shouted—nothing articulate, nothing comprehensible, just a sound for the rescuers to home on. The next moment, the door was flung open, the small shed was suddenly full of men and of light, and Henry slumped forward onto the floor in merciful unconsciousness.

Across the road, Mrs. Rundle-Webster removed her nose from the windowpane for long enough to remark to her obese tabby cat—"*There!* I *told* you so, Tabitha. Oh, I do hope that nice Mr. Smith isn't hurt."

When Henry opened his eyes again, he was in a small white room smelling of disinfectant. His head was aching, but there was no pain in his shoulder. However, a moment of experimentation showed him that his right arm was totally immobilized, being encased in plaster. The electric light was burning in the hospital room, and the streaks of darkness between the white slats of the venetian blind indicated that it was still dark outside.

Struggling back to consciousness, Henry marshaled his thoughts. The arrival of the squad car at 128 Parson's Drive remained, as far as he was concerned, an act of God. The idea that Mrs. Rundle-Webster might have been the Almighty's chosen instrument did not occur to him. The important thing was that he, Henry, was still alive—and that there were urgent things to be done. There was a bell-push on the wall beside the bed, and Henry reached out his left arm and placed a firm finger on the button.

After what seemed an hour, but was in fact less than five minutes, the door opened and a brisk, pretty, black nurse came in, her starched uniform rustling importantly.

"Ah, you're awake. Splendid. How do you feel?"

"Lousy," said Henry, "but that's not important. I've got to get out of here."

"Now, now, now." The nurse smiled indulgently. "No chance of that, I'm afraid. We're going to have the pleasure of your company for several days at least."

"That's what you think." Henry struggled to achieve a sitting position, and was humiliated to be returned to the horizontal by a firm but gentle pressure of the nurse's hand.

"Just lie back and relax. You're very lucky—the bullet passed clean through your shoulder without doing any serious damage. All the same, rest is what you need." The nurse smiled enchantingly, her teeth gleaming improbably white against her dark skin. She could hardly have been less like the pale, angular Nanny of Sandown Avenue, but Henry had the impression that they had been trained in the same school. She went on, "I'll just take your temperature and pulse, and if all is well, you may see a visitor for just a few minutes. There's a policeman waiting outside who's anxious to have a few words with you."

Henry opened his mouth to say that he certainly wished to speak to Sergeant Reynolds with all despatch—but he was silenced after the first syllable by the insertion of a thermometer and an injunction to lie still. The nurse's cool fingers closed over his wrist. A couple of hours later—or so it seemed—she released his wrist and removed the thermometer, which she studied gravely.

Then she said, "Good. That seems to be all right. I'll tell the young man he can have just five minutes. Then we can find out a few facts about you. Quite the mystery man." She was out of the room before the implication of what she had said penetrated Henry's tired brain. They didn't know who he was. Bates had evidently removed all Henry's identification papers while he was unconscious. Sergeant Reynolds, Emmy, Jane, Bill . . . none of them knew where he was or what had happened. The man waiting outside was not a C.I.D. Officer, but some plodding flatfoot from the local station. By the time the door opened again, Henry was ready to scream with frustration.

Young P.C. Hawthorn was feeling justifiably pleased with himself. If it had not been for him, and for his initiative, the squad car would have arrived in Parson's Drive too late—if at all. The sergeant, of course, was now claiming vehemently that he had always had every intention of investigating Mrs. Rundle-Webster's complaint, but Hawthorn had his own opinion about that.

As it was, however, Cal Smith was back behind bars after his short bout of freedom, nursing a lacerated right hand; and his unidentified victim was being cared for in the local hospital—in what the doctors called a satisfactory condition. Had the squad car not turned up, the man's condition would have been far from satisfactory. The driver's report stated that the injured man had been putting up a game fight, armed only with a garden fork, but he could not have held out much longer, and Smith would undoubtedly have killed him.

At least, Hawthorn reflected, the sarge had been decent enough to keep him on the case by detailing him to wait at the hospital and take a statement from the victim when he recovered consciousness.

"Now, be careful how you handle him, Constable," the sergeant had admonished him. "Smith says he is one of the Lawson mob, which means he's a petty villain himself—these small-timers are always getting into fights with each other. He'll like as not be scared silly when he finds a copper by his bed. Or worse, he'll be one of the sort that refuses to talk at all. Honor among thieves, dog doesn't eat dog, all that nonsense. It'll be quite a test for you, young man. You come back with the information we want, and I'll put in a good report on you. Your precious Chief Superintendent Tibbett might even get to hear of it. You were saying you wanted to transfer to the C.I.D., weren't you?" The sergeant smiled genially. "Off you go, then, and good luck."

With this briefing, P.C. Hawthorn approached the door of the hospital room in a mood of determination mingled with a certain apprehension. He decided that he would use a nice mixture of firmness and reassurance. He would gain the man's confidence, while at the same time giving no quarter. The iron hand in the velvet glove, reflected Hawthorn, who could turn a neat phrase with the next man.

Consequently, he was more than a little taken aback when, the moment he entered the room, the man on the bed said sharply, "There you are at last! What's your name? I hope you've got your notebook, because you're going to need it."

This, Hawthorn felt, was distinctly unfair. The man was asking him, Hawthorn, the very questions which he intended to ask the man. He wondered how the sergeant would have coped with this situation. For his own part, he sat down with deliberate slowness and took out his notebook.

"For God's sake, man, we haven't got all night!" There was

undoubted authority in the man's voice. Hawthorn had to remind himself firmly that this was, after all, only a petty crook.

He said, "We won't worry about my name for the moment. But I'd be interested to know yours." Pretty good, that, he thought. Establishes authority.

The man did not appear to have heard him. He was saying, "First of all, get to a telephone and contact Sergeant Reynolds at Scotland Yard, C Division. If he's not on duty, have them call him at home. Tell him he's to come here at once. Where is this benighted place, anyhow?"

"Coombefields General Hospital." Hawthorn only just prevented himself from adding "Sir." He pulled himself together. Remember he's more frightened of you than you are of him. "That's quite enough from you," he went on, miserably aware that he lacked the other's effortless air of command. "Your name, please."

"Tibbett, of course. Now, as soon as Reynolds is on his way—"

Hawthorn was making a note. "How do you spell—?" he began; and then, with a sickeningly unreal slowness, the awful suspicion dawned. He said, hesitantly, "Not . . . not Chief Superintendent . . . ?"

"Of course. Now, Constable, I want your name, number, and a brief report. After that, go and telephone Reynolds."

"But . . . sir . . ." Hawthorn was hopelessly confused and embarrassed, but he knew the rules. "I'm afraid I'll have to ask to see your credentials, sir. You see, you were brought in here with no papers of any sort—"

"I have gathered that much," said Henry tartly. "Now, stop wasting time. Give me your report."

Hawthorn was nearly in tears. All his instincts told him that this was, indeed, Chief Superintendent Henry Tibbett; on the other hand, supposing that the man was a very clever villain, with a very clever idea? He would first get all the information he needed, and then—while Hawthorn was telephoning—simply walk out of the hospital and disappear. Hawthorn could imagine only too vividly the attitude his superiors would take.

"I'm sorry, sir. Really I am. But I've got to establish your identity first. It's in the regulations."

Suddenly, Henry grinned. "You're perfectly right, Constable," he said. "The trouble is—how? We haven't much time."

Inspiration dawned on P.C. Hawthorn. "Earlier today," he said, "I was on duty at Wimbledon Station. I received a phone call—"

"Glory be," said Henry. "You're the chap I spoke to?"

"Yes, sir. So if you could just recall the conversation—"

Rapidly, Henry sketched out what had been said on the telephone. Hawthorn's honest young face broke into a smile of relief. "That's right, sir. Word for word. So since there's only you and me who could know what was said—"

Henry could not resist remarking, "Ah, but how can you be sure it was the real Tibbett you spoke to?"—and then, seeing dismay creeping back, he added, "I was only joking, Constable. You were quite right to demand proof of identity." Then, struggling to regain the sitting position from which the nurse had ousted him, he said, "The squad car. Was it you—?"

Hawthorn blushed. "I'd just come on duty, sir, and the sarge was talking about Mrs. Rundle-Webster's complaint, and saying it must have been a car backfiring. I remembered what you'd said—"

"God bless you and God bless Mrs. Rundle-Webster," said Henry piously. "What's your name?"

"Hawthorn, sir."

"You've done very well, Constable Hawthorn. I won't forget it. Now, one or two facts. You got Smith?"

"Yes, sir."

"Good. He's being held, I hope?"

"Yes, sir."

"Anything incriminating in the house?"

"Just the gun, sir. Several of them, actually—all unlicensed, of course. And a lot of money in cash and documents relating to house property. I believe the Fraud people are interested."

"Right," said Henry. "That's all I need to know for the moment. Now, do as I said and get hold of Sergeant Reynolds."

He paused. "On second thought, don't tell him to come here. Explain what's happened, and tell him to wait in his office at the Yard until I call him. By the way, what time is it?"

Hawthorn glanced at his watch. "Eleven forty-nine, sir."

"So late? Let's just hope it wasn't tonight."

"I beg your pardon, sir?"

"No—come to think of it, it couldn't have been. But it'll have to be tomorrow. Forty-eight hours. All right, Hawthorn, get to that phone. And when you've talked to Sergeant Reynolds, ring Gorsemere 387 and speak to my wife. Tell her I'm OK and ask her to get her sister to drive her up here at once. I've got to get out of this place."

The door had opened, and the colored nurse reappeared, her resemblance to Nanny now very marked. "I heard that," she said tartly. "Your wife may certainly visit you, but there is no question of your going home. And you—" to P.C. Hawthorn—"your five minutes is up." She took the constable's arm and led him firmly toward the door, at the same time saying in a lowered but audible voice, "Have you found out who he is?"

"Oh, yes, nurse. We know him. He's—"

"—known to the police, is he? Well, let me tell you that so long as he's in here, he's a patient like any other, and I won't have him bothered with questions or charges or—"

Their heads came together as Hawthorn, pink to the ears, evidently disclosed Henry's true identity in an indignant whisper.

The door was closing behind them as Henry heard the nurse saying, "Oh, he is, is he? Well, he could be the prime minister for all I care, he's staying here until the doctor says—" The door clicked shut. Henry lay back and closed his eyes. The interview had exhausted him more than he liked to admit, even to himself.

At midnight, Jane said, "Emmy, darling, I do think you ought to go to bed and try to get some sleep. There's really nothing else we can do. The sergeant at Scotland Yard said he'd let us know if there was any news."

Bill Spence, who had fallen asleep in his big armchair, with his spectacles awry and his newspaper on his chest, stirred, grunted, and sat up. "Must have dropped off. What time—goodness me, it's midnight. No sign of Henry?"

"No," said Emmy.

"Well, I daresay he knows what he's up to. I'll be off to bed. Coming, Jane?"

The sisters exchanged a quick look, and Emmy said, "Yes, I think we should all go to bed. There's no sense in waiting up."

Emmy had just undressed and was sitting on the bed wondering how best to pass the sleepless hours when the telephone rang. Seizing her dressing gown, she hurtled out of her room and down the stairs, dead-heating to the telephone with Jane, who had remained in the kitchen to finish some late-night task. Jane stood back. "It must be," she said. "You take it."

"Hello . . . yes . . . speaking . . . oh, thank heavens . . . where is he? . . . In the hospital? Oh, my God, is he? . . . Oh. Oh, good. Yes, I see . . . What happened? . . . No, of course you can't, I quite understand . . . Which hospital? . . . Coombefields? Where's that? . . . Oh, yes . . . yes, I know . . . he said *what?* . . . Now, this minute? . . . Well, I don't know if I . . . I'll ask her, but . . . what do the doctors say? . . . They do, do they? I might have known it . . . will you be seeing him again? . . . Oh, I see . . . well, if you can get a message through, tell him I'll be there at about . . ." Emmy glanced at the grandfather clock which ticked ponderously in the hallway . . . "between a quarter- and half-past one, with any luck . . . but tell him I don't promise anything . . . yes . . . yes . . . thank you very much, Mr. Hawthorn . . . yes, we were rather . . . good-bye . . ."

Emmy put down the receiver and Jane said, "Well?"

"He's in Coombefields General Hospital," said Emmy. "He's been shot."

"Oh, Emmy. How is he? What happened?"

Emmy gave an exasperated sigh. "He was shot in a fight. That's all I could get out of the policeman who called. As for how he is—he's ill enough for the doctors to say he's got to stay in hospital, and well enough for him to say that I've got to go and get him out."

"What—now? In the middle of the night?"

"That was the message. Actually, he asked if you would drive me to the hospital. Will you, Jane?"

Jane hesitated. "I don't know what to say," she said. "It sounds crazy."

"Of course it's crazy," said Emmy, "but if Henry feels so strongly about it, my guess is that it's important."

At the top of the stairs, Bill Spence appeared, yawning massively and tying the cord of his ancient dressing gown. "Thought I heard the phone . . ."

Before Emmy could reply, Jane said decisively, "It was the police, darling. Henry's had an accident, and is in hospital at Coombefields."

"Sorry to hear that. Is he—?"

"He's not in any danger," said Jane, "but the hospital would like Emmy to go there at once. So I'm going to drive her."

"But—" Emmy began.

Jane winked at her sister. "Go and get some clothes on, Emmy, and we'll be off. You may as well go back to bed, Bill. We'll be home for breakfast."

"Well, for heaven's sake be careful. Don't want you ending up in hospital, too." Bill yawned again, and shambled back to his room.

12

The hospital looked very large, dark, and forbidding. The bulky Victorian building stood on a tree-lined suburban road, and as Jane slowed the car down, the whole massive building seemed to be asleep. However, as they drew nearer, Emmy saw that some windows were dimly lit from within, and over one door a small electric light illuminated a sign with one word—"Emergencies."

"I suppose this must be the entrance we want," said Jane. "We're certainly an emergency." She parked the car by the curb, under a street lamp. "Shall I wait here, or come in with you?"

"Oh, come in, please. I just hope they'll let us see him."

In the stark, tiled hallway, an elderly porter was dozing behind his desk. He sat up with a jerk at the sound of the door, and glared suspiciously at the two women. Emmy said, "My name is Mrs. Tibbett. My husband was brought in this evening, after an accident. I'd like to see him, please."

The porter blinked at her, and then proceeded very slowly and deliberately to sort through some papers on his desk. At last he found what he was looking for. He adjusted his glasses and studied the pink, official-looking form. Then he said, "What was the name again?"

"Tibbett. Mrs. Henry Tibbett."

"Got any means of identification on you, madam?"

Surprised, Emmy said, "Yes. Here's my driving license." The

porter studied the document solemnly, then handed it back and said, "Room 319. Third floor, turn right out of the lift and it's on your left."

"Thank you so much," said Emmy. "Come on, Jane. We'll—"

"Wait a minute, wait a minute." The porter raised his hand. "Mrs. Tibbett only."

"But this is my sister. She drove me up from the country—"

"Your sister, madam? Well, in that case . . . she can go up with you, but don't blame me if she's not allowed to see Mr. Tibbett." And, having divested himself of responsibility, the porter returned to his desk.

Half an hour later, the man who had been watching the hospital entrance ever since Henry's arrival in the ambulance was in a nearby public telephone box, making his report.

"Well, they've been and gone . . . yes, two of them . . . must have been her sister, I reckon . . . yes, the car number checked with our info from Gorsemere . . . they got here at twenty past one . . . parked outside Emergencies, both went in . . . came out again at ten to two, and by the look of them I'd say things was going our way, all right . . . well, what I mean, the wife was all upset, weeping and so on . . . quite chirpy she was going in, too . . . left it to her sister to do the driving home, such a state she was in . . . I reckon the busy's in a bad way . . ." The man in the telephone booth sniggered unpleasantly. "Cal Smith's not half going to cop it this time, shooting a copper to death. I can hardly wait . . . no, of course I didn't mean . . . what d'you think I'd do, shoot my bloody mouth off? . . . I'll tell you where I'm going, and that's home for a bit of a zizz . . . yeah, I know . . . I'll be there . . ." He hung up, and pushed open the door of the telephone box. A passerby, had there been one, might have heard him mutter to himself the words, "Bloody women . . ."

The porter at the Emergency Door was really quite distressed. Such a nice lady, she'd seemed—couldn't have had any idea how bad the Tibbett character was. The porter had seen him being brought in on a stretcher, unconscious . . . but that didn't always mean it was a serious case. Must be, though, for a sensible lady like that to leave in floods of tears, with her coat just thrown anyhow over her shoulders and leaning on her sister's arm like she could hardly walk. Staggering, almost, she was. For a moment, the porter harbored an unworthy suspicion—but he put it aside at once. She'd been as right as rain when she arrived, certainly hadn't been drinking. Maybe the doctor had given her a slug of brandy to help her pull herself together, and being a lady unaccustomed to strong drink . . . The porter shook his head sadly, and went back into his cubbyhole to await the next emergency.

Bill Spence had slept only fitfully since the departure of his wife and sister-in-law. He was fond of Emmy, always had been, and he got on well with Henry. He was sorry the poor chap had had an accident. All the same, Bill's conservative soul resented the fact that Jane should be involved in these goings-on. He remembered only too vividly the night, some years ago, when he and Jane had sat up, gray with anxiety, in the Tibbetts' London apartment, waiting for news of their daughter. Oh, he knew it had been Veronica's own fault—she had insisted on indulging in some amateur sleuthing, against her Uncle Henry's express instructions, and had nearly got herself murdered as a consequence. He could not blame Henry. Nevertheless, lying there in the empty house, Bill remembered, and resented, and worried.

Twice during his sleepless hours, cars passed up Cherry Tree Drive—the sound of their engines raising his hopes, only to dampen them again as they roared past the house and faded into the distance. The third car, however, stopped. The engine was switched off, and Bill heard the sound of doors opening. He was out of bed in a flash, and pulling back the curtains to look down from his bedroom window onto the path which led to the front gate; and what he saw made his heart turn over.

Emmy was walking slowly up the path, supporting Jane. The latter was leaning heavily on her sister, and walking uncertainly and with difficulty, as if in pain. Her head was bowed and covered by a scarf, but Bill could see the glint of her golden hair drawn into its usual chignon; he could also see that she was holding a handkerchief to her eyes.

Bill took the stairs in a couple of flying leaps, and had the front door open before the two women reached it.

"Jane . . . !" he shouted, and then stopped dead. There was something extraordinary about Jane. Something altogether strange and wrong and . . . and then the two of them were inside the lighted hallway, the handkerchief was removed and the door slammed shut, and Bill found himself confronted by a transvestite brother-in-law.

"Henry! In the name of all that's holy, what on earth—?" In his surprise, Bill stepped backward, tripped, and found himself unexpectedly sitting on the bottom step of the stairs, gaping.

"It's quite all right, Bill," said Emmy. "Henry just borrowed Jane's clothes, you see—"

"And where's Jane, if I may ask?"

"Jane's in the hospital—"

Bill let out a bellow of fury and despair. "I knew it! I knew there'd be an accident! I told you to be careful—"

"There's nothing the matter with Jane," Emmy reassured him.

"Then what in heaven's name is she doing in the hospital? Have you all taken leave of your senses?"

"If nobody minds," said Henry, "I'm going to take off these hell-inspired shoes. I don't know how I made it up the path."

"Poor Henry," said Emmy sympathetically. "Lucky Jane's got largish feet, but they were a tight squeeze."

"Even if they'd fitted, how you women contrive to walk on these goddamned stilts—" Henry kicked off the offending shoes with a force which sent them flying across the hall. "And if you'd take this coat off me, darling—"

As Emmy slipped Jane's coat from Henry's shoulders, Bill said, almost accusingly, "You're hurt. Your arm. It's you should be in the hospital."

"That's right," Henry agreed cheerfully. "And so, to all intents and purposes, I am. You will read in your newspaper tomorrow that I have been seriously injured in a gunfight with a criminal, who is now in custody; that I am still unconscious, in critical condition, and that it is unlikely I shall recover. The hospital will issue more bulletins, each more gloomy than the last. Meanwhile, Jane has very kindly lent me her clothes—it's lucky she's tall, and was wearing a blouse and skirt. I don't think I'd ever have fitted into a dress. And by great good luck, my nurse remembered that one of the staff sisters had a false blonde chignon, which she borrowed for me. It looked quite convincing under the head scarf, didn't it? Jane's staying at the hospital tonight, and tomorrow she'll borrow some clothes from one of the nurses and come home by train. I'm sorry, Bill, but there was no other way of getting out of that hospital without being spotted. The place was certainly being watched, and there may well be somebody keeping an eye on this house. That's why I had to keep up the charade, right to the front door."

Bill shook his head in resignation. "Mad," he said. "Stark, raving mad, the lot of you." He looked at Henry and winced. "I wish you'd change out of those clothes. You give me the creeps. For heaven's sake, go to bed."

"Sorry," said Henry. "I can't just yet. There's work to be done."

"Work? Do you realize it's nearly three in the morning?"

"I do indeed. That's why the sooner I get on to Sergeant Reynolds at the Yard, the sooner we can all get some sleep. Mind if I use the phone?"

"I'm past caring what you do," said Bill. "Speaking for myself, I'm going to have a stiff drink. I've had a considerable shock." And he made his way to the drinks cupboard, averting his eyes as he went from the sight of his brother-in-law. Henry, his blonde chignon slightly awry, his floral silk skirt hitched up comfortably and his nylon-clad legs planted firmly apart, was sitting by the telephone and dialing.

As Bill poured himself an ample measure of Scotch, it occurred to him that he should perhaps be thankful that it was three o'clock in the morning. At least the Reverend Mr. Thacker was not likely to drop in at this hour for one of his impromptu visits. And yet . . . if he should do so . . . picturing the clergyman's face if confronted by Henry in drag, Bill Spence began to laugh, his good humor quite restored.

Emmy flopped into an armchair beside him, and Bill hastened to propose that she, too, should take a nightcap.

"No, bless you. I'm so tired, I just want to sleep, and it might keep me awake." Then she, too, started to laugh. "It really was awfully funny, Bill. The doctor was marvelous—entered into the spirit of the thing like mad, as soon as he was satisfied that Henry could leave the hospital without risking serious medical complications. We left him gleefully composing a bulletin to issue to the press tomorrow. The Sister was a bit more difficult—have you noticed how junior executive people hate breaking rules? People at the top and the bottom are much less law-abiding. Anyhow, we convinced her in the end. She's going to spend her time going in and out of the room with intravenous bottles and things, and the domestic staff have been told that Henry is too ill to be disturbed. So with any luck, there's absolutely nobody except the doctor and the nurse who know that Henry isn't still in there, very ill and unconscious. Except you and me and Jane, of course."

"All very ingenious, I'm sure," said Bill, dryly. "Worthy of the Boys' Own Paper. What I don't understand is—why? Henry's not some sort of free-lance private detective—he's a senior officer of the C.I.D. If he gets himself wounded in the course of an investigation, surely all he has to do is pass the facts along to some other officer, who will take up the case. All this fantastic play-acting—"

"I know," said Emmy sympathetically. "And I can't tell you very much, except that Henry's main idea is that the criminals should think he's not only seriously ill but also unconscious, and therefore hasn't been able to communicate with anybody. He says he knows too much—don't ask me what—and that if certain people knew he was very much alive and out of the hospital, there'd probably be another murder."

"Another? I didn't know there'd been one yet."

"Well, that's what Henry said in the car. Another murder, and the victim would be somebody here in Gorsemere. A friend of yours."

"That's ridiculous," Bill said flatly. "Who on earth would want to murder somebody here? We're just a quiet little country village."

Emmy shrugged. "Don't ask me. I'm only telling you what Henry said. He also said it was tremendously important for all of us to keep up the deception for a day or so."

"What deception?"

"That Henry's at death's door and hasn't recovered consciousness. I'm to creep around looking like death—in fact, I'm to stay indoors most of the time, and you and Jane are to talk in hushed whispers about the family tragedy." Emmy grinned. "At least," she added, "it'll probably get us all out of Mr. Thacker's fearful fête. He can hardly ask a prospective widow to run the Hoop-La."

From the hall outside, they could hear Henry talking on the telephone—talking and listening. Phrases and snatches of conversation drifted through the doorway. "Yes, it's bound to be tomorrow . . . hard to say, but I'd guess somewhere in the south . . . that's right, what they call a flapping track . . . I suggest you get hold of one of the sporting papers, to begin with . . . find out where races are being held tomorrow, then get hold of lists of runners, but be absolutely certain nobody knows which dog you're interested in . . . no, that's right, you don't, do you? All the better, I shan't tell you . . . just a complete list of all runners . . . yes, probably I could, but it's too risky . . . call me here tomorrow, and for heaven's sake remember to go round with a long face, because I'm supposed to be on the danger list . . . I don't think that remark was in the best of taste, Sergeant Reynolds . . . above all, let it be known that I'm still unconscious and you haven't been allowed to see me . . . and, by the way, don't let any fool of a magistrate let Cal Smith out on bail this time . . . now, I want you to listen very carefully . . . just a moment . . ."

Bill and Emmy heard the telephone being laid down on the table, and Henry's step in the hall. Then the sitting room door was closed quietly from the outside.

Bill put his drink down very deliberately, and said, "Well, I'll be damned." He was clearly not amused. "What does Henry think we are? Ruddy criminals or spies or something?"

Emmy smiled. "Don't worry, Bill," she said. "I'm used to it. The theory is that what you don't know can't hurt you. Whenever Henry has a bit of information that could be dangerous, he's always very careful only to give it to people who absolutely have to know it. It used to upset me at first, as if Henry didn't trust me—but I know better now. You and I know that Henry is out of the hospital. It's best if we don't know too much more."

"Don't worry," said Bill, a trifle bitterly. "I for one know strictly nothing, except that my wife, who is perfectly well, is incarcerated in a hospital somewhere in the suburbs, and that Henry is interested in lists of runners at racetracks tomorrow."

"And that," said Emmy firmly, "is plenty. Well, personally, I'm for bed."

Ten minutes later, Henry came upstairs. He sat down heavily on the bed, and said, "Help me out of these extraordinary clothes, will you, darling?" He pulled at the blonde chignon, which came off with a shower of hairpins. He smiled, a tired smile. "I must look pretty funny."

Emmy did not smile back. She said, "You look dead beat and ill. How's your shoulder?"

"It's OK."

"It's not. It's hurting you. I can tell."

"Well, the painkillers are beginning to wear off. It's bound to ache a bit."

"Hold your left arm up," Emmy ordered, "and I'll get the blouse over your head and then ease it round the bandage. The sooner you get to bed, the better. And tomorrow you're to stay absolutely quiet and—"

Henry, whose head was enveloped in the silken folds of Jane's shirt, made an inarticulate sound of protest. Emmy tugged, the blouse came free, and Henry said, "I'm afraid not, darling. Work to do."

"That's ridiculous," Emmy said. "Stand up, and I'll unzip your skirt. You can have the telephone by your bed and talk to anybody you want—but you're staying here."

"I wish I could," said Henry, "but it's out of the question. I'll stay in as long as I can, of course, but as soon as I know exactly where the action is going to be, I must go there."

"To a racetrack?"

"Yes."

"For heaven's sake, can't somebody else do it? Someone who isn't sick?" Emmy laid a hand on her husband's uninjured arm. "I'm sorry, darling. I do try not to interfere with your work, but this could be really serious."

"You're telling me," Henry said. "Somebody—maybe several people—could get killed. That's why I have to be there."

Emmy sighed. "I give up," she said. "Come on, I'll help you into your pajamas."

The publicity was very smoothly handled. The next morning, sitting up in bed and eating breakfast with one-handed awkwardness, Henry noted with satisfaction the paragraph in the mass-circulation daily paper:

> Chief Superintendent Henry Tibbett of Scotland Yard is in serious condition at Coombefields Hospital today, after a shootout with a gunman at a Wimbledon house last night. Police say a man is helping them with their inquiries. A hospital spokesman told me, "The Chief Superintendent is still unconscious, but we feel that he has at least a 50-50 chance. We will be issuing further bulletins on his condition." No other details of the shooting are available at this time.

Henry nodded approvingly to himself. The item was prominent enough to catch the eye of anybody interested, but it was deliberately unsensational. It would hardly grip the average reader. An officer of the C.I.D. was bound, after all, to tangle occasionally with armed criminals. The hospital, while scarcely cheerful, was not despairing. Most important, the gunman had been captured, so law-abiding citizens could sleep soundly. If the paragraph caused any comment, Henry reflected, it would not be so much on the incident itself, as its location. *Wimbledon,* of all places! What *is* the country coming to? Why, Aunt Mildred lived in Wimbledon for fifty years—you didn't get gun battles there in *her* day . . .

Henry's musings were interrupted by the ringing of the extension phone, which Emmy had plugged in by his bedside. He picked it up eagerly.

"Yes, speaking . . . You have? That's very good work, Sergeant . . . yes, at once, half a dozen copies . . . now, here's what I want you to do. Get on to Wimbledon, and tell them to recall Constable Hawthorn from Coombefields Hospital and post somebody else there instead . . . no, no, certainly not . . . he's to be told I'm too ill to be interviewed . . . it would be a good idea if Hawthorn and his replacement exchanged a few remarks to that effect when they change over—you never know who may be listening. Then I want you to put Hawthorn into a police car with a driver and send them down here . . . yes, to this address . . . officially, they've been sent as police protection for my wife, who has received a threatening phone call . . . no, thank God, but that's the story, and the driver is to be told no more. Hawthorn himself saw me at the hospital, so he must know I'm not at death's door . . . anyhow, I need him for my plan this evening. Try to have a word with him yourself and tell him the facts—he's a bright young man . . . yes, as soon as possible . . . and he can bring the lists with him . . ."

Henry's next move was to hold a bedside conference with Emmy and Bill. Jane was not expected back until lunchtime, as she would have to leave the hospital with departing midday visitors in order to remain inconspicuous. Her unavailability to speak on the phone during the morning was to be explained away by an RSPCA meeting in Middingfield—not an unusual occurrence, according to her husband. It was important, Henry stressed, to have the cover story well worked out, because calls were certain to come. He also gave instructions on how the various callers were to be handled.

And come they did. As the morning wore on, and more and more of the residents of Gorsemere found time to read their newspapers, enquiries and messages of condolence began to jam the line to Cherry Tree Cottage. Amanda Bratt-Cunningham was the first. Bill spoke to her, explaining that Jane was at a meeting and Emmy too distressed to talk. Yes, Emmy would be visiting the hospital later on, he thought. Well, yes, of course, she had wanted to go at once, but things were rather difficult . . . "Well," Bill went on, in a burst of indiscretion, "I suppose I shouldn't tell you this, but the fact is that Emmy had a threatening phone call early this morning . . . yes, very upsetting on top of everything else . . . well, the upshot is that Scotland Yard is sending police protection, and she's not to leave the house to go to the hospital till her escort arrives . . . if you ask me, probably a practical joker with a sick sense of humor, but one has to take these things seriously . . . no, we don't have any details about what happened . . . we thought he was at an Old Boys' Dinner . . . yes, thank God they caught the man, according to the paper, but that phone call could mean there was another one who got away . . . yes, of course I'll tell her . . . very kind of you to call, my dear . . . and—" Bill gave an embarrassed little laugh—"if you see a police car outside our house, you'll know we haven't fallen foul of the law . . . quite the reverse . . . good-bye, Amanda . . ." And that, reflected Bill, as he hung up, should ensure circulation for *that* particular story.

Close on Amanda's heels came the Reverend Mr. Thacker, and Emmy was persuaded to come to the telephone to receive the consolations of the Church.

"I do appreciate your thoughtfulness, Mr. Thacker . . . yes, well, all we can do is hope . . . it's most kind of you, but I really think I'd rather be alone for the moment . . . in any case, I'm hoping to go to the hospital again . . . oh yes, Jane drove me up to Coombefields last night, as soon as we got the news . . . not really, it was very disappointing, they wouldn't let me see him . . . yes, still unconscious . . . the doctors made it clear they didn't want me to stay, and there didn't seem much point in . . . yes, they're going to telephone me . . . no, we know no more than you do . . . as soon as there's any . . . no, they didn't give his name, just that a man was being questioned . . . and that's why we want to keep this telephone line free . . . no, I've no idea . . . I'm sure you understand . . . good-bye, Mr. Thacker." Emmy put down the receiver and turned to Bill. "Phew!" she said. "That man has missed his vocation—should have been a journalist. Ah, well, he got his tidbit about the hospital visit last night. I trust he'll make the most of it."

The next caller was Bella Yateley. So kind, distressed, and discreet was she that Bill Spence felt like a heel, having to lie to her. However, orders were orders, and he duly spun his yarn, but without embellishments. No mention of Emmy's imaginary threatening phone call, no word about police protection. He did not even have to refer to Jane's fictitious meeting, because Bella did not ask to speak to her. As Bella was about to hang up, Bill said impulsively, "It's so good to talk to you, Bella. Frankly, the atmosphere in this house is beginning to get me down . . . of course, nobody's more upset about old Henry than I am, but moping about here won't do him any good, and what with the Reverend Nosey-Parker Thacker on the phone every two minutes . . . no, not yet, but he'll turn up in person, don't you worry . . . look, by opening time I'm really going to need to get out of here and have a quiet beer somewhere cheerful . . . Why don't you and Simon meet me at the Bull at twelve? . . . Surely you can't be as busy as all that . . . you've got the kennel lad, haven't you, and it really would be an act of charity . . . bless you, Bella . . . see you later . . ."

Bella was followed on the line by a few of Henry and Emmy's closest friends from London—the handful of people who knew where Emmy was spending her holiday. Then, after a short interval, came a call from P.C. Denning. His wife, he told Bill, had seen the news item and was sure it was Mrs. Spence's brother-in-law, and they both wanted Mr. and Mrs. Spence to know how sorry they were. And the poor gentleman's wife too, of course. Meanwhile, P.C. Denning was hoping he could have a word with Mrs. Spence about a racing pigeon which had been picked up exhausted between here and Middingfield, and brought in to the station. If Mrs. Spence was about . . .

Bill explained about the nonexistent meeting, and assured the policeman that Jane would call him when she came home.

The next excitement was the arrival of the police car. The driver parked it conspicuously outside the gate of Cherry Tree Cottage, and informed Bill that his instructions were to remain in or near the vehicle.

"The very fact that the car's here," he explained, "that's the best protection the lady can have. Anyone with an eye on the house, they'll know better than to try anything with a squad car right here. My colleague," added the driver, indicating Constable Hawthorn with a certain amount of patronage, "will go in and interview the lady, and he'll stay in the house. But the important thing is for me to be outside here, with the car."

Bill agreed gravely, and escorted Hawthorn into the house.

Ever since Henry's telephone call to Wimbledon Police Station the day before, Police Constable Hawthorn seemed to have been living in a dazed dream. Mrs. Rundle-Webster's complaint, the chase to Parson's Drive, the hospital, the embarrassing interview with Chief Superintendent Tibbett, the further vigil in the hospital, the utterly unexpected summons to Scotland Yard and Sergeant Reynolds—all these events seemed rolled into an hallucinatory experience: a sensation which was compounded by the fact that the constable had had virtually no sleep for nearly thirty hours.

And now, here he was, being escorted into a cozy country cottage by an amiable, red-faced farmerlike character—a cottage which, if Sergeant Reynolds had not been romancing, contained not only Chief Superintendent Tibbett and his wife, but the makings of a dangerous and difficult murder case. For all his ambition to transfer to the C.I.D., Constable Hawthorn had joined the police force more as a steady job than anything else, and because he genuinely liked dealing with people and helping them whenever possible. He had to admit that he had not quite bargained for this sort of thing, and he was not sure that he liked it. As he followed Bill Spence into the hall of Cherry Tree Cottage, clutching the bulky envelope which Sergeant Reynolds had given him, and uncomfortably aware of the hard and unfamiliar outline of the gun under his jacket, he thought with distinct nostalgia of the station office at Wimbledon, the cups of tea and ledgers and parking tickets and traffic reports, and all the familiar routine that now seemed so far away.

Hawthorn followed Bill up the stairs, and found himself ushered into a cheerfully chintzy bedroom. In the bed, propped up on pillows and with his right arm bandaged, sat the now-familiar figure of Chief Superintendent Tibbett, with his sandy hair and disturbingly direct blue eyes. An attractive middle-aged woman, plumpish and dark-haired, came forward to meet him.

"You must be Mr. Hawthorn," she said. "I'm Emmy Tibbett. I think you know my husband."

"Er . . . yes. We have met," Hawthorn admitted uneasily.

"Certainly we have," said Henry. "How tall are you, Constable?"

"How tall?" In this Alice-in-Wonderland world, nothing surprised Hawthorn any longer. "Six foot one, sir."

The Chief Superintendent and his wife exchanged a quick glance. Then she said, "OK. I can do it if Jane will lend me her machine."

"Good," said the Chief Superintendent. Then, to Hawthorn, he added briskly, "All right, young man. Take off your trousers."

"But . . . sir . . ." Hawthorn was purple.

Henry grinned. "If you wouldn't mind, Emmy darling . . ." he said.

Emmy grinned back. "Of course. Don't be too long." She went out, closing the door behind her.

"Right," said Henry. "Now, look lively. Off with your trousers and your uniform jacket. My wife needs them. You can put on that dressing gown that's hanging behind the door. Then I think you ought to get some sleep. Oh . . . and I believe you have an envelope for me from Sergeant Reynolds . . ."

13

Eleven o'clock. Henry, with a look of grim satisfaction on his face, was consulting a map of southern England to determine the best route to a country town by the name of Bunstead. Emmy was busy at Jane's sewing machine. Constable Hawthorn, clad in underpants and an old dressing gown, was sound asleep on Bill Spence's bed. Bill was making a pretense of weeding a flowerbed, and wondering where Jane was. The police driver, lounging at the wheel of his car, was glaring suspiciously at the character in clerical gray and dog-collar—almost certainly a disguise—who was ringing the front doorbell of Cherry Tree Cottage.

Blasphemous but unsurprised, Bill Spence put down his trowel, wiped his earthy hands perfunctorily on his corduroy trousers, and went to open the front door.

"Ah, Mr. Spence . . . felt I had to come in person to present my condolences . . . how is poor, dear Mrs. Tibbett? . . . Such a very trying time for all of you . . ." Moving like an eel, and warding off discouragements by a smooth flow of pastoral patter, Mr. Thacker was through the front door and into the drawing room before Bill could do anything to stop him. In fact, the next thing Bill knew was that Mr. Thacker was comfortably ensconced in the best armchair, and accepting Bill's grudging offer of hospitality.

"Most kind of you . . . just a very small glass of sherry would be most refreshing . . . yes, I felt it was my duty to call . . . of course Mrs. Tibbett is not one of my parishioners, but since she is out of reach of her usual parson, I must do what I can *in loco rectoris,* if I may put it like that . . ."

Bill pulled himself together. "It's very kind of you, Mr. Thacker," he said, "but I'm afraid Emmy can't see anybody. She is resting at the moment. The doctor gave her a sedative," he added, with a burst of inspiration.

"Ah, yes . . . that would be the doctor at the hospital, I presume? She told me she had gone there last night . . . and then was not allowed to see her husband. So disappointing, a long journey like that for nothing."

"Yes, it was disappointing," Bill agreed stolidly. He measured the smallest sherry on record into a liqueur glass and handed it to Mr. Thacker.

"Thank you. So kind. Ah, well, I am glad to hear that your good lady wife is not feeling any ill effects after her night-time journey . . ."

"Eh? What?" Bill was taken off his guard. "My wife—?"

Mr. Thacker blinked over the rim of his tiny glass, like a surprised owl. "Pray don't misunderstand me, Mr. Spence. I simply meant that I can hear her busy at work on her sewing machine at this moment . . . the daily round, the common task . . . very sensible, and the best way to keep oneself from brooding . . . if I might perhaps have a word with her before I go . . . a few details to settle about the fête . . ."

Bill, thoroughly flustered, did his best. "Oh . . . no . . . no, that's not Jane . . . Jane's in Middingfield . . . RSPCA meeting, you know . . . no, that's . . . em . . . that's Mrs. Denning . . . she comes in and borrows the machine from time to time . . . making clothes for the kiddies . . ."

As a last-minute inspiration, Bill felt that it was not bad. It was well known that Mr. Thacker and the policeman's wife had not been the best of friends since the day when Mrs. Denning—who came from an extremely low-church family—

had denounced Mr. Thacker's altar candlesticks and vases of lilies as idolatrous. The memory obviously rankled still, for Mr. Thacker cleared his throat censoriously, and changed the subject.

"I couldn't help noticing, Mr. Spence, that there appears to be an *official vehicle* parked outside your house. I hope that does not portend further bad news?"

"An official—? Oh, you mean the police car. No, nothing sinister about that. Scotland Yard very kindly sent it, to take Emmy to the hospital as soon as the doctors say that—"

"The driver," said Mr. Thacker primly, "seemed an unprepossessing young man. He looked at me in the strangest way—as though he suspected me of some criminal intent."

"I really can't help it if you don't like the driver's face, Mr. Thacker. I didn't choose him." Bill, having negotiated the dangerous topic of the sewing machine, was back in his stride again.

Under this attack, Mr. Thacker immediately crumpled and became humble. "Of course not, Mr. Spence . . . pray don't think that I meant any . . . nothing could be further from . . . most delicious sherry . . . must really be going now . . . all my sympathy to the dear lady . . . trust you will have good news soon . . ." Mr. Thacker bowed himself out.

It was perhaps fortunate for Bill Spence's peace of mind that he was not in a position to follow the clergyman down the lane, round the corner, and along the road which led past the police station; or to hear his cheerful greeting—"Good morning, Mrs. Denning! Busy in the garden, I see!"—for Mr. Thacker believed that a soft answer turneth away wrath, and that one should turn the other cheek, even to a nonconformist.

Half-past twelve. Bill Spence, with a prodigious sigh of relief, had escaped from Cherry Tree Cottage on the stroke of noon, and was now happily leaning his elbows on the saloon bar of the White Bull, with a pint of the landlord's best bitter in front of him, and his good friends Simon and Bella Yateley on either side of him. Ex-Squadron-Leader Paul Claverton was busy behind the bar, mixing Simon's second pink gin, and the four of them were discussing Gorsemere's burning topic of conversation—the shooting of Chief Superintendent Henry Tibbett.

Jane was at Gorsemere Halt, using the public telephone to call Emmy, to announce her arrival and ask to be picked up and driven home. Emmy, her sewing job completed, was answering her sister's call, and promising to be at the station as soon as she had completed a few errands around the village. Constable Hawthorn was awake and feeling peckish. Henry, his plans securely laid, had taken a sleeping pill and was slumbering peacefully. Amanda Bratt-Cunningham, out walking Wotan, had stopped in a leafy lane for a brief chat with the vicar, who had just left the bedside of an ailing parishioner, having finished up her grapes. Sir Arthur Bratt-Cunningham was driving home from Middingfield, after a morning of dispensing justice at the Magistrates' Court. It was a quiet, uneventful, typical summer's day in an ordinary English village.

Jane, looking as elegant as ever despite an overlarge sweater and borrowed slacks, was in high spirits as Emmy drove her back from the station.

"It went like a breeze," she said. "No trouble at all. I attached myself to a huge family party who were leaving the maternity ward after their first glimpse of a new baby—they were all so excited and talking at once, I don't think they even noticed me, and I'm sure nobody else did. How did Henry manage last night? He looked to me as though he was having trouble with those shoes. Oh, by the way, I've a message for him from the doctor. He says to remind Henry that he only took the plaster off against his better judgment, and that he's to stay in bed for at least two days and not—"

"You can save your breath," said Emmy. "I've managed to keep him in bed so far, but this evening he's going off on some adventure or other, and nobody can stop him. And while we're on the subject, there's a policeman asleep on your bed. I thought I'd better warn you."

"A policeman? That sounds very reassuring."

"Well, you wouldn't know he was a policeman," Emmy

amended, "because he's in what you might call civilian clothes. Not to mince words, he's in his underpants."

"Good heavens," said Jane mildly, her eyebrows only slightly raised. "Why?"

"Because," said Emmy, "I've pinched his trousers. And his jacket."

"Oh," said Jane. "I see. Well, thanks for telling me."

Emmy took her eyes off the road for long enough to exchange a fleeting glance with her sister, and they both grinned. Ever since nursery days, they had had a pact—often difficult to honor—that they would never demand from each other any explanation of even the most bizarre facts. Jane was playing the game according to the rules.

Emmy said, "I'll explain. His name is Hawthorn, and Henry's idea is to . . . no, wait a minute, I'll have to go back a bit. This is how it all started . . ."

By one o'clock, Jane was in her own clothes again, and presiding over the kitchen. A substantial snack had been sent out to the driver of the police car, who staunchly refused all inducements to leave his post and come in for lunch. Constable Hawthorn, rigged out in a pair of Bill's pants which, although the right length, were far too ample in seat and waist, was enjoying a preprandial beer in the drawing room. Emmy was carrying a tray up to Henry. And Bill Spence was making his way back to Cherry Tree Cottage on foot, having parted regretfully from the Yateleys in the pub yard, and refused their kind offer of a lift home, as he knew it would take them out of their way.

Jane, Emmy, Bill, and Constable Hawthorn were in the middle of their meal when the telephone rang. Jane looked at Bill questioningly, and he said, "Yes, you'd better answer it. Just as well to establish as soon as possible that you're here."

"OK," said Jane. "Help yourselves to more, everybody." She went into the hall and picked up the telephone. "Hello?"

"Oh, Jane. It's you. I'm so glad. This is Bella."

"Nice to hear from you. Bill said you'd been having a drink together."

"Yes, we've just got home. And found the most extraordinary thing."

"Really? What sort of a thing?"

"Well . . . an envelope, actually, pushed into the letter box by the gate while we were out. Nothing at all written on the outside, and inside, a cutting from a sporting paper, with one item ringed in red ink."

Jane laughed. "You're making it sound very sensational, Bella," she said, "but is it so extraordinary? I mean, if it's about greyhound racing and everybody knows how interested you are—"

"But wait. I haven't told you. The item that was ringed was the 8:30 P.M. race this evening at Bunstead."

"Bunstead? Where on earth is that?"

"Oh, not too far from here. There's quite a big track there—what we call a flapping track, not a NGRC stadium, but pretty posh. A proper indoor course and restaurants and everything."

"I still don't see—"

"One of the runners in the 8:30," said Bella impressively, "is listed as Mr. Henry Heathfield's Lady Griselda."

"But Bella . . . that's not possible, is it?"

"Of course it's possible. With poor Harry in prison and certainly not able to see any racing papers, whoever stole Griselda must now feel sure enough of himself to start racing her. What he doesn't know, of course, is that she's just not a runner and will come nowhere—if she even bothers to start, which is doubtful. But the important thing is, Jane, that we know where she is. Or at least, where she'll be this evening."

"So—what are you going to do?"

"Go there, of course. Go there and get her back. We can keep her until Harry's free—we've plenty of room in the old kennels. Only—Simon and I were wondering . . ."

"Wondering what, Bella?"

"Well, it's going to be tricky. I mean, confronting these characters who've had the nerve to enter her for a race, and proving she doesn't belong to them. So we thought . . . well, you did go to Harry's house to fetch her on behalf of the RSPCA, didn't you? You know she's been reported as stolen? What I mean to say is—couldn't you and Bill possibly come along with us this evening to Bunstead?"

Jane hesitated. "I don't know what to say, Bella. I'll have to ask Bill. At the moment, we're all so worried about Henry—"

"Of course you are," Bella said quickly. "And naturally you couldn't leave Emmy alone. But perhaps she'd like to come along, too? She needn't get involved in any of the business with Griselda, and it might be an amusing evening out for her. Take her mind off things a bit."

"Hold on a moment," said Jane. "I'll talk to Bill."

Jane went into the dining room, closed the door behind her, and said, "Bella Yateley."

Bill looked up from his plate. "Does she—?"

"Yes."

"Well, I'm damned," said Bill. "Emmy, too?"

"As an afterthought. Might amuse her and take her mind off her troubles."

"What did you say?"

"That I'd ask you. She's holding on."

"Well," said Bill, taking a large, loaded forkful to his mouth, "give her a minute or so to think we're discussing it. Then go and say 'Yes, we'd be delighted.' But you'd better explain that Emmy is going to the hospital with a police escort, so she won't be able to join the party. After that, you can go up and tell Henry for me that he's a ruddy miracleman. How on earth did he know what would happen?"

Jane was back in the dining room within minutes. "That's settled," she said. "Bella wanted to drive us there, but I said we'd rather take our own car. So she and Simon are coming here for a drink at half-past six, and then we'll drive to Bunstead in convoy." She sat down at the table and resumed her meal. After a moment, she added, "I just hope Henry knows what he's doing."

"I wouldn't worry about that, Mrs. Spence," said P.C. Hawthorn cheerfully. "The chief superintendent is right on top of this case, believe you me."

"It's all very well for you," Bill remarked. "You're not going to be where the action is."

Hawthorn flushed. "That's the chief superintendent's idea, sir. Not mine. I'd give anything to be there, you know that."

Bill grinned at the young man. "I know, Constable Hawthorn. And speaking personally, I wish you were going to be one of our party. I'd feel a whole lot safer."

At five o'clock, Emmy came out of Cherry Tree Cottage, escorted by the stalwart constable. Jane walked with them to the waiting police car. As the constable climbed into the front seat beside the driver, Jane said anxiously, "You'll take care, won't you, Emmy?"

Emmy smiled, a strained smile. "I should be all right, with the strong arm of the law to protect me."

"I was going to say 'Give our love to Henry,'" said Jane, "but if he's still unconscious—"

"Maybe he'll come round while I'm there," Emmy said. "He must be better, or they wouldn't have sent for me."

The two sisters exchanged a quick kiss, then Emmy got into the car and it drove off in the direction of the London road. Jane was still standing in the lane, waving, when she became aware of a large, dark presence at her heels.

"Why, hello, Wotan old man." She bent to caress the great dog. "Where's your mistress, then? Ah, there you are, Amanda. Giving him his evening run?"

"Yes. I just thought—" For some reason, Amanda sounded nervous. "I was just passing . . . wasn't that your sister, going off in the police car?"

"Yes," said Jane. "The hospital called. They say she can see Henry."

"Oh, I am glad. So he's regained consciousness?"

Jane allowed her brow to cloud. "I'm afraid not. They told Emmy he was better, and that she could see him, but she mustn't expect him to talk or even to recognize her. I'm just so afraid that—"

"Oh, Jane. You mean—they may have called her because he's worse?"

"I'm trying not to think so," said Jane.

A small item on the six o'clock radio news bulletin mentioned that Chief Superintendent Henry Tibbett was still unconscious in a London hospital after a shooting incident, and that his condition was reported as only fair. A man was still helping police with their enquiries, but no charges had been made as yet. This news item was listened to with varying degrees of interest in several houses in Gorsemere and in various districts of London. It also came through loud and clear on the radio of the police car.

Punctually at six-thirty, the Yateleys arrived at Cherry Tree Cottage, accepted a drink each, and then suggested they should be on their way to Bunstead if they were not to miss the first race, which was scheduled for seven-thirty. Soon, the Spences' elderly sation wagon was following the Yateleys' sparkling new Rover along the winding country lanes which led from Gorsemere to Bunstead.

Some twenty minutes later, another car from Gorsemere took the same route. Meanwhile, from the direction of London, a nondescript blue van had already made the journey to Bunstead. By seven o'clock, three more vehicles worthy of interest were on the London–Bunstead road: an old but flashy Jaguar, with Marlene Lawson at the wheel and Mrs. Bertini —dressed in the style which she imagined suitable for the owner of a racing greyhound—in the passenger seat; a purring black Rolls Royce, driven by Mr. Albert Pennington, who was set for another evening of slumming with his amusing chum, Major George Weatherby; and an inconspicuous green family saloon, driven by an ordinary-looking, square-set young man in civilian clothes, who was very much afraid that his face was too well known to deceive any but the most law-abiding patrons of Bunstead Stadium into thinking that he was there for an evening's amusement. The more suspect characters there would recognize him as Sergeant Reynolds of the C.I.D.

14

Bella Yateley had not exaggerated when she decribed Bunstead Stadium as pretty posh. It was a large, oval structure surrounded by an acreage of car parks and outbuildings, and only the most knowledgeable of its patrons would have been aware that it was a nonregistered track. As far as Jane and Bill could see, it might have been Wembley or Romford.

The meeting was obviously a popular one, for the place swarmed like a cheerful, noisy anthill. As well as the steady stream of patrons flowing from their parked cars to the entry gates, a tributary of pedestrian humanity made its way up the road from the local railway station to swell the flood. Outside each turnstile, raucous-voiced men selling racecards shouted their wares under the arc lamps, while tipsters did their noisy best to persuade the public to part with twenty pence in return for an envelope containing the name of a guaranteed winner.

As they walked toward the turnstiles, Simon explained to Bill that there were several different admission prices. It was possible to get in for as little as 10p, which entitled you to roam on foot on the unroofed, ground-level area surrounding the track. For this modest sum, you could also buy snacks in the buffet and drinks in the bars, and lose your money to the bookmakers like everybody else.

A 25p ticket gave the additional privilege of admission to the first covered tier, thereby enabling you to keep dry if it rained, as well as the right to pay rather more for identical food and drink at a higher altitude; whereas the top price of 50p threw open the enclosed, centrally heated top story, with its luxury restaurant and cocktail bar, and its ranks of comfortable seats—steeply raked like those in a theatre—whence you could gaze down through a plate-glass partition, not only on the brilliantly lit oval of the track itself, but also on the lesser beings braving the elements down below. The possessor of a top-price ticket, Simon explained, could go slumming in the lower areas if he wished, but the 10p man was strictly forbidden to climb above his station. The Yateleys and the Spences agreed to do the thing in style, and bought four 50p tickets, together with racecards. Soon they were enjoying a drink and a sandwich at the plushy bar, consulting their cards and mapping their plan of campaign.

The first thing to do was to make a formal check of the racecard: sure enough, there was the entry among the runners for the 8:30 race—the principal event of the evening. Mr. Henry Heathfield's Lady Griselda, trained by Mrs. Bella Yateley. Bella and Simon then became involved in a somewhat technical discussion as to which official to approach and how to set about it, so that Bill and Jane were able to look around them and study some of their fellow-racegoers.

It was Jane who first noticed the two women, and drew Bill's attention to them. They appeared to be on their own, without male escorts. The younger one was strikingly attractive, with her fine features, deeply tanned complexion, and jet-black hair. She was slim and petite, and very elegant in a black and white pants suit, and she was also very cross. The object of her displeasure seemed to be her companion—a middle-aged, blousy lady with improbably golden hair and too much makeup—who was startlingly dressed in a creation of brilliant purple liberally interwoven with glittering silver threads. The two of them were perched on stools at the bar, and they were quarreling in fierce, audible whispers.

"No, you may *not*, Mum—just get that into your head. I don't know why I ever let you wear that silly dress." The girl was doing her best to keep a social smile on her face, but it was wearing thin.

The older woman pouted. "I suppose you're jealous, just because somebody gives me a present of something nice for a change. And I've a right. I'm an owner, aren't I?"

"No, you are *not* and you'll kindly shut up before you get us all into all sorts of trouble."

"Well, I am, so there—and that being so, I've a right. She said—"

"Heartless, I call it," said the girl, suddenly switching her attack. "I'd have thought you'd have been more interested in what she told us about Larry and that woman. But oh no. Never think of me, only of yourself."

"That's not fair, Marlene."

The girl slammed her empty glass angrily onto the counter. "For God's sake, finish your drink and go and put your money on. That's what you're here for. Then I've a good mind to take you home."

"You can't do that, and well you know it." The older woman drained her glass with deliberate slowness, her little finger extended like a butterfly's wing. Then they both got down from their barstools and made their way toward the betting windows.

"Surely that woman can't really own a greyhound, can she?" Jane whispered to Bill, much amused.

"Oh, I don't know. All sorts of unlikely people—" Bill broke off suddenly and said in a different tone, "Look. Over there. It's them."

"Who's what?" Jane swiveled round on her stool.

"Those two men who've just come in—the thin fair chap and the big red-faced man."

"What about them?"

"They're the two who gave evidence at Heathfield's trial—I remember them from the committal proceedings. The red-faced fellow is the London publican whose car was pinched."

"What's that?" Simon Yateley suspended his discussion with Bella and turned to stare at the newcomers, who had emerged from the restaurant and were now installed in ringside seats, studying their racecards.

"So those are the villains of the piece, are they? According to Jane, anyway. They look pretty harmless to me."

"All the same," Bella remarked, "isn't it a bit odd that they should turn up here on the very evening that Griselda's running?"

Simon shrugged. "Just coincidence, I expect. After all, several thousand other people have also turned up, and if they're in the habit of making evening excursions to the country . . ." He looked at his watch. "Come on, drink up, love. And you, too, Jane, if you don't mind. Time we were off to find Griselda."

As he spoke, the lights in the gallery dimmed, throwing the illuminated track into even greater prominence, and an amplified voice announced the imminent start of the first race. Within seconds, the bar was deserted as people made their way toward the plate-glass window to watch the race. Struggling against the tide of humanity which was surging toward the best vantage points, Bill and Jane followed the Yateleys with some difficulty, occasionally colliding with another racegoer intent on finding a seat near the front. On one such encounter, Jane found herself entangled with a tall, slim female in corduroy pants and a white silk shirt, who was heading determinedly toward the window.

"So sorry," Jane muttered, "we're just trying—" And then, with a gasp of amazement, "Amanda! What on earth are you doing here?"

Amanda Bratt-Cunningham looked equally taken aback. "Jane! I didn't know you were interested in the dogs."

"I'm not, really," Jane admitted. "Simon and Bella brought us. Emmy's gone off to the hospital to see Henry, and they thought an evening out would cheer us up."

"Oh, I see." Amanda sounded relieved. "Well, you're going the wrong way. You won't see anything of the first race unless you get nearer the window. Come with me."

Jane could see, glimpsed through the crowd, the bobbing heads of the Yateleys and Bill getting steadily further away, as they made for the stairway. She said, "Terribly sorry, Amanda . . . for some reason, Simon wants to watch from down below . . . must go . . ."

Amanda seemed about to protest, when a voice from behind her said, "Why, if it isn't young Amanda! All alone, are you? Come and sit with us—" And Jane recognized the fair man whom Bill had pointed out as a witness at the Heathfield trial.

Amanda wheeled round. "Oh, hello, Bertie." She sounded less than enthusiastic. "All right. See you later, Jane."

"You've met old George Weatherby, haven't you . . ." The voices were lost as Albert Pennington steered Amanda toward the front row of seats. In the hush of expectation which preceded the start of the race, Jane slipped quietly through the outer fringes of the crowd to join Bill and the Yateleys, and the four of them started down the concrete stairs at the exact moment when a roar of excitement told them that the greyhounds were off.

It was quickly obvious that the Yateleys were well accustomed to stadium geography. Even though it was their first visit to Bunstead, they seemed to know by instinct which passage to follow, and which door—inevitably marked "No Admittance"—to go through. Several times they were challenged by white-coated officials. Each time, they identified themselves as trainers, and asked to see the racecourse manager. At last, they found themselves outside a door which, in addition to the usual "No Admittance" sign, bore a neat plaque reading "Racecourse Manager." Simon knocked briefly on the door and then walked in without waiting for an answer.

It was a small office, and at the cluttered desk sat a small, balding man, who said, without looking up, "Go away."

"Well, I'll be damned," said Simon. "Pat Murphy, or I'm a Dutchman!"

At this, the small man looked up, whipped off his reading glasses, and exclaimed, "Simon Yateley! And Bella!"

In the warm reunion which followed, it emerged that this Pat Murphy had known the Yateleys some years ago, when he had been assistant manager at some other track. He abruptly ceased to be too busy to be interrupted.

"Well, it certainly is good to see you both again. I was wondering if you'd be along tonight—I see you've a bitch running in the 8:30. Plenty of time to have a quick drink and then watch her run."

"Maybe later on, Pat," Simon said, "but for the moment, I'm afraid I'm here on business."

"Well, of course you are, but no harm in mixing it with a little pleasure, surely?"

"You don't understand, Pat. Our business is to do with that bitch in the 8:30, and I'm afraid it's all rather unpleasant."

After a split second of silence, Murphy's Irish temper flared like a petroleum flame. "Now, I'll have none of that, from you or anyone else, Simon Yateley! If you think this place isn't properly and honestly run, you've another think coming, and I'm the one to give it to you. We may be technically a flapping track, but by God this place is run right, and run straight, and it's going to be registered very soon—"

"Keep your hair on, Pat," said Simon—not, perhaps, very tactfully. "I'm not accusing you personally of anything."

"You're making insinuations—" shouted Murphy, and was off again.

It took some time to calm him down, but in the end Bella and Simon between them managed to convince Mr. Murphy that there was a strong suspicion that the said bitch had been stolen from her rightful owner; and that they, the Yateleys, having bred and trained her, would be able to identify her positively. Jane, they explained, was a witness to the fact that the greyhound had been reported missing.

Resignedly, Murphy agreed that they had all better go and take a look at Lady Griselda, to identify her positively. Then, after the race, the villains who had entered her would come to collect her, and could be apprehended.

"There are always plenty of bobbies about, as you know," Murphy added. "On the lookout for pickpockets and so on. I don't mind telling you, I'm unhappy about the whole thing. An affair like this could get the stadium a bad name, even though it's not our fault. Still, there's nothing I can do but cooperate."

He sorted out Lady Griselda's identity card from the pile on his desk, and led the way to the locked door which separated the kennels from the rest of the building. Here it was obvious that security was extremely strict, and the Yateleys and Spences got a number of suspicious looks from track officials, even though they were now escorted not only by Murphy, but also by the paddock steward—the man whose responsibility it was to see that each greyhound was housed in its correct kennel while waiting to race, and in its correct trap for the actual start. The paddock steward consulted a typed list, and directed the party toward a kennel on the far side of the big enclosure.

Suddenly, Bella grasped Simon's arm. "Look! There she is! I can see her!"

She broke into a run, and by the time the others arrived she was on her knees beside the kennel, calling, "Griselda! Griselda, girl!"

The greyhound bitch, who seemed extremely placid and unexcited by the whole procedure, was taking her ease, stretched out with her back to the bars. At the sound of Bella's voice, she reacted by no more than a faint twitch of the ears, indicating mild annoyance at having her nap disturbed. Then, reluctantly, she heaved herself into a sitting position and turned to locate the source of the nuisance. For a long moment, Bella and the greyhound stared at each other through the bars.

Murphy said, "Well?"

Slowly, Bella sat back on her heels, and shook her head. "I just don't understand," she said.

"What do you mean, Bella?" Simon's voice was sharp.

"She's the same color and size . . . identical markings . . . but that's not Griselda."

It was shortly before the start of the second race at eight o'clock that an announcement came over the loudspeakers, reaching every part of the great building.

"Ladies and gentlemen, may I have your attention please? Will the owner of the bitch Lady Griselda, or his representative, come to the Racecourse Manager's office at once? I'll repeat that. Will the owner of Lady Griselda, entered for the 8:30 race, kindly come to the Racecourse Manager's office?"

Mrs. Bertini and Marlene Lawson were in the snack bar eating hot dogs when the announcement was made. Mrs. Bertini dropped her sausage as if it had bitten her, and jumped up.

"Oh, my Gawd! I knew there'd be trouble—"

In a furious whisper, Marlene hissed, "Don't be silly, Mum. Sit down and pull yourself together."

"But Marlene—"

"It was always on the cards there might be trouble. She warned us, didn't she? Now you know what you have to do. Just go quietly and slowly to the ladies' room and stay there. Say you've got a headache or something. Then when the next race is on and nobody will notice, come down to the car park. You remember where the car is?"

"I don't remember nothing, I'm that upset," said Mrs. Bertini, with a sniff. "I think I ought to go and—"

"You'll do as you're told. The car's in number 2 Park, Row G. Got that?"

"I suppose so."

"Tell me, then. Where's the car?"

"Number 2 Park, Row G—if you say so."

"Right. Now, off you go to the ladies', and when you hear the start announced over the speakers, you come to the car. I'll be waiting. OK?"

With a bad grace, Mrs. Bertini got up from the table and headed for the door marked "Ladies." Marlene watched her go impatiently, then got up herself and made her way unconcernedly down to the 10p enclosure. Since she had not habitually shared in her husband's criminal activities, she was not even aware of the fact that she was being followed; and had she been, she would not have been able to identify her shadow as Sergeant Reynolds, for she had never met him. Nevertheless, Reynolds took more than usually careful precautions not to be spotted, for he had a shrewd idea of whom Marlene was going to meet, and Shorty Bates was an old acquaintance of his.

Amanda Bratt-Cunningham heard the announcement as she sat in the front row of seats upstairs, chatting to Albert Pennington and George Weatherby, who were seated on either side of her. The conversation came to an abrupt halt as all three listened to the message. When it ended, Albert Pennington stood up, without haste, and said, "Excuse me, my dear. I think there may have been some stupid sort of confusion that I can help to sort out." He and Major Weatherby exchanged the briefest of understanding glances. Then Pennington, too, made his way to the stairs.

Amanda turned to Weatherby. "What's all this about?" she demanded. She sounded nervous.

Weatherby grinned in what he imagined to be a reassuring manner. "About? My dear young lady, what should it be about? Just some incompetent official getting things muddled up, I suppose, as Albert said. No concern of yours or mine, I'm sure."

"But Lady Griselda—" Amanda began, and then stopped. She bit her lip. "I wonder where Simon and Bella are?" she added.

"Simon and Bella?"

"Friends of mine. I'm told they're here tonight. I think I'll go and—"

"Now, now, now, no need to panic." Weatherby's voice was smooth, but the hand which he laid on Amanda's arm was very firm. "Albert will be back in a moment. Now, what d'you fancy for the eight o'clock, eh?"

"I—I really don't know. I haven't looked at the card. Major Weatherby, I really think I'll go and look for—"

Amanda, appearing definitely nervous now, began to rise from her seat; but Weatherby was between her and the aisle, and he showed no signs of budging. In fact, he was leaning forward to study his racecard, and short of climbing over him—or over the back of the seat—there was no way out.

He said, "Merry Mick is supposed to be a good runner. But

I see Albert's marked Storm Signal. Better take his advice, I reckon—that boy knows a thing or two."

"Major Weatherby . . . if you don't mind . . ."

"Or there's Miss Mischief. I rather fancy her, myself." George Weatherby settled his considerable bulk even more firmly in his seat, barring her way out.

"Please . . . I'm sorry to disturb you . . . if you don't mind . . ."

It was at that moment that a voice behind Amanda said, "Excuse me, miss . . . sir . . . would you be Miss Amanda Bratt-Cunningham?"

"That's right." Amanda turned to see a small man standing in the empty row of seats behind her. Pinned to the lapel of his suit was a badge with the word "Steward" printed on it.

"Sorry to bother you, miss," he went on, "but Mrs. Bella Yateley asked me if I'd come and fetch you."

"Fetch me?"

"That's right. She and Mr. Yateley are in the Racecourse Manager's office—something about the bitch called Lady Griselda. Mrs. Yateley thinks you can help, and wonders if you'd be kind enough—"

"Of course. I'll be delighted. I was going to look for her anyhow." Amanda beamed at the steward, and then said, with an air of triumph, "So, Major Weatherby, *if* you don't mind—"

"Not at all, not at all. Going to place my bets anyway—have to get them on pretty damn quick, they'll be off in a minute." Weatherby heaved himself to his feet and preceded Amanda down the aisle. "Shall I put a bit on for you, my dear?"

"Oh . . . no . . . no, thank you very much . . ."

"As you wish. I expect you're right. If you don't know a really good thing, hang on to your money." With which words of wisdom, Major George Weatherby lumbered off toward the bookmakers' windows.

"This way, miss." The steward led Amanda downstairs. "I'll go first, shall I? It's a bit tricky to find the way—"

Amanda and her escort had just reached the lowest level of

the stadium when the lights were dimmed and the start of the race announced. A surge of humanity, larger, tougher, and less mannerly than the patrons of the 50p lounge, swirled toward the track. In a momentary panic, Amanda lost sight of her guide in the darkness of the milling crowd. For a moment, she caught a reassuring glimpse of a blue-helmeted policeman—one of the anti-pickpocket patrol. She had begun to fight her way toward him when she felt a hand tugging her arm. She gave a little cry of alarm and clutched her handbag more closely.

"It's only me, miss." With relief, she saw the steward beside her. "Sorry if I scared you, but we don't want to lose each other, do we? Not in a crowd like this. Come along, then . . . this way . . . it's a bit dark, but . . ."

He propelled her through a swing door, and as Amanda passed through it, she heard the crowd's excited roar celebrating the "Off." The corridor beyond the door was a dimly lit concrete tunnel which led to yet another door. Following her escort through this second door, Amanda was surprised to find herself in the open air. The surge and bustle of the stadium came faintly to her ears, like the rumble of traffic through double-glazed windows. Here, outside, it was very dark—but she could make out the hunched shapes of parked cars standing in patient rows. She remembered that the area in which she had left her own car had been brightly lit by overhead arc lamps. She stopped for a moment, and then realized that the steward was vanishing between two parked cars ahead of her.

She called out, "Hey! Just a moment!"

The figure ahead stopped and turned. "What is it?" he asked.

"Well—are you sure we're going the right way? I thought you said the Racecourse Manager's office—"

"That's right. This is the staff car park, and the office is over on the other side."

"Oh. I see."

The small, dark figure was off again before Amanda spoke. He seemed to her to be moving faster, dodging between the cars, and suddenly he was nowhere to be seen, and Amanda realized with a stab of mingled annoyance and alarm that she had lost him. Oh, well, she thought. He said the other side of the car park. If I keep going this way . . .

The faint sound of a stealthy step behind her stopped her in her tracks. She peered into the gloom. Nothing. Must have been imagination. Wish I had Wotan with me, Amanda thought—and then laughed at her own timidity. What on earth was there to be frightened of? All the same . . .

And then, suddenly, she saw the steward again. He had not gone straight across the car park, but was standing outside a door leading back into the building on the right-hand side of the parking lot. He waved, and called out, "This way, Miss!"

"Oh . . . so sorry . . . I lost you . . . coming . . ." And Amanda half-ran out across the open yard between two rows of parked cars.

The shot split the air with shocking impact, deafeningly loud in the deserted courtyard. Instinctively, Amanda jerked back and dodged down behind a parked car, just as the second shot thudded into its bodywork. Both shots had been aimed at her, no doubt about it. The steward had disappeared. Somewhere in the darkness, somebody with a gun was stalking her, hunting her down. With difficulty, Amanda suppressed a scream of panic. Quiet. Must be quiet at all costs. Must get away from here . . . move . . . but in which direction? The shots had come from ahead of her, to the left—but the gunman was capable of moving, too. In this maze of darkness and obstacles, she was as likely to run full-tilt into her attacker as to escape. Her legs felt as heavy as lead, but she knew that the one thing she must not do was to stay still.

Amanda sidled around the car, keeping her head low. The car to her right afforded the nearest shelter, and she allowed that fact to determine the direction of her move. A quick dart across the shadowy space between the cars, and she was protected by the mass of a great Bentley. From here, she could see the door which led back into the stadium. If she could get there alive . . . She made another dash, and a third shot came simultaneously with a sharp, shattering pain in her right leg.

Amanda fell and lay like a wounded bird, her white shirt glimmering in the gloom, an easy mark for the final close-in, the *coup de grace*.

She heard the footsteps approaching, and closed her eyes, trying to pray. To pray for forgiveness, because she knew what she had done and why this was happening to her. To pray that she might atone with her life for the weakness which had led her step by step into the spider's web of crime. The footsteps were closer now. Another minute . . .

And then, suddenly, there were more footsteps, and shouting and another shot and then another. Amanda stopped praying abruptly and opened her eyes in time to see a bizarre sight. Within a few yards of where she lay, a police constable was grappling with a woman, fighting as though for his life and apparently getting the worst of it. This seemed curious to Amanda, until she realized that the policeman was, as it were, fighting with one hand tied behind his back. His right arm was clearly useless. She could also see that the woman was holding a gun, and that the constable's whole strength, such as it was, was devoted to preventing her from using it, either on Amanda or himself.

It flashed through Amanda's mind—"He's got one arm and two legs, I've only got one leg, but by God I've got two arms"—and despite the agonizing pain from her injured leg, she started dragging herself as fast as she could across the concrete. A moment later, and she had flung both arms round the woman's legs, jerking them from under her. As she fell, Amanda had a glimpse of a shimmering purple and silver dress under a dark raincoat—then another shot went off, at random; the world seemed a melée of flailing arms and legs highlighted by exquisite pain—and then there were more people, people running, men in uniform. A voice said, "Are you all right, sir? I came as soon as I—"

Another voice. "The young lady's hurt. Better call an ambulance, quick!"

The woman in the purple dress was quiet now, on her feet again, her arms pinioned by a burly, dark young man who was securing her wrists with handcuffs. A young, fresh-faced constable knelt down beside Amanda, and said, "How are you, miss? Is it bad?"

"I don't think so. Just my leg. I'll be all right."

"The ambulance'll be here in no time, miss. Just you lie quiet." The policeman took off his blue serge jacket and wrapped it around and under Amanda's shoulders. She lay back gratefully in its warmth, and closed her eyes.

A moment later, she had them open again, as wide as they would go in astonishment. Because she could have sworn that she heard Henry Tibbett's voice, and that it was saying, "Albert Pennington, I am arresting you for the attempted murder of Miss Amanda Bratt-Cunningham, and for conspiring in the murder of Lawrence Lawson. I warn you that anything you say will be taken down and may be used . . ."

Another voice chimed in. "Got her, sir. In the other car park. Trying to make a getaway, by the look of it."

With an effort, Amanda turned her head toward the source of the voices, looked up—and decided that she had developed double vision. There, standing side by side, each held firmly by the arm of the law, were two women—both equally tall and blonde, both dressed in gaudy purple and silver.

"I give up," said Amanda aloud, to nobody in particular. "Better hurry up with that ambulance and take me straight to the nuthouse."

The loudspeaker system at Bunstead Stadium was efficient and comprehensive. Its disembodied voice reached even into the quiet confines of the staff car park. As gentle hands lifted Amanda onto a stretcher, and not-so-gentle ones propelled the prisoners into a Black Maria, the unseen announcer informed them boomingly of the winner, second, and third in the eight o'clock race. It added, "Here is an announcement. Number 4, Lady Griselda, will not be running in the next race, the 8:30. I repeat, Lady Griselda, number 4, has been withdrawn and will not run . . ."

15

The formalities seemed to take forever, although in fact they were expeditiously managed. The race program of the Bunstead Stadium wound its way to a close—as a matter of interest, the 8:30 race was won by the favorite, Lucky Strike—who was lucky indeed, for he would not have stood a chance against Marlene's Fancy, alias Lady Griselda, had she been running against him. Her odds, which normally would have been astronomic, had shortened to fifteen to one after her surprise win of the previous day, but her backers would have stood to clean up a sizable fortune had the race taken place according to plan.

Long after the last of the crowds had departed, long after the vast car parks were deserted, even after the canine competitors had been collected by their owners or trainers and driven away to their home kennels, Jane and Bill Spence sat with Pat Murphy in his office, waiting for a word from Henry.

Around ten o'clock they were joined by Emmy, who had accompanied Amanda Bratt-Cunningham to the hospital, and was glad to be able to report that she was in no danger, and was now sleeping the sleep of the gently tranquilized. However, as to where Henry was, or exactly what was going on, Emmy was not able to enlighten them. All she knew was that Albert Pennington, improbably dressed in a purple and silver lamé gown and blonde wig, had been arrested; that Mrs. Bertini and her daughter were "helping the police with their enquiries"; and that, predictably, Major George Weatherby had vanished at the first sign of trouble like a drop of morning dew under the sun's first rays. Emmy also reported that Henry had put through two telephone calls to Gorsemere—one to P.C. Denning and the other to the Spences' house—but she had no idea of what had been said. She did not know where the Yateleys were.

On this point, Pat Murphy was able to throw light. "Simon and Bella? They're round at the kennels, waiting to see if anybody arrives to pick up Lady Griselda—or whatever her real name is. If, as we strongly suspect, nobody turns up, then they've very sportingly agreed to take her back to Hilltop and care for her until this business is cleared up."

Sure enough, it was not many minutes later that Simon and Bella arrived in the office, accompanied by the paddock steward leading a beautiful beige-colored greyhound bitch, with a white star on her forehead and white forelegs.

"Just as we thought, Pat," said Bella. "Every other hound claimed but this one." She fondled the bitch's ears, and was rewarded by a prodigious yawn. She added, "You may look like Griselda, but you're as different as chalk from cheese when it comes to temperament. I hope you're not as lazy on the track as off it. Does anybody know who she is, by the way?"

Emmy said, "I only got a garbled account from Henry, but I think her name is Marlene's Fancy."

There was a short silence, as significant looks were exchanged between the Yateleys, Murphy, and the steward. Emmy said, "Have I put my foot in it, or something? I'm very ignorant about greyhounds. I just heard Henry mention the name."

Murphy said, quickly, "No, no, Mrs. Tibbett, of course not. It's just that . . ." He looked at the steward, who nodded. "Marlene's Fancy is way above the class of the runners in the 8:30 here. She'd have licked the pants off them. She's never run here, of course—always been up north. I knew she was beige and white, but—"

Bella said, "I've never seen her before, either. But of course I know her by reputation."

And Simon added, "By God. Of course. Anybody who cottoned onto the fact that there was another bitch, virtually identical to look at, but a lousy runner . . ."

Murphy said, with a touch of ice, "Somebody did cotton on, Yateley. And since Lady Griselda was born and bred at your kennels, it looks very much like an inside job."

"Now, look here, Pat—" Simon began, blusteringly.

"I'm not accusing you of anything," said Murphy—a patent misstatement; the whole incident had reflected badly on the Bunstead Stadium and on Murphy personally, and he saw his chance of getting a little of his own back. "I'm merely pointing out that somebody at Gorsemere who knew both greyhounds must have given the tip-off."

"Or somebody up north who knew Marlene's Fancy—" Bella began indignantly, and then stopped.

Murphy smiled, not a very friendly smile. "It won't do, will it, Bella dear? Marlene's Fancy is a well-known, up-and-coming runner. Plenty of people know her or have seen pictures of her. Lady Griselda, on the other hand—"

"Wait a minute." Simon was interested, and had forgotten to be angry with Murphy. "If the two bitches are the same age, Marlene's Fancy may well have run her novice race up at Doblington, at the same time as Griselda." He turned to his wife. "You took Griselda up for the Novices' Silver Collar, didn't you, darling? Can you remember?"

Bella shook her head. "I couldn't get away," she said. "I've always wondered if Griselda mightn't have done better if I'd been there—on the practice track, she'd race her heart out for me, and nobody else. But I absolutely had to go to Wimbledon with Black Prince that evening. It was Tommy took her up to Doblington."

"Where somebody saw her," Simon went on, "and realized he could pull a sweet swindle and clean up a packet." To Murphy, he said, "Nobody came to claim Marlene's Fancy—if it is her—but somebody must have delivered her here."

Murphy shook his head. "No," he said. "She was sent here direct from Kevingfield, where she won the day before yesterday. As Lady Griselda, of course. Complete with identity card. If the same dog is raced twice in forty-eight hours," he added to Emmy, in explanation, "the manager of the first track is responsible for delivering the card direct to the manager of the second track—it doesn't have to go back to NGRC headquarters in between."

Emmy exclaimed, "Now I understand! That's why Henry said it had to be tonight—"

Murphy nodded slowly. "That's right," he said. "They—whoever they are—they let her win at Kevingfield, had it all entered on her card, and sent the bitch and the card straight here for what was to be the big killing, financially speaking. The fact that she'd won before made her record seem in order, and she was put in a race which she'd have won easily, but which wasn't so far below her apparent form as to cause comment. Kevingfield's a smaller track altogether, and they wouldn't have checked as carefully as we would. If a complete outsider had won the second race of her career here, having come last in her first and only other one, we'd have smelt a rat. There'd have been an enquiry. And I dare say the NGRC would have cast a fishy eye on that identity card if it had been sent back to them between the two races."

"Wait a minute." Bella frowned. "This can't be Marlene's Fancy. I read that she's in whelp."

"I read that, too," said Murphy. "Obviously, it was just a story handed out to the sporting press to account for the fact that she happened to disappear from the track at the same moment that Lady Griselda made her comeback."

"Then what about the real Griselda?" Bella asked, anxiously. "You don't think they've—"

Simon rubbed his chin thoughtfully. "That would depend," he said. "If things had gone according to plan, and they'd got away with the substitution, they'd need to be able to produce both dogs to keep the record straight for the future. But now that the lid's blown off—well, the fewer greyhounds the better, I imagine, as far as the gang is concerned. They've simply abandoned Marlene's Fancy, for obvious reasons, and

I wouldn't be surprised if they didn't dispose of Griselda as fast as they can."

Jane burst out indignantly, "You mean that Henry's prepared to let them murder that beautiful creature, just to expose a fraud and catch a few petty crooks?"

"Not so petty, Jane," said Emmy. "He had a good try at killing Amanda, and Henry seems to think there's been one murder committed already."

"All the same—" Jane began.

Bill said, "Oh, for heaven's sake, Jane. You're just plain demented when it comes to animals."

And Bella added, "I do know how you feel, Jane, but what can anyone do? We've no idea where Griselda is—"

"Oh yes, we have." Henry, still in the uniform of a police constable, stood in the open doorway, with the sturdy figure of Sergeant Reynolds hovering in the passage behind him. Henry looked exhausted, and carried his right arm in a sling provided by Amanda's ambulance crew; however, he sounded cheerful as he said, "Sorry to keep you all waiting. So there were no takers for Marlene's Fancy? Just as I thought. Right. Let's get going."

"Where to?" Jane asked.

Henry looked surprised. "Back to Gorsemere, of course."

"But Griselda . . . you can't just abandon her. You said you knew where she was . . ."

"My dear Jane," said Henry, "unless I am gravely mistaken, Lady Griselda is in Gorsemere. In fact, she's back home, and she's been there for some time."

So the convoy made its way back along darkened country roads to Gorsemere, but in a somewhat amended form. Sergeant Reynolds, together with the police car, remained at Bunstead Police Station, acting as a liaison between Henry and the various detainees. As might have been expected, Albert Pennington—who knew his rights as a citizen, in or out of drag—was creating maximum nuisance value, refusing to make a statement and demanding to see his lawyer. Marlene Lawson was displaying every bit as much stubbornness as Pennington, sitting on a hard chair in the charge room like a small, evil-tempered statue, her pretty mouth clamped shut and her dark eyes blazing with anger. Mrs. Bertini was having hysterics in the rest room under the kind but firm eye of a competent W.P.C. The local Bunstead force was doing its best, but not being in full possession of the facts, it was difficult for its members to feel in control of the situation. Sergeant Reynolds had been extremely reluctant to let Henry go back to Gorsemere without him, but had eventually bowed to discipline and common sense. At any moment, one of the suspects—voluntarily or involuntarily—might divulge some important information, and somebody had to be there to hear it.

Consequently, Henry was being driven back to Gorsemere by the police driver in the small saloon car in which Reynolds had driven from London, and which was capable of a turn of speed quite belied by its modest exterior. It had easily outstripped even the Yateleys in their Rover, on the back seat of which Marlene's Fancy slept with her usual philosophic acceptance of whatever life might bring. She was an easy-going bitch, and asked for no more than two good meals a day, a warm dry kennel, and the occasional thrill of a race—although she had found from experience that she could outmatch her rivals without really trying, so the excitement was minimal.

Some way behind the Rover, the Spences in their station wagon bowled sedately along, with little conversation. Bill was brooding on the unspeakable complications which his sister-in-law and her husband always seemed to bring into his life. And Jane was worrying about Griselda.

Last of all came Emmy, on her own and driving cautiously, because the controls of Amanda's MG were still unfamiliar. Amanda had pressed the keys on Emmy at the hospital and begged her to drive the car back; in fact, before the nurse arrived with her hypodermic full of sedative, Amanda had pressed something less acceptable on Emmy—her confidences, or, to be blunt, her confession. As she drove, Emmy pondered on what Amanda had told her, and wondered how much of it

Henry knew, or had guessed, and what she should do about it. At least, certain mysteries were now explained, and Emmy felt confident that Harry Heathfield would soon be a free man, back in his little house with Tess and Ginger . . . and Griselda? Emmy wondered about that, too, and wished that she had put up more of a fight when Henry had issued strict orders that she was to go straight to Cherry Tree Cottage with Jane and Bill, and stay there behind locked doors until he, Henry, arrived. Henry was exhausted, and his right arm was useless. Emmy had great faith in and affection for Sergeant Derek Reynolds, but he had stayed behind at Bunstead. In Emmy's opinion, the combined efforts of Constables Denning and Hawthorn would be a poor substitute. And so she worried.

The village of Gorsemere at eleven o'clock on an early summer night was not exactly a hive of activity, but at least it still showed signs of life. Ex-Squadron-Leader Paul Claverton was putting up the shutters at the White Bull, and the last of his customers were still chatting and laughing in the pub yard. A few lights burned in cottage windows, and in a few cars, a few smartly dressed commuter couples drove home to their ramblers on their new housing developments, having dined with identical couples in identical houses on identical developments on the other side of the village. By contrast, the road which wound up from the village green toward Hilltop Kennels seemed darker, lonelier, and more deserted than ever. There was no moon, and the tall hedges overshadowed the narrow lane like prison walls.

As the driver swung the car around the final bend, the hedges fell back and the trees thinned out—and there on the open ground at the top of the hill Henry could see the buildings of the Yateley establishment, the low, whitewashed kennels clustered around the tall, ugly, red brick house. He also saw the stout wire fence, the padlocked gate—and the small blue van which was parked outside it. Henry told the driver to stop, let him out, and return to Gorsemere Police Station. As the engine noise of the departing car dwindled, silence came flooding back. Nothing stirred, no dogs barked—to all appearances, Hilltop Kennels were asleep. Henry walked slowly toward the gate and the parked van.

A shadow detached itself from the darker recesses of the trees and came toward him. A square-cut, homely, reassuring shadow, which quickly resolved itself into P.C. Denning, uniformed and helmeted and pushing his ubiquitous bicycle.

Henry stopped. Softly, he said, "Denning?"

"That's right, sir. Chief Superintendent Tibbett, isn't it? Glad to see you, sir."

"Where's Hawthorn?"

"Back under the trees, sir, keeping watch. Like you said. We might join him, if you agree."

"Right, constable." Henry glanced toward the blue van. "When did our friend arrive?"

"About an hour ago, sir." The two men retreated into the blackness of a wooded copse. Denning propped his bicycle against a tree and whistled softly. A moment later, Hawthorn appeared as if from nowhere. He was wearing a sweater and an old duffle coat of Bill Spence's, as well as the latter's voluminous trousers, which were being kept vertical by faith and a stout leather belt.

He greeted Henry deferentially, and, prompted by Denning, took up the story. "That's right, sir. Just like you said it would be. About an hour ago, the van drove up and parked outside the gate, like it is now. P.C. Denning and I were keeping watch from here. A man got out of the van, a small chap, not much over five-foot-four, I'd say—"

"Shorty Bates," said Henry. "Direct from his success at impersonating a racetrack steward at Bunstead. He must have slipped away when the shooting started, lain low in the car park, and then nipped into the van and driven down here when he realized we'd got Pennington. That would fit in nicely. Well, what happened then?"

"Like you said, sir, he rang the bell on the gate. We weren't close enough to be sure, but I guess he gave some sort of signal by the way he rang. Anyhow, the dogs all started barking and yelping—nobody to hear them except us, of course—but they shut up right away. Somebody inside recognized the signal, quieted the dogs, and came to the gate within a matter of seconds. I thought it was a girl at first, but Mr. Denning here says it was the kennel boy."

"That's right, sir. Young Tommy. Mr. and Mrs. Yateley leave him in charge if they're both out of an evening," Denning added. "I did notice he didn't put any lights on, which I thought was a bit odd. Anyhow, he obviously knew the visitor—the short chap. They whispered together for a moment, and then Tommy opened the gate and they both went in."

"And they're still there?" Henry asked.

"Yes, sir," Denning answered. "That is, I did like you said, sir. After ten minutes or so, I pushed my bike out onto the road and up the hill, like I was on an ordinary evening beat, and I rang the Hilltop bell."

"And what happened?"

"Well, nothing for a minute or two, sir. Then all the lights went on, and young Tommy come out. He didn't unlock the gate. He spoke to me from the other side, like. Nervy, I thought he seemed. I said like you told me—that Mr. Yateley had asked me to keep an eye on the kennels, and that I'd seen this suspicious vehicle without lights—the blue van—parked at the gate, and thought I'd better investigate."

"Good work, Denning," said Henry. "What did he say?"

"Well, it was really comical, sir." Denning was his usual genial self. "I could see the poor lad didn't know what story to tell. Fair tongue-tied, he was. Didn't know whether to admit he'd got a pal in there, or to deny he knew anything about the van. He's only a lad, after all," added Denning, always ready to give the benefit of the doubt. Then he looked quickly at his watch, and said to Hawthorn, "You'd better take the tale on from there, son. I'm off on my beat." He wheeled his bicycle out onto the road, got it rolling with a few running steps, threw a nimble leg over the saddle, and pedaled off in the direction of Hilltop Kennels.

As soon as Denning had gone, Henry said, "Well, did you bring the suitcase?"

"Yes, sir. It's here, sir."

"Then I'll start changing," Henry said, "while you regale me with the story of P.C. Denning and his beat. If I heard right."

Hawthorn grinned in the darkness. "That's right, sir. Before the boy had decided what to answer the constable, this other character comes out from the kennels. Bates, I think you said his name was. 'That's all right, Constable,' he says. 'I'm a friend of Tommy's and that's my van. Just visiting my young pal for the evening,' he says, smooth as you like. So P.C. Denning says—he's not nearly so slow as he looks, sir—he says, quick as a flash, 'Oh, is that so?' he says. 'Well, I'm glad to hear it because there's a lot of valuable dogs in here, and I've been tipped off about suspicious persons in the neighborhood, and I know as how Mr. and Mrs. Yateley is both away at a race meeting. So I reckon—' he says, 'I reckon I'll just patrol around hereabout until Mr. Yateley gets back. Well, young Tommy and his friend didn't seem to think much of that for an idea. Assured Denning it wasn't necessary, and so forth, but he insisted and there wasn't a lot they could do. So he's been cycling past the gate every ten minutes or so, regular. Got them bottled up in there all right."

While Hawthorn had been speaking, Henry had not been idle. He had divested himself of his uniform jacket and trousers, and, with some help from the constable, had climbed into a pair of comfortable old gray flannel trousers and was halfway into a thick knitted sweater. In a muffled voice, he said, "Pull the sweater down over my head, will you, Constable? This blasted arm of mine . . . ah, that's better." Henry's head appeared like a jack-in-the-box from the enveloping knitwear. He shook himself, and added, "They didn't try to get a greyhound out and away?"

"That they did, sir. After Denning's first patrol, as it were. They must have been watching, and as soon as his bike disappeared down this way, out they come to the gate, with

Tommy leading this dog. Well, of course, Denning hadn't gone pedaling off on his beat like they thought—he was right here with me, watching—so straight away he's on his bike and back again before Tommy can get the gate unlocked. So Denning greets them again, all friendly like, as if he's no notion of anything being wrong—and Tommy says something about exercising the hound, and Denning says as how he can see it's a champion dog and it wouldn't do if it escaped, would it? So that puts a stop to *that* little lark, and they haven't tried again."

"There's just the one gate, I trust?" Henry said.

"According to P.C. Denning, yes, sir. And anyhow the van is here and—well, have you seen that fence, sir? Solid iron mesh and about two foot of barbed wire on the top. No, they're inside all right, and—ah, here comes Mr. Denning back, sir. Perhaps you'll give him his instructions, sir?"

"What instructions would those be?" Henry asked.

There was a small, embarrassed pause. Then Hawthorn said, "Well, sir, you didn't say anything on the telephone except what we were to do, up till the time you arrived. But now you're here, I'd have thought it'd be the moment for P.C. Denning to tell the Hilltop lot that he's knocking off for the night . . . give 'em the all clear, in fact . . . and then wait here and nab them when they come out with the dog."

"Hawthorn," said Henry, "I couldn't have put it better myself. Did I hear a rumor that you're keen to transfer to the C.I.D.?"

"You did indeed, sir. And if—"

"I can't promise anything," said Henry, "but you can rely on me for a reference. Ah, here comes Denning now."

The whispered conference did not take more than half a minute, and then P.C. Denning was pedaling his way back to the formidable gate of Hilltop Kennels. From their vantage point among the trees, Henry and Hawthorn could not overhear what was being said, but they watched the pantomime as Denning rang the bell and Tommy appeared—no sign of Bates this time—and Denning announced his intention of retiring for the night. Even at that distance, it seemed to the watchers that Tommy relaxed, became less nervous and merrier. At least, they could see that he sped the constable on his way with a light-hearted wave of the arm. Denning mounted his faithful steed and directed it downhill, around the first bend in the road, and back through the copse to his waiting companions.

"Right," said Henry. "Come on, Hawthorn." He linked his good left arm with the constable's right one. "Here we go." Raising their voices in unmelodious harmony, the two marched out unsteadily into the road.

Inside the Hilltop compound, Shorty Bates was growing impatient. "Come on, for God's sake. Simple Simon'll be back in no time—the last race at Bunstead's the ten o'clock."

"Gotta be sure the fuzz 'as gone," Tommy whispered. His hand tightened on Griselda's collar, and she nuzzled his leg gently. They were old friends. Something in the pit of Tommy's stomach turned over, and he felt sick. He said, "What'll happen to her?"

"To who? Miss Bloody Amanda? She's had her chips."

"I meant . . . Griselda."

Bates sensed trouble. "Nothing. Nothing for you to bother about. She'll be OK. Now, for God's sake, get that gate open. I got to get out of here, and fast."

Tommy was just seventeen. Nothing that he had done up till now had worried him—what's the difference, put a few extra quid in your pocket, what's Yateley ever done for you, lad? Little bit of info here and there . . . what's that to worry about, eh? That's how you get on in life, boy. You'll learn. Well, he was learning. He hadn't bargained for the rough stuff, like that poor sod in the van yesterday evening, laid out cold. Shorty had explained . . . just the result of a business disagreement, had to rough him up a bit, he was all right. Well, Tommy knew he was alive—could hear him breathing. Just have to help me get him home, lad, Shorty had said. Leave him in his own garden shed, he'll be OK. Tommy had recognized the man—he'd been at Hilltop, talking to the Yateleys while Black Prince was exercising. That's right, Shorty said.

Hanging round where he wasn't wanted, sticking his nose into other people's business. You take his shoulders, don't let him see your ugly mug. And keep your trap shut.

Tommy had kept his trap shut, and the twin pressures of greed and fear had combined to help him rationalize his role in that particular caper. After all, he'd only seen the man once. A business rival of Shorty's. These things happened.

But this—this was different. This was Griselda. Tommy had been there when Griselda was born. He'd fed her and exercised her and helped to train her. He'd taken her up to Doblington for her first race, all on his own, as proud as a young father entering his offspring for a baby show—and he'd watched her lope in a bad last, with that endearing expression on her silly face. He knew she could have won if she'd wanted to. She just didn't choose to. That was Griselda.

In the excitement of the race, not many people had even noticed such a hopeless nonstarter as Griselda—all the attention had been focused on the winner, Marlene's Fancy, a champion in the making if ever Tommy had seen one; so Tommy was one of the very few to notice the extraordinary similarity between the two bitches—the white star on the forehead, the white forepaws. When Tommy got back to Gorsemere, he'd happened to mention the curious resemblance between the two bitches to . . . well, that was when it all started.

And now, it was ending. Ending with the ultimate betrayal. He, Tommy, was handing Griselda over to Shorty Bates, to be shoved into the little blue van and driven off to die. Tommy knew that very well, no matter what Bates said. Griselda was "hot." Griselda had to disappear. They reached the compound gate, and Tommy began fumbling reluctantly in his pocket for the key. And then, with huge relief, he said, "Listen!"

"Get that gate open, for Pete's sake!" snapped Bates.

"Listen—somebody's coming. Better get back."

For a moment they listened. Then Bates said, "That's nothing. A couple of drunks going home from the pub."

"You are my he-e-art's desire . . . I le-e-rv you . . . Nelly De-e-a-a-n!" warbled a couple of discordant male voices.

"They're coming this way—they'll see you!" Tommy whispered urgently.

"So what? They're not capable of seeing anything, the state they're in." Bates stiffened. "But what I do hear is a car. Bloody Yateley, that'll be. Get that gate open!"

Miserably, Tommy produced the key. The iron gate swung open. The two drunks were lurching across the road, arm in arm, oblivious to everything. No help to be had from them.

Bates opened the back door of the van and turned on Tommy. "Right. Help me get the bloody dog in the van. And look sharp about it."

He put a hand to Griselda's collar and wrenched it savagely out of Tommy's grasp. The bitch gave a yelp of pain and alarm, and something in Tommy's brain snapped. He flung his arms around the greyhound's neck and began to scream. "No! Leave her alone! No! Help! Help!"

It was no good, of course. Bates sent Tommy sprawling with a well-aimed kick to the groin, and dragged the whimpering dog toward the van. So occupied was he that he did not even notice that the drunks had stopped behaving like drunks. In fact, Hawthorn had him handcuffed before he fully registered that something was wrong. Tommy was still rolling on the ground, clutching himself and moaning. And, as the powerful headlamps of the Rover came roaring around the corner to illuminate the strange scene, a beige and white greyhound bitch streaked away into the darkness of the trees, her tail between her legs. Lady Griselda of Gorsemere was going home.

They found her sitting patiently as her namesake outside the shed in Harry Heathfield's backyard. She had negotiated the fence without difficulty, and was now waiting for her master. She wondered vaguely what had happened to Ginger and Tess, but a dog's brain is somewhat limited in capacity, and for some time now Griselda had had just one object in life—to return to the place where she had been so happy, until the day when her master went off in the morning and never came back, and a dark-skinned man had broken into her shed and dragged her away to a waiting car. Since then, life had been a nightmare of strange sheds, of uncomfortable rides in cars and vans, of unfamiliar voices and harsh treatment.

Her return to Hilltop and Tommy had delighted Griselda at first, but she could not understand why Bella never visited her, why she was not exercised or allowed to mix with the other dogs, but was kept by Tommy shut up in the damp darkness of one of the old kennels on the far perimeter of the compound. This, in Griselda's opinion, was a poor exchange for her highly satisfactory life as the apple of Harry Heathfield's eye. Consequently, she had come home.

Of course, she could not be allowed to stay there, and of course it was Jane who offered to take her in, together with her old pals Tess and Ginger, until the majesty of the law had seen fit to extract Harry Heathfield from Middingfield Jail and send him home with an apology.

At Cherry Tree Cottage, seeing her new charge for the first time under adequate lighting in the kitchen, Jane suddenly said, "Well, Marlene's Fancy may not be in whelp, but Lady Griselda certainly is."

The conversation, which had been confused and unsatisfactory in any case, stopped abruptly as Emmy, Henry, and Bill turned to look at Griselda, who was sensibly getting her nose down into a bowl of biscuits.

"But—how can she be? She's been with Harry until just recently—" Bill began.

"Yes," Jane pointed out. "In the company of another bitch *and* a male."

"Oh, Ginger," said Emmy. "Oh, Ginger, was it really you?"

Ginger sat back on his haunches and scratched his ear. There was no mistaking the complacent smirk on his ill-bred face.

"Ginger," said Emmy. "I'm ashamed of you."

16

"Well," Henry said, "they almost got away with it. I suppose I should have guessed sooner, but—" He leaned forward and caressed Marlene's Fancy behind the ears, whereupon Lady Griselda, resenting this show of favoritism, pushed her muzzle against his knee, demanding equal attention.

Seeing the two greyhounds together, it was obvious that they were not so much like identical twins as sisters; and, indeed, it transpired that they had been sired by the same dog, Lord Jim, and each bore a strong resemblance to her father. The differences between them—obvious to the eye but not to the identity card—were the shape of the head, the set of the ears, and, most importantly, the shade of beige in the overall coat color. Griselda was most noticeably lighter in color than Marlene's Fancy, which was why only Tommy's sharp eyes had spotted the similarity at Doblington; but on an identity card, beige is beige, and with their identical markings it was no surprise that racetrack officials, in all good faith, had accepted the one for the other.

The grandfather clock in the Spences' hall had just struck two o'clock in the morning, but still Henry and Emmy, Bill and Jane, lingered over a nightcap. Henry would dearly have liked to go to bed, but he knew that he would be in a whirl of official proceedings the following day, and it seemed only fair to give his sister- and brother-in-law a rational explanation for the goings-on into which he had led them.

"It's hard to know where to begin," he said. "At first, I was just mildly intrigued by the story of the third dog who was missing. Then, hearing about the Heathfield case, it reminded me of the so-called accidental death of one Larry Lawson, a notorious dog track gambler and petty crook. When I checked and found that Lawson had been the accident victim, I got really interested. Of course, coincidences do happen, but it's highly unusual for a man like that to die a death that's both violent and accidental . . . and what would he have been doing on a country road near Gorsemere late at night? Then, one of the chief witnesses at the Heathfield trial turned out to be an old enemy of mine—a shady publican from London who consorts with gamblers, keeps his own nose clean, but has a way of cropping up as a convenient witness in the courts. I can assure you, I didn't want to get involved or to drag you in—but the smell of rats was too strong by then. I couldn't let it drop. Besides, there was Heathfield himself."

"They'll let him out of prison now, won't they?" Jane asked.

"Certainly," said Henry. "The formalities may take a few days, but he'll get a free pardon."

Bill Spence moved uneasily in his chair. "Look here, Henry," he said, "that's all very well, but don't forget I heard the Heathfield committal proceedings. The thing may have been stage-managed—doesn't surprise me to hear it—but you can't get away from the fact that he was drunk and he was driving that car."

"Yes and no," said Henry.

"What do you mean?"

"He was certainly drunk," Henry agreed, "and probably drugged as well. After all that whiskey, it wouldn't have taken much to knock him right out, and it was agreed that he 'came over queer' quite suddenly, just before he left the pub."

"Nevertheless, he drove that car—"

"No."

There was a moment of incredulous silence. Then Jane said, "But he did, Henry. Everybody knows that. The two other men stayed in the Bull, and the police found Harry slumped over the wheel after the accident."

"I know that," said Henry, "but the fact is that there was, in the classic phrase, a third man. A man who waited hidden in the car until Heathfield came out into the pub yard, who bundled him into the car, made sure he had passed out cold, and then drove to Heathfield's house, where he knew very well that Lawson would be waiting, by appointment, leaning up against the front wall. He deliberately ran Lawson down, arranged the unconscious Heathfield artistically behind the wheel, and left the scene of the crime with all speed."

"Wait a moment," said Bill. "The woman next door heard the crash and looked out of her window—"

"She was in bed and asleep," Henry pointed out. "The crash woke her. She had to get out of bed, put on a dressing gown, go to the window, and draw back the curtains. The road isn't lit, you know."

"Still, surely she'd have seen the other man—"

"I doubt it. You see, he was a black man. And a black man in a black suit can disappear very effectively in the dark."

Jane had been looking worried. She said, "But Henry, Amanda's evidence was . . . what's the matter, Emmy?"

"Nothing."

"Of course something's the matter," said Jane, with a sisterly lack of finesse. "You've gone as red as a beet root."

Henry said, "She told you, did she, darling?" Emmy nodded. To Jane, Henry said, "I'm afraid your friend Amanda perjured herself in court. She was in a difficult position. She had met this delightful young Mr. Pennington in London—and he had some sort of hold on her. I imagine it was money, wasn't it?" He looked inquiringly at Emmy.

"Yes," said Emmy. "Oh, I suppose it doesn't matter telling you. Amanda asked me to, anyhow. It seems she's always been keen on racing, and liked to have a bit of a flutter—nothing terrible, but you know Sir Arthur's views on the subject. She met Pennington, and he gave her a lot of so-called tips, some of which paid off but others didn't. She gradually got thoroughly enmeshed—you know how it happens—and found she owed a great deal in gambling debts. Far more than she could afford. She didn't dare tell her father. Then Pennington came to the rescue. He not only paid her debts—feeling guilty, he said, because she'd taken his advice and it hadn't worked—but he also lent her money to start up her market-garden business. Funnily enough, Pennington's philanthropy—well, his interest in Amanda—blossomed just after she had mentioned to him something that Tommy, the kennel lad at Hilltop, had told her—"

Bill and Jane exclaimed in unison, "About Marlene's Fancy and Griselda!"

"That's right," said Emmy. "Apparently, Tommy took Griselda up to Doblington for her one and only race, and he noticed that the winner was a dead ringer for Griselda. He told Amanda, and she passed it on to Pennington, and—"

"And so," Henry said, "he asked her—very politely, I'm sure—if she'd do him a small favor."

"That's right. It sounded perfectly innocent, Amanda said. He asked her to drive her car to a crossroads near the Bull at a certain time on a certain evening, and watch out for a certain other car going past. Weatherby's car. He described it and gave her the license number. He said he was having some sort of legal wrangle with the owner, and wanted an independent witness who could testify that the car was in Gorsemere that evening. Amanda said it sounded a bit odd, but not in any way illegal—and she could hardly refuse when he'd been so generous to her."

"Generous!" Bill Spence snorted sardonically.

"Well, she thought he had. Of course, it was the evening of the Heathfield affair. Amanda saw the car go by, all right. She says it was being driven fast and very competently, and that she couldn't see the driver—he just looked like a shadow, she said. It doesn't seem to have occurred to her that he might have been a black man, but of course that would explain it.

"Next day, she called Pennington as promised and told him

what she had seen—and it was then he broke it to her that she was to testify in court that the car was being driven in a slow, drunken, weaving way, and that she had positively recognized Harry Heathfield at the wheel. She was horrified and refused—whereupon he brought out the big stick. It appears he hadn't paid her gambling debts at all . . . I didn't quite understand how he worked it . . ."

Henry said, "I can explain. Pennington's occupation is listed as Company Director, and I had Sergeant Reynolds look him up. His companies are bookmakers and money-lenders—not under his own name, of course. When he so kindly put on Amanda's bets for her, she had no idea that he was, in effect, taking them himself. Of course, he could suspend them and tell her he'd paid them. Equally, he could bring out all the documentation of unpaid debts and threaten to sue."

Emmy said, "I think if Amanda had had only herself to think of, she might have said, 'Sue and be damned.' But there was her father. Sir Arthur, fourth baronet, squire of the village, Chairman of the Board of Magistrates, and a well-known anti-gambler. Think what the *Daily Scoop* would make of it—'Baronet's Daughter in Gaming Debt Scandal'—just the sort of thing they love."

Jane nodded, slowly. "It would have finished Sir Arthur," she said.

"Well," Emmy went on, "that's why Amanda finally agreed. Pennington seems to have half-persuaded her that Heathfield was guilty anyway and that it was him she saw at the wheel. Anyhow, once she'd been idiot enough to give perjured evidence, Pennington had a real stranglehold on her."

"And yet he tried to kill her this evening, if I understand aright?" Bill remarked.

"Yes," said Henry. "You see, she was the only person left who could identify Pennington and tie him in with Lawson's murder and the business of the greyhounds. She was too dangerous. That's why we had to get him tonight before he got her, and it was a near thing."

Jane said, "All right, that seems to take care of Amanda and her part in all this. But there's a whole lot more to explain. Who is this Pennington, anyway, and how does he come to be mixed up in all this?"

"That's a very good question, Jane," Henry said, "because it goes right to the heart of the matter. Once you understand who Albert Pennington is, it becomes very much easier to understand why he did what he did."

"Well, who is he?"

"He's the son of the late Sir Humphrey Pennington, a larger-than-life, hard-drinking, heavy-gambling character from the fifties, who ran through most of his considerable inheritance—largely thanks to his string of thoroughbred horses. Albert inherited what was left of the money—still enough to leave him a rich man by most standards—together with tendencies to compulsive gambling, transvestism, homosexuality, violence, and—above all—slumming. He couldn't compete in the really wealthy world of horseracing, so he turned his attention to the humbler dog track. For some years now he has been amusing himself by assuming two personalities. On the one hand, the mustachioed, upper-class Mr. Pennington, crony of Major Weatherby, acquaintance of Sir Arthur Bratt-Cunningham and his charming daughter, and behind-the-scenes Mr. Big of the Red Dicky Marsh dogtrack mob. On the other, and always in drag, a formidable, foul-mouthed female—the mysterious, unnamed boss of the Larry Lawson gang. With his warped sense of humor, he must have had a lot of giggles, turning one gang against the other and watching the fun from his elegant Chelsea house."

Emmy said, "I don't know how you can be sure of all this, Henry. Well—perhaps you know it now, when Scotland Yard's been mobilized to investigate Pennington—but what made you suspect it?"

Henry said, "For a long time, I didn't. I tried to make logical deductions—but certain facts simply wouldn't fit into the pattern. There had to be somebody in the know on both sides, manipulating both gangs, pulling the strings. Well, given a set of facts like that, my rule is always to assume the impossible—or at least the unlikely—and look around to see if the cap fits. As soon as I visited Albert Pennington, I could see that this cap was tailor-made for him."

"That's as clear as mud," said Emmy succinctly. "Try going back a bit, or something. Tell us what happened to the greyhounds."

"All right," said Henry. "That's as good a starting point as any. The trouble really began when Larry Lawson bought Marlene's Fancy, and she turned out to be a champion." The bitch in question, her sleeping attention perhaps caught by the mention of her name, rolled over onto her back and yawned hugely. Henry grinned at her. "Yes, you started it all, young lady. You, and your namesake, Marlene. The fact of the matter was that Larry Lawson was getting above himself. Before, he'd been a little third-rate crook, and easy for Pennington to twist round his little finger. Then, a couple of years ago, things changed. Larry Lawson met and married Marlene Bertini, who is an intelligent and formidable girl. He also bought this greyhound bitch, registered in his mother-in-law's name, and began to rake in money. Marlene demanded a large house, and of course Pennington—or rather one of his companies—financed the buying of the Lawson house in Finchley, which gave him a hold of some sort on Marlene and Larry—but it wasn't enough. They were doing well, and they certainly weren't going to go on taking orders from any unidentified female on the telephone. It soon got so that only Shorty Bates and poor Mrs. Bertini were really impressed by Pennington's ridiculous *alter ego*."

Jane said, "So that's the mysterious 'she' that the girl and her mother were talking about in the bar at Bunstead."

Henry was interested. "You mean you overheard a conversation between Marlene and Mrs. Bertini? That could be important. What did they say?"

"I can't remember word for word. It started with Mrs. Bertini swanking about being an owner, and her daughter shutting her up. Then they started on about the purple and silver dress, which I gathered had been a present from 'her'—and then

Marlene said something about 'she' having told them some scandal about Larry and another woman. That must sound pretty garbled, but it's as near as I can remember."

"It sounds one hundred percent accurate to me," Henry said. "It completes the jigsaw neatly. Pennington was in the process of liquidating both his gangs, which had ceased to be amusing and had become an embarrassment. He intended to clean up financially on Lady Griselda's win, and that was to be the end. However, there were some awkward loose ends hanging around. Amanda, who knew there was something shady in Pennington's connection with the Heathfield case. And Marlene and her mother."

"And Bates?" Emmy suggested.

Henry shook his head. "Too small a fish for Pennington to worry about. Bates had never seen him, even in drag—and with the gang thoroughly dispersed, Bates would simply have disappeared back into the mud, where he came from. No, it was the women who worried Pennington, and so he thought up a typical scheme. To murder Amanda and frame Mrs. Bertini for the crime. He made sure she would be wearing a most conspicuous outfit, which he duplicated for himself and hid in his car. He made sure she would be in or around the car park at the time of the shooting. And to provide a motive, he fed Marlene and her mother with a tale about goings-on between Larry Lawson and that attractive girl who gave evidence at Heathfield's trial. What—he must have asked Marlene—did she think her husband was doing down in Gorsemere anyway? It's clear Marlene didn't know. If he'd got away with it—slipped off and changed back into his city-gent clothes and false mustache, having made sure that somebody got a glimpse of the purple dress—what chance do you think Mrs. Bertini would have had of being believed when she protested her innocence?" Suddenly, Henry hit his forehead with the palm of his hand. "Of course. Weatherby. Major George Weatherby, the eternally convenient witness. Weatherby would have served a double purpose—he'd have provided an alibi for his friend Pennington, who never left his side all evening, and he'd have conveniently happened to notice a blonde woman in a striking outfit hurrying toward the car park. Thank God I was there."

There was a moment of silence, and then Bill said, "Well, I'm as much in the dark as Marlene. What *was* Lawson doing in Gorsemere that evening?"

"He was being set up to be murdered," said Henry grimly, "but he imagined that he had a date with Harry Heathfield to discuss the purchase of Lady Griselda. Once Pennington heard from Amanda about the virtually identical greyhounds, he worked out a scheme which was designed with a double purpose. To make a lot of money, and to dispose of his unwanted minions by setting them against each other. Heathfield had no appointment with Lawson, of course, but Pennington assured Lawson it was all arranged. In that way, he knew exactly where Lawson would be, at what time. They had, of course, mapped out the substitution plan. Lawson imagined he was on to a good thing, and agreed enthusiastically. So far, so good.

"Pennington's next step was to go to the rival mob—Red Dicky Marsh and the West Indian Cal Smith—and tip them off. He outlined a most attractive scheme whereby the Marsh gang could not only dispose of Lawson permanently and be sure of pinning the blame on an innocent man; as a bonus, the man in question, the owner of this potentially valuable hound, was certain to be hauled off to prison—at which moment, what could be easier than to steal Lady Griselda? Whoever would notice if a dog was missing?

"Pennington knew from Amanda that Heathfield always took a pint or so in the White Bull, and he undertook to make sure he passed out at the appropriate time. Cal Smith, of course, was waiting in the car outside and did the actual killing of Lawson. That disposed neatly of him, too, because it gave Pennington an absolute hold over him. Like the ten little Indians, Pennington's potentially awkward associates were being rubbed out at a satisfactory rate."

"And I suppose it was Smith who stole Griselda while Harry was in court?" said Jane.

"Smith or Marsh or both," said Henry. "In any case, they hid her in the shed of the house they shared in Wimbledon. Their next move was supposed to be to take her up north to the kennels where Marlene's Fancy was boarded, and do a swap. Lawson was out of the way, and neither Mrs. Bertini—the so-called owner—nor her daughter had ever seen the greyhound. Bates was too stupid to matter. It would be in the bag, and they could clean up a packet once they had possession of both dogs. It all sounded very attractive—but it didn't work out like that. The very next evening after Griselda was stolen, Marsh was in the hospital and Smith was in prison."

Emmy looked at her husband, her eyes widening. "Henry, you don't mean it was Pennington—?"

"Of course it was. The only honest witness we could lay hands on after the Runworth shooting gave it as his impression that the shots were fired by a tall, blonde woman. Does that remind you of anything?"

"Pennington's not particularly tall," Jane objected.

"Not for a man," Henry pointed out. "He's five-foot-nine. That's pretty tall for a woman."

"And of course," Emmy added thoughtfully, "Smith and Marsh knew him as Albert Pennington, the company director of Chelsea."

"That's right. For once, Dicky Marsh was speaking the truth when he told the police afterward that he had no idea who had shot him."

"You're making my head burst, trying to follow all this," Bill complained. "We seem to have reached a point where the Marsh–Smith setup is out of action. Right?"

"Right. Whereupon, the mysterious 'she' calls up Shorty Bates and tells him that he can collect Lady Griselda at his leisure from the Wimbledon garden shed. Armed with a letter from Mrs. Bertini authorizing him to remove Marlene's Fancy from her Yorkshire kennels. Bates—not to mention Marlene and her mother—will be sitting pretty, with both greyhounds in their possession. All they have to do is to make the switch and run Marlene's Fancy in Lady Griselda's name, and everyone'll be rich."

"I don't see how you can be sure of all this," Jane said. "It must be guesswork."

"Not really. Thanks to the vigilance of a certain Mrs. Rundle-Webster and the conscientiousness of Constable Hawthorn, I definitely established that Bates turned up in his blue van at the Wimbledon house the evening Smith was arrested, which means he must have taken Griselda. He then arranged with Marlene to board her temporarily at the Lawson's empty house in Finchley, where I as near as dammit caught up with them. Bates literally whisked Griselda out of there from under my nose, and there wasn't a thing I could do about it. Pennington, meanwhile, had arranged with Amanda and Tommy to have her boarded quietly at an old kennel at Hilltop."

Bill whistled. "I say," he said. "Amanda was pretty deep into all this, wasn't she?"

"She had no choice," said Henry. "As I explained. As for Tommy, the kennel boy, they used a mixture of stick and carrot—bribes and threats. It wasn't difficult to hide one extra greyhound in that vast establishment."

"Simon and Bella didn't know, then?"

"No, I'm sure they didn't." Henry smiled, a little ruefully. "There we all were, scouring the countryside for Griselda, and all the time she was sitting quietly at home."

Emmy, who had been calculating days of the week on her fingers, said, "But there was a delay of several days before they raced Marlene's Fancy as Lady Griselda for the first time. Why was that?"

"It was the minimum time possible," Henry explained. "Marlene's Fancy had to be collected from Yorkshire, and then reboarded at a perfectly respectable training establishment in the Midlands as Lady Griselda. She was then entered from this kennel for the Kevingfield race, which of course she won. That was to give an air of respectability to her big win at Bunstead, and also to ensure that her card didn't have to go back to the NGRC between the two races. Meanwhile, Pennington, Bates, and the two women were quietly placing large numbers of smallish bets under various names on Lady Griselda to win the 8:30 at Bunstead. Everything seemed to be going according to plan. And then I got too close behind them."

"That was the day they kidnapped you?" Emmy said.

"The same. The day of 'Griselda's' first win. I visited Pennington for the first and only time that day—I'm ashamed to say that up to then I hadn't considered the possibility that he might be the missing link I was looking for. Stupidly, I imagined that he'd been taken to Gorsemere by Weatherby to provide a nice, innocent, unimpeachable witness. Of course, it was the other way around. Similarly, I was thinking that Lady Griselda—the slow runner—was to be substituted for Marlene's Fancy, the champion. I had it all backwards.

"The moment he saw me, Pennington knew he'd have to act fast to keep ahead of me. He knew from Amanda that I was staying in Gorsemere, but this was his first inkling that I was on the warpath. He must have called Bates the moment I left him, to set up the reception committee at Gorsemere station."

"No," said Jane, suddenly.

Henry looked at her, surprised. "What do you mean?"

"I mean, it must have been Amanda he called—in the first place, anyhow. I had quite forgotten, she came here that afternoon, walking Wotan, but it never occurred to me that she was fishing for information. She worked the conversation around to you, and I told her that you were in London and expected back for supper. Come to think of it, she actually offered to meet you at the station, but I said I didn't know which train you'd be on, and that you'd be walking back here."

"So that's how Bates knew exactly where and when to find me," said Henry. "He only had to wait in the station car park until I arrived."

"I thought you said Bates had a girl with him," Emmy said. "Was that Marlene?"

"No. Not a girl. Bates took young Tommy along to help lug the body around—which was the first time Tommy realized just what he was mixed up in. Well, you know the rest. It was a nice touch of Pennington's to tell Bates to dump me in Smith's garden shed. That way, even if Smith were released on bail—which in fact happened—he wouldn't stay free for long once I'd been found. And if he wasn't released, the chances were I wouldn't be found—at least, not alive. Heads I win, tails you lose.

"As it was, mercifully, the Hawthorn–Rundle-Webster team turned up trumps again, and I was found. That was why we had to go through the charade at the hospital—my only hope of catching Pennington was to make him think I hadn't been able to tell anybody what I knew. I reckoned he'd think it worth the risk of disposing of Amanda and the Bertini woman, as well as cleaning up financially. After that—with any luck I'd die quietly, and still incommunicado. If not, all this would have been virtually impossible to prove. I had to be there at the stadium, I had to catch him red-handed and in his ridiculous transvestite getup. It meant taking a fearful risk with Amanda's safety, even though Sergeant Reynolds and I were never more than a few paces away from her. Well . . . that's it, and I'm glad it's over."

There was a silence, and then Emmy said, "And they really will let Harry Heathfield go home again?"

"I'm sure of it," said Henry.

"Because," said Emmy, "I was going to say . . . that is, if Ginger needs a home just for a few weeks . . . till Harry comes back . . . I'm sure we could always . . ."

"NO!" said Henry.

As it turned out, Ginger quite enjoyed his ten days in the Tibbetts' Chelsea apartment; but even Emmy was forced to agree that he was happier in the country, and his reunion with Harry Heathfield was extremely touching.

Epilogue

It was a chilly evening in October, and Paul Claverton had lit the big log fire in the Saloon Bar of the White Bull. The crackling flames leapt merrily in the hearth, flickering over the venerable polished tables and glinting off the horse-brasses. In his usual inglenook, Harry Heathfield sat, deeply content, with a pint of mild and bitter in his hand. At his feet, Lady Griselda, Ginger, and Tess slumbered peacefully, making a sort of beige, brown, and black fur rug.

Across the table from Heathfield sat a young, fresh-faced man and a pretty, auburn-haired girl. They were strangers in these parts, as they freely admitted. Had just driven down from London and seen this awfully attractive-looking old pub . . .

Lady Griselda stirred in her sleep, and Harry said, "I see you're admiring my greyhound bitch."

"Er . . . yes. That's right," said the young man hastily.

"Lady Griselda of Gorsemere. That's her name. Very fine runner in her day. Of course, I don't race her anymore now. Just keep her as a pet, like."

"You mean—you used to race her?" The girl was impressed. "That must have been exciting."

"Ah, well . . . we owners, you know . . . we take it all in our stride." Harry glanced quickly around the bar. Mr. and Mrs. Spence were over in the corner, but they had been hunted down relentlessly by the Reverend Mr. Thacker, who was now haranguing them, probably about the church roof. They could not possibly hear. "Of course," Harry went on, "it's always a thrill if your dog wins."

"Oh, it must be!"

"Yes . . . I keep a few cuttings . . . just as a memento of the old days . . . happen I might have one here . . ." Harry fumbled in his pocket. "Yes, funnily enough. Here's one." He unfolded a grubby, much handled page from a cheap sporting paper and indicated a paragraph with a stubby forefinger.

"See? There. Where it says 'Surprise Win for Outsider' . . . see? '. . . romped home in the 1:30 race to beat the 2-to-1 favorite . . . The surprise winner was Mr. Henry Heathfield's Lady Griselda, trained by Mrs. Bella Yateley.'" Harry looked fondly at the paper. "Yes," he said, reminiscently, "that was a thrill. That was a day I'll always remember . . . thank you very much, sir, a pint of mild and bitter . . . yes, up in the Midlands it was . . . all the excitement of the crowds . . . the bookies shouting the odds . . . nobody thought Griselda had a chance, but I knew better . . ."

Lady Griselda opened one eye, looked at Harry, and closed it again in a long, slow wink.